# *Murder Egyptian Style*

by

**Gerhard Behrens**

Grosvenor House
Publishing Limited

The right of Gerhard Behrens to be identified as the author of this
work has been asserted in accordance with Section 78
of the Copyright, Designs and Patents Act 1988

The book cover picture is copyright to Gerhard Behrens

This book is published by
Grosvenor House Publishing Ltd
Link House
140 The Broadway, Tolworth, Surrey, KT6 7HT.
www.grosvenorhousepublishing.co.uk

A CIP record for this book
is available from the British Library

ISBN 978-1-78623-237-3

Cover design by Nonno Leonidas

A stubborn heart will come to a bad end,
and whoever dallies with danger will perish in it.
*(Old Testament, Book of Jesus Sirach 3/27)*

## Note to the Reader

While the events unfold upon the background of Egyptian society in the second decade of the 21$^{st}$ century, my book only aims to entertain the reader; it is not about politics. For anyone interested in the rather harsh realities of modern Egypt I recommend Robert Springborg's admirable analysis in his book 'Egypt'. (Cambrige/UK, 2018).

I am indebted to Rosalind Wade-Heddon for her invaluable work to improve style, grammar and consistency and to my wife Doris for her contribution to the plausibility of the story.

It goes without saying that any remaining inconsistencies or mistakes are my responsibility alone and that any similarity of fictitious persons or institutions like the British Orient Bank and the auction house of Chrosby's with real ones would be sheer coincidence.

## London

Things had not been going well recently for Dina. She was often gloomy, irritable and at times even bitter.

Her marriage to Alistair was in tatters.

He had met a much younger woman and had decided to live with her as his companion in a belated spring of new erotic fulfilment.

Their marriage had been in decline for several years already, especially after Alistair had retired and was around all the time. When she met him all those years ago in Cairo, he had been a dashing young man, working for the British Orient Bank as their local branch manager, full of enthusiasm for his career, his comfortable expatriate life with golf and horse riding and a love for his new and exotic country, Egypt—in short, a master of the universe, who had no difficulty in conquering the all too impressionable young Egyptian girl she had been then.

All went well for quite some time, but passion slowly faded away and was replaced by boredom. It was only after Alistair's retirement and his continuous presence at home, where TV watching became their main pastime in common, that she seriously began to think of leaving him. It never went beyond that stage though—a separation would be too costly, too complicated, too painful—and she was not sure if she could adapt easily to a life alone without a new partner in sight.

It came as a shock therefore that it was he, not she, who broke up their marriage. To assume that their long marriage—a happy one as both used to say almost automatically—would have prevented Alistair from making a fool of himself was wrong. There is no fool like an old fool, and Alistair had become one. Well, in her opinion but not his.

It all began, when Alistair started to play golf not just once, but twice a week or more. He did not even object, when she declined to join him, because she had never liked the game. His tolerant acceptance of her repeated refusals should have made her suspicious though, because in the past he had always insisted that playing together was much more fun. This certainly continued to be true, but the fun part was now found in other quarters.

Not long before they had met an attractive woman in her thirties at the bar of the golf-club. She had a charming Scandinavian accent, blond hair and big slightly protuberant teeth. She exuded vitality, and Alistair seemed quite impressed by her healthy looks.

They had started the usual golf conversation about handicaps, the missed and the successful drives and putts, the difficult bunker at hole 13, the forthcoming tournament, etc.

Dina had soon lost interest, while nudging Alistair discreetly a few times under the stool as a hint to go home. When she shot sideways glances at him she saw an overeager bald man with a puffy face, trying to impress their new acquaintance with witty remarks Dina had heard so many times before.

She had become increasingly aware that the Alistair she had married so long ago was no more the young dashing and attractive man she had fallen in love with; now he was an ordinary, aging husband with all the deficiencies old men have. As Dina had decided a long time ago not to expect too much from her married life, she attached little importance to Alistair's attention to this young woman.

When they were in their car on their way back, she only made a mocking remark about the impression their new acquaintance had obviously made on Alistair. He took the remark in good humour, but his constrained and artificial laughter should have alarmed her.

In fact, she never suspected anything until Alistair in his well-measured banker's voice gave her the news after an unusually silent dinner at home.

"Dina, you know that I have always loved you and I still do," he opened the subject. "But I am at an age now, when I have to grasp new chances and opportunities, before it is too late."

"What new opportunities?" she laughed. "Let me guess: you want to go to Abu Dhabi to manage the finances of an Arab oil sheikh? But what does that have to do with loving me?"

"You do not take anything I tell you seriously," he protested," and that is one of the reasons why I have decided to live with Birgit. I would have liked to break the news more gently, but you leave me no choice."

"Birgit? Who the fuck is Birgit?" Dina was so shocked that she forgot her good manners and used the f-word which she would never tolerate from others.

"You have met her yourself recently. You remember that lady we talked with at the bar of the golf club. I have seen her quite a few times since, and I am sure now that we have so much in common that I want to live with her permanently."

"You mean that stupid blonde, who had no subject to talk about except golf? Alistair, tell me you are not serious!"

"I am deadly serious. That 'stupid blonde' as you so nicely put it, is nothing less than the vice-president of a bank. With her I can relate in many ways that I never could with you thanks to your obsession with Islamic art and culture and nothing else."

"Ordinary vice-president, executive vice-president or senior vice-president?" asked Dina.

She knew a lot about bank hierarchy. She had not been married to a banker for so long for nothing. It had been a comfortable life for Lady Trevelyan, as she was known in society, because her Alistair had been knighted for some reason no one quite knew for sure except he himself and his political friends to whose election campaign his bank had contributed through mysterious channels that somehow had been opened by Alistair. She had learned to judge people by their title, rank and professional jargon. She had also acquired a taste for gossiping, which in good society is accepted as a sure sign of belonging to good society.

"Just vice-president, as if that were of any importance," Alistair replied. He was no more apologetic but clearly annoyed now.

"So not much more than a middle-rank bank employee! Even someone like you ranked higher. At least that explains why a young woman would be prepared to live with an old man. Money is always a good substitute for other talents."

Alistair's face reddened. He was justifiably angry now.

As a true member of his class he had always been a bit dull, something Dina did not mind because Islamic art and history provided her with the intellectual satisfaction that neither banking nor golfing ever did. Yet Alistair was also well-mannered and methodical and had thought of everything. He had already found a buyer for their home, an expensive mews house in a posh neigh-bourhood of London.

"In spite of your sarcasm I shall leave you half of the proceeds of the sale of our house and half of my other assets," he said with his eyes averted. "There is still enough for me after that. You can be assured that even with your own moderate income you will be no worse off financially, if we act as civilized people, which we surely will. In case you are interested, I have even found a com-fortable and sizeable flat for you to live in with enough space for your precious library that you love so much."

He planned to live with Birgit in her native country Sweden. In winter in her flat in Stockholm and in summer in a house she had inherited from her parents on a lake with a golf course near-by and a small sailing boat moored on the lake, where they could enjoy a quiet and none too exciting country life with a lot of nature and without unnecessary intellectual challenges.

"It's a small red clapboard house typical of local architec-ture," he added quite unnecessarily, as if that would be of interest to someone dealing in art. And yes—they even had a private sauna from which they could jump naked into the lake. And they would also have a dog, because Birgit was mad about dogs.

"Fortunately we have no children, who would suffer from a separation."

"It was not my fault! You never wanted to check if something with your sperms is not quite right," she interrupted him.

"It is quite unfair to put the blame on me," he replied with a hurt expression. "We had always agreed that we could live without children, who could have prevented you from fulfilling your professional ambitions that I have always supported, as you well know."

Their conversation had taken a nasty turn indeed.

They continued to blame each other for insensitive behaviour, for not caring for the other's interests and with all the reproaches that are part of a marital dispute. It continued until both of them had slung all the mud that had accumulated over the years at each other. Small bits of annoyance or disappointment, which had never been a problem for long in the past, were now feeding their duelling pistols with lethal bullets. They had to realize that the small irritations and the increasing ennui that both had felt but never mentioned or wanted to admit before, had now culminated in a serious break-down of their marriage. This was no longer a 'domestic' as they used to call their previous quarrels. They had reached a point of no return; even a future reconciliation after sobering up would not last long. Too many insults and dirt had been exchanged between them, not to forget casual, but nevertheless hurting remarks about their sex life or the lack of it.

When they were too exhausted to continue their unpleasant conversation they went to bed. She stayed awake for a long time, while he had no trouble falling asleep. She realized that her life had taken a dramatic turn, although she was unable as yet to decide if it was to the worse or to the better. In any case she would make sure she was known as Dina Ghalib in future by adopting her maiden name again. Chrosby's would not be happy about this change of course, as some of their more snobbish clients were surely more impressed by a Lady Dina Trevelyan, a member of the Cornish gentry, rather than by a simple Dina Ghalib of unknown Middle Eastern origin. Dina herself had not been averse to being called Lady Trevelyan, but under her new circumstances: no more! Her pride was stronger than her vanity.

It was not only Alistair who was leaving her, but she had also lost her father recently after a severe heart attack. Her brother Maguid in Cairo had phoned her to give her this sad news. She could not even attend his funeral, because he had been buried immediately according to local tradition.

Her father was the only person besides Alistair who really mattered to her, and Dina felt lonely for the first time in her life after losing both. Her father had been a successful surgeon during his active life, whose services had been in demand from ministers, rich businessmen and once even from the Egyptian president himself. Dina owed him a lot, a critical mind and also her stubbornness, which she inherited from him; he had also instilled in her a love of art. Her parents had often taken her out, driving along the street leading to the pyramids at Gizeh, where at a very early age she developed a love for Egyptian antiquities. She still remembered vividly her surprise that the small pictures called hieroglyphs were letters and could be read and understood. "I want to read hirglifs myself when I am older," she exclaimed and her father patted her head approvingly: "You will, darling, you will," he said.

It was only Dina they took out regularly for excursions with some cultural ambition. Their father—never patient with lethargic colleagues nor with bored children—usually left her siblings in the care of their nanny watching TV, whenever they went out to something more demanding than eating ice-cream or going to the beach. It was perhaps not a method approved by modern pedagogues for raising children in an equable manner, but the Ghalib children were never much alike anyway.

Their separation went quite smoothly, as Alistair had predicted. They were civilized people after all. Dina became the owner of a large flat on the fourth floor of a Victorian building in Chelsea. At that height it was much airier than their old mews house, which commanded a rather depressing view across a closed court to another mews house with its garage. In the freakish London property market the sale of their home still left them with a comfortable surplus after purchasing her new flat.

"Much nicer than the view from our house," Dina remarked to Alistair, combining a compliment for his choice with a critique of their old home, of which he had always been proud.

There were no delays, the kind experienced by people less affluent than the Trevelyans. They were cash buyers—estate agents' most favoured clients—and did not have to wait for the sale of their marital home in order to secure the money for Dina's apartment.

Alistair also had the good taste of never bringing Birgit home. Dina had almost forgotten what she looked like, when the moment of separation came.

One morning at breakfast, which Alistair had prepared as usual, he told her that he would catch a plane to Stockholm that afternoon. Of course, his departure should have been expected at any moment, because all the preparations for relocating to his new country had been made. But it was still rather a shock for Dina.

"Is this the moment of separation then?" she asked.

"Yes, I am afraid so," he said. Dina almost laughed. It was the quintessential British phrase for expressing something unpleasant. Unable to be straightforward, she thought, they always have to be afraid or sorry of saying or doing something—even Alistair in these final moments of their marriage.

When she was ready to leave, she stopped at the door and turned around. They looked undecidedly at each other, as if they thought of exchanging one last kiss. Then Dina said with a firm voice: "Well, good-bye then and the best of luck to you both. Just email or write to me to let me know where you are."

"Of course, we shall stay in touch," Alistair promised. She shut the door behind her. Alistair could not have known then that he would never see Dina alive again!

Dina had been staring absentmindedly for a while at the metal object on her desk. Her mind was distracted by unpleasant thoughts concerning her private life. The sudden turbulence caused by her husband's infidelities had affected her more than she ever wanted to admit.

Concentrating on something else was the best remedy for personal sorrows, and she knew that. She was even more determined not to neglect her duties as the head of Chrosby's Islamic sales department. To achieve this she was now spending more time at her desk in Mayfair, working overtime for her employer.

She had a lot to attend to anyway. Reports and painstakingly researched catalogue entries had to be written, when she was not meeting with clients in her office or with the important ones in their Pall-Mall clubs, in restaurants or in their homes, where they frequently bored her with their homespun theories about Islamic art. But this was still better than thinking of Alistair.

She suddenly became aware that her mind had wandered off at a tangent once more and blamed herself for this. She never liked to succumb to weakness and loss of control—this was unworthy of the 'control-freak' that Alistair used to call her.

...

The bronze basin with its silver inlaid inscriptions had for some time been a source of irritation, and all she wanted to do was to return it and then forget about it. The owner—a well-known collector of Islamic art—was a very good Chrosby's customer. He deserved respect and had therefore to be treated with the utmost courtesy. She could not afford to annoy him and to have him take his custom elsewhere, possibly even complaining about her lack of assistance, when all he wanted was to enter his precious object into the next auction with the highest estimate possible. The problem was that his ideas were all wrong. His basin was utterly worthless, except possibly on eBay.

Disappointing hopeful collectors was the unpleasant part of her job. Some of her colleagues were not as conscientious as Dina and had no qualms about revaluing cheap items or—worse—to auction fake or stolen objects in order to make money for their employer. Dina was different, she had not accepted her position at

Chrosby's for their modest salary, but because it offered her the chance to combine the perks of socializing with interesting and largely rich people on an equal level while indulging her love for Islamic art. Fakes and lies about provenance were not part of that deal in her understanding. When an envious colleague had once dismissed her as having a 'holier-than-you' arrogance, Dina even took that as a compliment.

She tried to convince the collector that his basin was a modern copy, but he would have none of it. He explained that he had bought it a long time ago as an original 15th century vessel from an unscrupulous dealer and did not want to accept that it should be redated to the 20th century.

She had to tread carefully now. She finally decided to ask an outside expert for an opinion, who she knew would certainly describe the item as an example of modern bazaar ware that it was. At least that would redirect the flak from herself to the specialist.

She took a sip of the cold coffee on her desk, mumbling an exasperated 'merde, merde alors' to herself. Her education at the Lycée Français in Cairo had not only taught her about Racine and Balzac, but also swearing in the French way.

She reached for her phone and called the owner.

The collector was none too pleased, when she said she needed a second opinion. That could delay everything, especially because there was only one expert of Islamic metal ware available, who moreover had retired to his home in France, where he could only be reached, if he bothered to open his mailbox.

"You must be patient," explained Dina, "he will reply, but he cannot be rushed. Perhaps he will prove me wrong, so this could be to your benefit." The humble fee Chrosby's were ready to pay their experts was not a real incentive to lure him away from his local golf course or from the beaches in sun-drenched Provence.

After swearing once more in a low voice she decided to call it a day and to return to her solitary flat.

After a long day in the office Dina was longing for a shower at home.

She looked at herself in the long mirror facing the shower cubicle, and in spite of her usual scepticism that had proved her right so many times in the art world she could not find a reason why Alistair should have preferred another woman to keep him company. She was slim after a rigorous regime—perhaps a bit too slim now—barely any wrinkles on her skin, although perhaps not as smooth as Birgit's; her legs were well shaped, although probably not as long as Birgit's; and her breasts still firm. Well, possibly also not as firm as Birgit's. Moreover, she was a brunette with some assistance from the hairdresser's colouring and not a stupid blonde! And her position as the head of Chrosby's Islamic section was certainly higher than that of a non-executive and non-senior vice-president of a bank. What she saw in the mirror was a still very attractive woman and definitely a more interesting one than that Swedish blonde.

"Alistair, you are a fool," Dina muttered, which made her feel infinitely superior.

She poured herself a double Chivas Regal on the rocks with a little soda added to make it a bit fizzy and with the bathrobe wrapped around her nestled in the comfortable leather armchair in front of the large TV screen.

A whisky and watching TV had become part of her pre-bedtime ritual, after Alistair had gone. The solitary evenings without a partner—even a partner like Alistair—to talk to and with whom she could exchange thoughts, even banal ones, had been more distressing than she wanted to admit at first. Being alone can be a form of mental torture just as noise can be used as a physical torture. The whisky helped to relax, and watching TV provided the soundtrack to break the silence as a distraction from painful soul-searching.

The film she was watching now was about a serial killer, who chose his victims in alphabetical order. The story came to a climax, when the police tried to protect a frightened woman called Georgina (the letter 'G' was next in line). Coincidentally she happened to be the estranged former wife of the police inspector, whose personal involvement had him eliminated from the case. This had been assigned to his assistant, who continually intrigued against him, because he was after his job. Before turning the TV off Dina knew that movie tradition required that the police inspector and not his intriguing assistant would solve the case.

This scenario was too idiotic to distract her from her thoughts though.

"I need human company," Dina thought, "or I will go crazy."

She decided to call Jürgen over for dinner and a chat.

It was always good to have Jürgen around, her old and faithful admirer. She had several things on her mind that needed competent advice, and Jürgen was always a good listener, who had proven on more than one occasion to be an excellent advisor as well.

When Dina called Jürgen Rietberg, professor emeritus of Islamic history at the School for Oriental and African Studies in London, he was also relaxing in an armchair with a glass of red wine, reading a book written by a Lebanese historian. It was about the original home of the Jews before their Babylonian exile. The book was very scholarly, very controversial and also rather dry, so Rietberg was delighted to be interrupted by Dina's call.

He had met her many years ago in Cairo, when he was there on a sabbatical researching the archives and she had been writing her MA-thesis on Islamic architecture at the American University. From the first moment he fell in love with her, although his affection never passed the platonic stage. Dina was married then to Alistair and Rietberg was always too inhibited for an attempt to seduce her into an extramarital affair. Even if he had tried, he could not have been sure of success. He was never very impressive, certainly not as dashing as the young Alistair. He always had the looks and the demeanour of a bookish and rather grey professor, more at ease with his books than with women. During his stay in Cairo he had no suitable accommodation to serve as a love nest either, a fact that he used as a lame excuse for his lack of courage and initiative towards Dina.

Rietberg had recently remarried, after his first much earlier marriage had failed completely. His new wife, Marie-Anne, was the widow of a murdered colleague. Their relationship had begun shortly after the murder and during a time when Rietberg was not only consoling her but also helping to solve the murder case. The circumstances were not exactly propitious for a love affair, but such affairs do not always follow a standard pattern. For the first time in his life Rietberg had found his ideal partner, who also let him forget his unfulfilled dreams about Dina, a woman he never possessed, partly because of his timidity and lack of macho courage.

Yet he and Dina had formed a strong bond of friendship that had even become stronger after Alistair had left her. They shared scholarly interests—Islamic and Arabic history and culture—, while Alistair was always excluded from their animated discussions they had when they met at her home. They still even flirted with each other from time to time—innocently and jokingly, but nevertheless.

He was therefore much looking forward to a dinner with her in her new home. Recently her dinner invitations had become more frequent. Although Rietberg was always glad to see her, the frequency of her calls troubled him. Dina was obviously unhappy with her solitary life and needed company, much more than she admitted after her divorce. He pitied her, a sentiment he never had reason to feel towards Dina before. She had always been the glamorous and successful society lady—admired, even envied—anything but pitied.

Marie-Anne was never part of their private meetings. Even if she had been invited, she would have declined. She did like Dina, as everyone did except Dina's own family. But she knew her Jürgen. Both were mature persons, and as such they never spoiled their relationship by intruding into spheres that even close partners prefer to remain exclusive; and Dina was an exclusive part of Rietberg's earlier life. Marie-Anne was a successful medical doctor and would certainly not have Rietberg around in her surgery or at a medical congress. There was no need to burden Jürgen's animated scholarly discussions with Dina by artificially trying to join in their conversations.

"I want to show you something that might be interesting for an historian like you," said Dina, "after we have had our dinner."

Eating food prepared by her was always a delight shared by both Alistair and Rietberg, as there was nothing more exciting that Rietberg could ever have shared with Alistair. Her special cuisine was a fusion of the best kind. It combined the solid stuff of Egyptian cooking with the refined seasoning she had learned in her long experience as hostess to the many dinner parties organized by the Trevelyans in both Cairo and London, which had done a lot for the social standing of her banker husband.

During the recent unpleasant exchange with Alistair, Dina had thought of reminding him of her role as the hostess for their successful dinners. She even wanted to predict a complete culinary disaster with Birgit, the Swedish blonde, preparing food in their country retreat. Dry meatballs were the pinnacle of Swedish cuisine, as she remembered from a trip to Stockholm. But, such a remark would have painted her role as being that of a mere cook and housewife, not as an attractive companion and lover, so she had decided against it.

Also Dina enjoyed the dinner with Rietberg—mainly for other stimulants than the food, however. Cooking for her friend helped to overcome the bitterness that had crept into her solitary life.

After their usual lengthy dinner Dina produced her laptop and showed Rietberg an image of a wooden panel someone had sent her as an email attachment.

"A well-known Syrian collector, who is living in Lebanon now to escape the war, has mailed this. This object has been offered to him, and he wants my advice as to whether he should buy it."

"But I have no knowledge of art—Islamic or Western —as you well know," protested Rietberg.

"Ok, then let me tell you that the style and execution of the inscriptions on this panel point clearly to Egypt in the Fatimid period, *i.e.* to the 11th century. They are quite rare now like most artefacts of this period. Their early date and their material were not propitious for reaching old age. Most of these panels have been eaten by worms, termites or were otherwise destroyed."

"If it is so rare, why don't you just tell him to go ahead and buy it? Do you know how much it would cost, by the way?"

"Hundreds of thousands. Not Lebanese lira, but dollars."

"Wow," said Rietberg, "your man must really be loaded to contemplate such a purchase. The panel is not even particularly beautiful."

"This remark proves that you know nothing in fact about art and its market," said Dina, "I find Rubens' fat nudes and much of contemporary art unattractive, to say the least, but that stuff is worth many millions nevertheless. Think also of Indian shrunken heads in Latin America, a big collector item for the Victorians, which are positively disgusting."

"If I am so ignorant in the field of fine art, including shrunken heads, I do not understand why you need my advice here. You are the art expert, I am not."

Dina looked at him maliciously.

"I want to demonstrate that I am not a greedy dealer, just because I am working for an auction house. I know what you think about auction houses, which according to your quite unfounded opinion peddle in all kind of goods without paying due attention to legal niceties, in particular when we deal with stolen or otherwise illegally acquired objects."

Unperturbed by his sceptical smile, she continued:

"My main duty in my job at Chrosby's is to sell and not to research of course. Still no one among us can ignore serious doubts about the provenance of art offered for sale. I have refused other items before, when I had serious doubts about them, even when others would have called me an over-legalistic pedant. Therefore, for this panel as well I have consulted the international database for lost or stolen art, the Artloss register. I found no trace of it there, however."

"Well, no problem then," said Rietberg.

Dina was still not reassured.

"If it were just an ordinary piece of art, even an expensive one, I would agree. But I happen to know that Fatimid wooden panels of this quality are very rare and do not appear on the market usually. Most of them are part of museum collections anyway, and if any of them was offered for sale, the museums would raise hell and try to stop the sale. But no museum has come forward yet, as far as I know."

Rietberg hum-hummed a while as was his usual professorial habit when he had to think of a reply.

"So, in spite of the absence of contrary proof you have doubts about the provenance, yet you still intend to give the collector the green light to buy. For that decision you need my moral support—correct?"

"Yes, probably something of that sort," sighed Dina.

"Before doing that I would try to establish that it is not a fake," Rietberg ventured after a while. "To advise your friend to buy a fake would not be good for your reputation. I happened to read something about another incised object, a so-called Aztec skull made of rock crystal that even fooled museum curators that turned out to be a modern fake. It left many shamefaced scholars as victims of this hoax."

"Bravo," said Dina, "you do still know something about art. That skull was not carved with the traditional tools available at the time, but with modern lathe-mounted rotary wheels, so-called jeweller's wheels, that carve the incisions at a different angle than hand tools would do. Of course a similar test was done here to know if the incisions are of Fatimid origin or made by modern tools. This panel has passed the test successfully, according to a certificate shown to my collector."

"If that is so, you have to make a second step," Rietberg said, "but don't be offended by your Egyptian patriotism, if I mention something you know already. Pilfering and thefts of art always happened in the Middle East, but now on an unprecedented scale. The media are full of reports about it, as you certainly know. In fact, the whole cultural heritage of the Middle East is up for sale at present or—worse—for demolition. Just start by browsing through Egyptian museums' catalogues, the Islamic Museum in particular. Perhaps you will find the treasure offered to your Syrian collector there. Perhaps also not, but it's worth a try. I suppose you or Chrosby's have these catalogues, and if not, there is always the British library."

"Of course; I have had the same idea already," snapped Dina.

"Meaning that my well-intentioned advice was not needed after all."

"Oh, come off it. I did not know that you would take offence so easily. I have that catalogue in my office and intend to check it first thing in the morning."

She laughed:

"Of course, following your advice!"

## Damascus

She had first met Radwan Sabunji several years earlier at a reception given by him in Damascus for an international delegation of museum staff visiting Syria in more peaceful times. *i.e.* before much of Syria was destroyed in a bloody civil war.

He wanted to show them his famous collection of Islamic art. Dina, although only a tourist then on a trip to Syria together with Alistair, was invited as well, after she had previously contacted Radwan to see his treasures, one of the biggest private collections of Islamic art in the world. Alistair did not attend, preferring instead to meet an old banker acquaintance, who was working for the Bank of Syria. After an initial show of interest in Dina's work, when he was courting her, he had since made no pretence to have more than a financial interest in art.

During the reception Radwan showed the delegation around in the Sabunji villa, a marvel of Syria's domestic architecture dating to the Ottoman period. Radwan had furnished his home in a tasteful combination of modern with traditional Syrian wooden inlaid furniture. One of the rooms was similar to the famous Aleppo room that had been shipped in 1912 to a museum in Berlin, where it has been the pride of their collections ever since.

"You know," he said, standing in front of an exquisite mosque glass lamp worth a million and without looking at anyone in particular, "I want to leave all this to my country—only I do not know who represents it."

Those who knew Radwan smiled the way people usually do when a friend mentions a personal weakness—with sympathy and tolerance. Radwan—a good-looking middle-aged man with a well-trimmed black-coloured moustache and full salt and pepper hair, who always dressed impeccably in a formal dark suit— had no children and no wife either, because he was gay. Not that he flaunted his homosexuality—he was much too discreet for that— nor did his partner ever show up at social events, although everyone of Radwan's many friends in Syria knew him as his secretary. It was also certain that his lover would never inherit Radwan's treasures. Apart from being handsome he had no other interests than passing his free time in a gym to groom his body in order to become even more handsome. It was unthinkable that Radwan could leave his priceless collection to a man, who had not the slightest interest in history or culture.

Radwan smiled. It was a sad smile.

Dina had never met a man like him. A collector with a sense of patriotic duty—she admired that, having dealt with too many of them, who were only interested in amassing as many pieces as possible for their own private delight, like stamp collectors. Both belonged to the rapidly diminishing old Middle Eastern world, where identity was less defined by religion than by class and common culture.

While they were strolling around, someone amongst the delegation accosted Dina.

"You must be Madame Dina," he said. "Do you remember me?"

She looked at an unassuming man of about her age, with the looks and the dress of a small bureaucrat, an Egyptian bureaucrat to be precise, of the sort she had often met in her country. Egypt had always been run by such bureaucratic looking men in the service of the real power moguls. She scrambled her brain to identify him. She had definitely met him before—that was sure—but where and when? Just before admitting defeat and disappointing her hopeful interlocutor by asking him who he was, she remembered.

"Of course, you must be Mustafa," she said, "how could I ever forget?"

She was so pleased with herself that Mustafa mistook her sudden expression of relief at remembering him for an expression of her joy at meeting him again.

He beamed and tried to buttonhole her for the rest of the evening.

Mustafa—she could not even remember his surname—had studied Islamic art with her at the American University in Cairo until she had passed her MA. With his own MA he later landed a job in the Islamic Museum in Cairo as a deputy curator.

"Our museum has assigned me to be a member of this delegation," he said with obvious pride. To be sent on a mission abroad was always one of the most coveted perks in public service and depended mainly on having good relations with someone influential. He also mentioned that he expected a promotion soon to a more important job in the Department of Antiquities. Mustafa was well connected, no doubt about it, and wanted to demonstrate his importance to Dina, who had scarcely taken any notice of him during their studies.

She was much more interested in talking to Radwan, their host, and managed to escape Mustafa after a while. She forgot about him almost immediately, not knowing that she would have to deal with him and his influential superiors again, with serious problems for both her work and for herself.

Her private discussion with Radwan after the delegation including Mustafa, the important man without a surname, had left, was long and sad.

"What did you mean, when you said that you do not know who is representing your country?" she started.

"Well—who are those whom I can trust here? Tell me—museums, foundations or the government? I have been around for too long to have any illusions about any of them. With a few exceptions they only want to fill their pockets, even by embezzling my beloved treasures. as soon as they get hold of them."

His smile was even more melancholy than before.

"I should probably sell all of it myself in London or other places, while I am still alive, at least to secure a safe place for them in a Western museum or even in private collections. Our Middle East is finished—only destruction and corruption everywhere, not to mention the religious fanatics whose ideas about Islam are only killing, forbidding innocent pleasures and destroying everything we inherited from the past."

"Still, I know that my own country, Egypt, has a repatriation office that managed to retrieve several stolen objects and repatriate them. You can certainly find something similar in Syria," she objected.

Radwan laughed.

"Of course, of course. For Melina Mercouri to request the return of the Elgin marbles and for your own Zahi Hawas to want

Nefertiti's bust back proves their patriotism. But does it not strike you as strange that all these patriots are only concerned about thefts that happened long before their time? They present themselves as idealistic campaigners in a crusade against thieves who are long dead. When it comes to recent thefts, which happen during their own time in office and for which they themselves could be blamed, directly or indirectly, they are strangely silent."

Dina had no response. She went to school during Nasser's time when she learned of Saladin, Bismarck, Garibaldi and Nasser and other nationalists that had made her a patriotic Egyptian herself. On the other hand, she had also frequently auctioned antiquities from war-torn Afghanistan with a doubtful yet officially undisputed provenance. Was it so wrong to place them into the possession of responsible collectors instead of having them destroyed for their metal value, or was it? Or should they be given to a museum in Kabul with a government known to be one of the most corrupt in the world?

## London

During their long discussion Radwan and Dina had become friends. For a while she had no news from him, but he had contacted her recently after moving from war-torn Syria to Lebanon for help with a Fatimid wood panel.

As a service to Radwan she had to find out more about the provenance of the item that she had already discussed with Rietberg. She ordered a strong coffee from her secretary—the third one that day—and started by probing if the panel had been stolen from the Islamic Museum in Cairo.

In her well-stocked library she did find two relevant catalogues.

The first one was recently published after the turn of the 21st century. It was a glossy thing with splendid colour illustrations, yet more a general guide than a detailed catalogue. None of the illustrations showed a wooden panel.

An unsatisfactory result indeed.

The other catalogue was older, dating to the 1930s, with only black-and-white illustrations. It included several wooden panels of different periods. One of these was similar to that one offered to Radwan. It was still difficult to say if it was the same one. The illustration in the old catalogue was not very clear and whereas the catalogue entry indicated the size of its panel, Dina did not know what size Radwan's panel was. Moreover, the benedictory inscriptions on both panels were more or less standard and did not allow for a clear identification either.

As a true expert of Islamic art with a detective's talent to spot even the most insignificant details on her objects, she set herself to examine the catalogue entry meticulously. She took out a magnifying glass in true Sherlock Holmes style and compared both panels in detail. She was not sure what she really wanted, though—proof of theft or the opposite. The first would be a reason to be proud of her investigation, the latter a reason not to doubt the integrity of the museum curators.

Finally, she was rewarded.

One vertical letter—an Arabic *alif*—in the catalogue inscription had a dent at its top, possibly caused by a slip of the engraver's hand. That particular *alif* in Radwan's panel had the same dent! There was no doubt anymore.

It had to be the same panel. Radwan's panel had been part of the museum's collection in the 1930s, after which it mysteriously disappeared!

"Gotcha!" said Dina to herself. Finally her detective spirit had won over her love of honesty

She phoned Radwan immediately to share her triumph with him.

He was very grateful for the disclosure.

"Of course, I will not touch it," he told her on the phone. "In fact I had had my own doubts already, which I see confirmed now. Congratulations for your forensic work."

"Who was it that offered it to you then?"

It took Radwan some moments to reply.

"I will give you his name and address if you wish, of course. But I suspect it won't help you very much, Dina. I suppose you want to have the panel returned to the museum in Cairo, which is also my wish. The dealer, a Syrian living in Dubai, is not the owner, however. He has offered it to me representing an anonymous owner, or rather possessor. As soon as I tell the dealer that it was stolen, what will he do in your opinion?"

Dina sighed audibly.

"He will return it to the owner or owners—sorry, possessors!"

"Bravo, Dina, you know the rules of the game of course. And that will not be the end of it. Both—owner or the dealer—might keep it, while pretending to know nothing about it and will remain silent for a while, waiting for an opportunity to offer it to another collector, who is not as honest as I am and who seeks advice from someone not as knowledgeable as you are. But I do not have to tell all this to someone working for Chrosby's."

"They can go into hiding only if there is no proof linking your dealer with the offer," objected Dina.

Radwan laughed.

"Exactly, and he made sure that it could not happen. He came to me in person with the photograph and nothing else. I had to scan the panel myself to mail it to you with no trace of origin. He could always deny everything,"

Dina had an idea.

"You could do something about it, however. Send him an email asking him any question related to his offer. You have his email address, I suppose. Preferably a mail with a subject line like 'wooden panel.' If he answers that we have the written proof for his involvement."

"Well, well! You like to play Miss Marple, it seems. But you will also understand that I do not want to be part of a legal dispute between him, the present owner or whoever might be accused of handling a stolen object. If that becomes known, no other dealer will offer me anything in future. There is a limit to civic duty, even for me."

"Never mind that," said Dina. "He has no reason as yet to doubt your interest in his offer. He will reply, I am sure. After that he will eventually be obliged to disclose the whereabouts of both artefacts if he wants to avoid legal steps against him. The repatriation office can take it from there to coerce him or the present owner of the stolen good to hand it back. There is no need even to mention your name. Our info could have come from a jealous colleague, a family member or someone else who has a grudge against him or the owner. Agreed?"

Agreed it was. The dealer sent the exact dimensions of the panel as requested by Radwan—, proof enough to link him with his offer, just as Dina had intended.

After moving to her new home Dina always took the number 19 bus to a stop near Chrosby's. She had to use public transport, because with no affordable long-term parking facility near her office her own car was useless for commuting.

Public transport in London is quite frequent and convenient, but it has its own negative side, particularly for over-sensitive and intolerant customers like Dina. To be forced to use buses while squeezed together with the usual bus crowd composed of mobile-phone using, backpack swinging and pram pushing customers was bad enough. It was summer now and it had become worse with the smell of often scantily dressed and sweating people during rush hour. Dina had recently tried to resolve this unpleasantness by taking the bus a little later, when the worst was over, or simply by taking a taxi.

One day in July, midway between the spring and autumn sales, she had a visitor, an old acquaintance, who came sufficiently early to be kept waiting for Dina's late arrival.

Martin Laird wanted to see her for a chat. He was a well-known collector and had learned all the tricks of the trade during a lifetime of buying and selling art in London's auction houses and elsewhere.

After she had been served her usual coffee and Martin his usual cuppa he pulled out some photographs from his briefcase and put them on Dina's desk.

"I have been offered these beauties, but I need competent advice as to whether I should buy them," he said. "My bank has no objections although the price is obscenely high, but I am lacking a trustworthy expert's opinion. With all your experience in handling Islamic art objects you can probably help."

Dina did not trust her eyes looking at the photographs. They represented not only one, but five extremely valuable objects—two enamelled mosque lamps dating to the 13th/14th centuries, two early Arabic papyri and a curious silver chessboard with black and white squares—all on sale.

The truly sensational piece amongst them was the chessboard. According to Martin a radiocarbon test that had been made of the ebony wood used for the black squares pointed to the 10th or

11th century as the years of production, roughly the period, when the Fatimids, a Shia dynasty, ruled Egypt. The impurities in the silver confirmed a pre-modern manufacture—a modern forgery would have used pure silver. A Fatimid origin seemed probable, because the dynasty was known for having produced singular objects uncommon at other times, like rock crystal in different shapes, including chess sets. The white squares on the chessboard showed the crackles typical of old ivory. From its looks it must have been a luxury item commissioned by a rich chess player.

"Just look at the inscription on the silver frame," said Martin, giving her a photograph from his pocket. "It's a dedication to a judge who is mentioned amongst other Fatimid dignitaries in the biographies of the period."

Dina had never seen an object as unique as this one.

"Are you really sure it's not a modern forgery?" asked Dina. "If no other authentic piece like this is known, I would have some doubts."

"Just the opposite," disagreed Martin. "Forgers always try to imitate originals, with some modifications in order to make their own piece more credible. Creating something unheard of raises doubts, which an intelligent forger tries to avoid. At any rate the tests done point clearly to its manufacture in the Middle Ages."

"Well, unless we know of its exact provenance, we cannot be absolutely sure," said Dina, cautiously as ever.

Her passion for Islamic art objects made her want to see the objects themselves, to touch and to research them, but she could not give him a detailed expertise in exchange. Radwan had to remain an exception for doing something forbidden by her employers.

"My dear Martin, you seem to forget that I am paid to generate business for Chrosby's. If these items were auctioned I'd have to assess them of course, including their provenance. But put them into auction you cannot, because they do not belong to you. I am not paid to give independent expertise, however."

Martin grinned. His grin displayed a row of large teeth and added more creases to his wrinkled round face, with shrewd and slightly slanted eyes looking mischievously at Dina. Somehow his grin always reminded her of the Cheshire cat grinning at Alice in Wonderland.

"I could offer you money for your expertise, but you will certainly give me one more legalistic excuse that your work contract prohibits you from giving opinions not connected with Chrosby's. Now, what about just helping a friend in your free time? Surely, even your employer can have nothing against that."

"I admire your subtle distinction, which still has not really persuaded me," she sighed. "But I will do you the favour, although I cannot promise anything, especially as you can only show me the photos and not the objects themselves. It could well be that I find nothing out about them."

"You will, you will, because I know you!" purred the Cheshire cat and faded away, not without promising another visit to see the results.

During the following days, Dina tried to repeat the success she had had with Radwan's wooden panel by researching the authenticity and provenance of Martin's pieces.

After her investigations she decided that she needed Rietberg once more to discuss her findings, so she invited him to one of her now customary dinners. There was no one at Chrosby's whom she could trust with her findings, largely because she did not want her colleagues to discover that she spent considerable time during office hours pursuing some 'hobby' of hers, searching catalogues, articles and the internet for clues. She even had to delay writing entries for an auction catalogue that was scheduled to go to press.

Rietberg used Karl's Jaguar for driving to Chrosby's. Marie-Anne usually left it for him, because she preferred public transport for the commute to her surgery.

In the beginning he had a feeling of indecency using the car left by Karl, his murdered colleague. All right—he had slept with Marie-Anne just after Karl's murder and had even moved into her flat, which meant that in many ways he had adopted Karl's role and even assumed his identity. Yet driving Karl's Jaguar was something more intimate than sleeping with his widow. To sit in front of the steering wheel where Karl had once sat, while either he or Marie-Anne was in the passenger seat, was an uncanny experience. He had heard joking remarks about the love relationship between cars and men in particular, which had not meant anything to him because he never felt the need to own one with SOAS being within walking distance from his bachelor flat. But there was in fact something rather erotic in sitting in the driver's seat of a car used by his new lover's former partner, even pornographic, as if the three of them were sharing the same bed together. It took Rietberg a while to laugh off his discomfort as the dreams of a dirty old man, not worthy of a solid professor and husband.

Yet the car was sleek, elegant and fast, and he got used to enjoying his short rides in the city.

He parked in the car-park near John Lewis and walked to Dina's office, where she broke the news about the antiquities.

When Dina told him about her meeting with Martin, proudly announcing her successful research into his objects, Rietberg frowned. For the first time he did not agree with her. He warned her about the danger of what is known as inner resignation, *i.e.* distancing herself from her job without tending a formal resignation.

"If you continue like this, trying to help collectors in office time, who are not even clients of your employer, you risk losing both—your job and your hobby, because only your job at Chrosby's allows you to do what you call your research."

His remark, in particular the bit about 'your hobby' and 'what you call your research', upset her. His higher academic degree did not make him superior—she protested angrily. Rietberg had never imagined that she could have an inferiority complex, with only her Egyptian MA to match his academic credentials obtained in prestigious European universities. Dina, who he had always admired, even envied, had changed recently, and not for the better. It seemed that her disappointment with Alistair and her extended office hours had led to a certain fatigue and he sensed that her present occupation no longer satisfied her. Perhaps deep down she wanted an academic career, which she could have pursued at a considerable sacrifice, but it was too late now. Painstaking research into the authenticity of art objects and even of their provenance, which she had done for Radwan and apparently now also for Martin, came as close to art historical research as possible—doing her job by selling them did not.

Seeing her anger, he realised he had to pacify her.

"Look, Dina, you know as well as I do, how much I admire you and your passion for Islamic art, where you are so much more knowledgeable than I am in spite of my academic credentials. Your MA-thesis alone could have made a PhD at SOAS. So please forget my insensitive words and tell me about Martin's treasures."

She was too eager to report what she had discovered and was instantly mollified by his remark.

"Well I accept your apology," she said smiling. "First, let me tell you about the lamps. They are obviously Egyptian or Syrian mosque lamps of the 13th to 14th centuries."

"I have of course seen such lamps in museums, but I never understood how they functioned," remarked Rietberg.

"They were not actually lamps themselves but transparent containers for actual oil lamps that were mounted inside and have mostly disappeared."

Dina was glad to teach her friend, the university professor, something new to him.

"They were typical for their period, having a fine transparent round glass body with an upper cone-shaped part. As you can see, their silhouette somehow resembles a huge upside-down keyhole. Their enamelled inscriptions enhance the aesthetic value of the lamps that shed a magical light into the dark interior of the mosques. They are truly splendid objects."

"One of his lamps has clearly been stolen from the Islamic museum in Cairo at some time after 1930," she continued. "You remember Radwan's wooden panel with an accidental dent equal to the one depicted in the catalogue of 1930? Well, Martin's lamp has a similar flaw, which is proven by a small break to its foot that is identical to one on the lamp in the catalogue."

"Congratulations," said Rietberg, eager to please her hurt ego.

"I have not managed to find a provenance for Michael's second Mamluk lamp, however. Alistair once saw one in the entrance hall of a bank and told me about it; that was when he was still pretending to be interested in my work. On his second visit it was no longer there. That particular bank is in charge of administering all estates for unidentified heirs, which are automatically inherited by the state, or to give the heir of last resort its traditional name, the *bayt al-mal*. The lamp was therefore without a physical owner and without protection. Yet the possibility that the bank's lamp had also gone to the art market does not prove of course that it was Michael's lamp."

"It would have been the easiest bank heist ever," laughed Rietberg.

"I could not find anything untoward either concerning the papyri. At first sight they could be originals dating to the 7th to 8th centuries, long before parchment and paper became generally used. As far as I was able to decipher them, which is very difficult, they record commercial transactions. But I doubt that they are authentic. They can easily be faked, you know.

The chessboard presents the greatest puzzle, however."

"Which, I presume, you have solved," said Rietberg with a smile.

"Just listen to this story—it is truly remarkable."

Dina's expression was triumphant.

"As I said, it was a complete mystery at first. An object like this, dated to the Fatimids, is truly unique. I know of Islamic chess pieces made of rock crystal; we have auctioned a few of them ourselves. But a chessboard of this exquisite quality: no! I know of none like this one in the art world, neither in a museum collection nor a private one. It can therefore be easily fenced or sold on the open market; because no one can come forward to claim it as the legitimate owner."

Rietberg digested this information, then came up with a critical remark:

"I cannot see then why it's so outrageous to offer it for sale. If it has not been stolen, let the highest bidder win—a museum or a freak chess fanatic. I could well imagine this mad American chess player—Fischer or whatever his name is—buying it with his prize money in order to display it at home and hug it in bed when he goes to sleep."

"But you have not let me finish my story," Dina said, still with a triumphant grin.

"OK, then let's have it then," resigned Rietberg, "you have discovered that it has been stolen!"

"Yes, I have indeed!" said Dina, "but it was more by luck than anything else, I have to admit."

"Of course I did not bother to search in catalogues where nothing like this kind can be found," she continued. "Instead, I relied on my memory, which is very good, as you well know."

She waited for Rietberg's agreement.

"Yes, I know, you always remember every time I spilt my glass at your table, but go on for heaven's sake."

"While I was still a student at the American University in Cairo, ages ago, I had an older friend in another Egyptian university, who participated in archaeological digs near Aswan."

She stopped again.

"So?"

"Doesn't that ring a bell? Aswan was one of the main Fatimid centres in Egypt. Therefore, the late Aga Khan is buried there, because he was a sort of Fatimid prince himself. I remembered vaguely that my friend told me about a Fatimid mansion, probably the palace of a governor or a judge, full of household items that they found buried under sand, garbage and the human refuse of later generations near Aswan."

"I think I know about that find," said Rietberg. "I read an article about such a palace. If I remember correctly, it was published by an Egyptian scholar. Was he or she your university friend?"

"No," said Dina, "it was not her. After much effort I found my former friend again—she is now a professor at a university in the US—and she told me that the head of that Egyptian archaeological team had forbidden everyone else from publishing anything about it. Publishing was his exclusive right, he said, true to form as an Egyptian boss."

"Now comes the interesting part," she continued. "My friend remembers clearly that among these household belongings was a chessboard with ebony- and ivory-inlaid squares. Yet it was never published! My friend asked the team leader later, but the only reply she received was: firstly, the chessboard was still being restored; and secondly, that this was none of her business. As things are in the academic world she could not risk angering him, because she needed him for academic references when she applied for a job. She kept quiet and the chessboard remained invisible."

"So you think that yours is the same chessboard?"

"Of course I do."

"And what now?" asked Rietberg. "What will you do with this information?"

"Well, first of all I will tell Martin to go ahead and buy the one non-suspicious mosque lamp and the papyri, if he thinks they are authentic, but not to touch the remaining objects."

"And then?"

Her expression suddenly became very serious.

"You know what?" she said, no longer smiling as before. "I have enjoyed myself all my life without doing anything I can be proud of. Yet recently my beloved father died, who was the first to awaken my interest in the arts and Egypt's cultural heritage."

"My sincerest condolences," said Rietberg. Dina's eyes had gone misty.

"Something should be done against the theft and embezzlement of these artefacts, and I see now my chance to do something useful at last and also to repay my father for his love and my education.

"I will do my best to have them repatriated to Egypt, where they belong. The art market is where I make my money, but that is no excuse for not trying to do my duty in protecting our cultural heritage, if only on the small scale available to me."

He looked at her, and he did not exactly like what he saw. She sounded like a crusader with a missionary zeal completely alien to the usually relaxed Dina he had known for many years. He suspected that not only the death of her father was responsible for this change, but also Alistair's humiliating betrayal.

"You are right of course," Rietberg said cautiously, He did not want to alienate her once more by openly contradicting her." But you have to see these things in perspective. I read an article recently about globalized crime. Do you know where most illegal money is made? First of course with drugs, followed by art thefts and lately also by computer crime."

"I know that of course," snapped Dina. "What's your point?" She had clearly become defensive again.

"Well, billions of dollars' worth of art goes missing every year, according to the FBI. In the same article I noted that art and antiques worth £300m-500m are stolen every year in the UK alone. Artworks present a better investment than bonds or shares since the financial crash. You cannot possibly succeed in fighting your own war against this global crime wave, just as all efforts to stop the drugs trade have been in vain. Let me remind you of the prohibition era in the US after WWI. Even the mighty American administration with all their law enforcement powers had in the end to accept defeat by the booze addicted public."

"I don't care about any global phenomenon," protested Dina. "I leave it to God to change the fate of humanity. My ambition is much smaller. I want these few stolen treasures returned to Egypt and the culprits punished, and I have decided to devote my spare time to this task."

"But you will make enemies, possibly even dangerous enemies if you go on a campaign like that. With a lot of money at stake, you'd better be careful."

There was nothing else that he could do. Dina was adamant in her resolve.

"I know you, Jürgen. You have many talents, but courage is not one of them. I am different and I am not so easily frightened. I still want to know your opinion as to how I should proceed—only do not try to dissuade me."

"Well, if you insist. But don't say I didn't warn you," he said. "Writing a full report to the Egyptian restitution department alerting them of the thefts should be your starting point. That is certainly necessary, but not enough to push them into action. As you will be dealing with Egyptian bureaucracy I have one more piece of advice: make sure they do not ignore your messages or pretend that they were lost in the mail. You need to ask a trustworthy friend in Cairo to follow-up, meaning to get on their nerves by repeated reminders in person to do their duty. You certainly know a suitable candidate."

Of course she did. Dina knew many people, many more than Rietberg anyway. Mahmoud al-Allamy was an old acquaintance from her study days, who now worked for a private newspaper, which made him the ideal man for the task of motivating bureaucrats, their main concern being to please the minister in charge. Nothing could be more harmful to their career than the anger of His Excellency the Minister, when he had to read negative reports in the press about negligence and corruption in his own department, and Mahmoud was known for his sarcastic comments about corruption and inefficiency at all levels of government—except at the level of the president and his cronies of course. He was enthusiastic to be set on a track for a new article about his favourite target—Egyptian officials. After sending a detailed

report about all three invaluable stolen artefacts to the repatriation committee Dina could relax and wait for the results that
would surely follow.

"Thanks for your tip. Jürgen," she said. "Your advice is
always welcome."

Everything then went according to Dina's expectations. At the
beginning at least.

As soon as Dina reached her office the next morning, her secretary told her that she had a visitor.

"He has been waiting for you since early morning. It must be quite important, because he was already at the front door, when I arrived."

Her secretary had learned to be very punctual in order to humour Dina in the morning, when she was never in the best of moods before she had had a strong coffee. Dina had her own way of dealing with people, by bossing them around in her most charming and most steely manner.

"Did he give his name?"

"No, he will only talk to you. He is waiting in the visitors' room, where I served him a cup of tea."

"Well done," said Dina. "In fact I have other things on my mind right now, but if it's that important tell him that I will see him now. And bring me my coffee, please, if you don't mind."

She hoped that her visitor would not be the same one, who had announced his visit on the phone a few days earlier.

Unfortunately, he was the very same one.

A well-dressed middle-aged man of decidedly Middle Eastern appearance, slightly corpulent with frizzy hair, entered her office with a big smile.

"Dina, how nice to see you after such a long time," he said in English, and without waiting for an invitation sat in the visitor's chair in front of her desk, looking at her with an expression of brotherly love.

"Oh, Halim, it's you," was Dina's none too enthusiastic welcome.

It was her cousin Halim freshly arrived from Egypt. He was in the tourist business and travelled regularly to London for talks with travel agencies, but previously he had never bothered to pay her a visit.

Dina's relations with her family, except with her father, had cooled off after living in London for a long time, and after her mother had for some time inexorably sunken into a demented state. Dina's infatuation and professional work with Islamic art had not particularly endeared her to her other Coptic relatives.

They were all more or less successful in their careers, but had little in common with her anymore. None of her siblings and cousins was interested in anything but money, family squabbling and their children's education, all of which bored Dina. In politics they tended to be in favour of any government on condition that it was against the Muslim Brothers. Understandable with Copts, Dina had to agree, but she was too much of an Arab spring rebel and not a sufficiently devout Copt to have much sympathy with people who saw no harm in a dictatorship that persecuted Muslim fundamentalists and liberals alike.

Of course she had also often disagreed with Alistair's political views, but he was at least well-informed and could defend his opinions with reasonable arguments. Her own family was simply too ignorant of political and historical facts to make their cases convincingly. As patience was not one of Dina's virtues she always became angry listening to her relatives' political opinion. Fortunately, politics were rarely discussed while her father was still present. They had all lived in awe of him and dared not contradict him, because he had always tended to take the side of his favourite daughter.

In fact, nothing bound her to them anymore except almost forgotten childhood memories.

After her father's recent death something had arisen that drew the whole Ghalib family, including Dina, together into a sort of nightmarish quagmire. It was about inheritance, and that can reanimate family relations as well as destroy them forever.

Halim was eager to see her to discuss this particular case—that was clear, although he had not mentioned it yet. He was a master at hiding his true intentions under a veil of superficial friendship.

Dina did not want to make it easy for him.

"Halim darling, I am so pleased to see you. Unfortunately, I am very busy at the moment and have not the time to entertain you as I should and as I would want. Perhaps you can tell me now what is on your mind that is so urgent."

Halim was embarrassed. Under the circumstances he could no longer hide the true purpose of his visit after his extended display of brotherly affection.

"Well," he said, "because you force me to be so direct, it's about your late father's building. We have to do something about it, and we need your approval as one of his heirs."

Of course, it had to be their late father's building or *imara* as they called it in Arabic, even when speaking English. It was located near the centre of Cairo in Dokki. It was worth a lot of money now with real estate having appreciated greatly in value. Their late father had been a successful surgeon and had invested his considerable earnings in property, when it was still affordable for the well-to-do and not just the oligarchs. Cairo had seen property values multiplying considerably recently, although not as much as in London, which made the Ghalib heirs millionaires without any merit of their own.

"I am aware of that. Still, as my cousin you are not an heir yourself, according to my knowledge. Or did father include you in a last will?"

"No, but your brothers wanted me to be their messenger during my visit to London. They think that the matter cannot wait much longer."

"But can't it wait until *arbaeen*?"

"Will you come to Cairo for our celebration then?"

"Yes, I owe it to Baba, and I will certainly join all of you for that occasion," she replied, while shuffling some papers on her desk as a sign for Halim to leave, which he did, without forgetting to say how sad it all was for the family.

A week before she was due to travel to Cairo, Mr Edmond Darcy-Hunter, one of Chrosby's directors, invited her out of the blue 'to do him the favour of having lunch with him'. The invitation left Dina wondering what it was all about.

As superiors seldom invite lower ranking employees to have lunch with them without some hidden agenda, Dina decided to remain on her guard in order to pick up the meaning of even the subtlest signs emitted by her host.

D.H., as he was usually called, was one of the less stuffy board members, affable and always very relaxed. Dina had met him a few times before at Chrosby's staff meetings and occasional receptions. His role at Chrosby's was a bit mysterious, as was that of other board members, but he was known to be rich and to have an impressive collection of Japanese netsuke, the exquisite miniature figures used as pouch and kimono fasteners. She had never exchanged many words with him, because she knew nothing of Japanese art and presumably he knew nothing about Islamic art either.

She was sitting at the lunch table in one of the prestigious Pall-Mall clubs together with her host. He had courteously helped her to her seat, a rare courtesy nowadays.

The lunch started with the usual rituals, with his recommendation of particular dishes 'for which our chef is famous' gladly accepted by Dina. As it was in the middle of the day and she had to return to the office later, the choice of drinks was tricky. Of course in America only soft drinks would do with a boss as the host, but this was England. D.H., a true man of the world, made it easy for her. He insisted on opening a bottle of German Riesling to go with the fish, 'because certainly both of us are not like the Americans who will drink mineral water or even Coke with good food.'

D.H. and Dina laughed, and everything started well.

He was a good host; he told her about his hobby of angling in the wild waters of the world, and some innocent stories of his professional work that seemed to be mainly liaising with the great and the good.

Politely he then changed the subject from him to her, asking her about her experiences in Chrosby's, not forgetting to compliment her on her invaluable work that everyone knew about.

"Our biggest problem is to find a correct way of handling art, always with our clients' interests in mind," he confided in her. "I heard with admiration that you have helped important collectors establish the authenticity and provenance of individual pieces in order to avoid serious mistakes."

That was it! Exactly as Rietberg had predicted. Someone in her office must have informed the upper echelons that she spent too much time helping Radwan and Michael instead of working for Chrosby's. D.H. had mentioned only 'important collectors' and not 'important clients'! It was a warning—a very discreet and very polite one, but a warning nevertheless not to spend her office hours on outside work.

She understood and reacted in the best way she could.

"Just a few hints to encourage them to buy from a trustworthy auction house like ours instead of being deceived by shady dealers," she laughed it off, making the service to her two friends look like part of her official duties.

Yet there was more to come.

"I recently met Michael Laird, a very good friend of mine, who sold me a few netsukes for my collection. He is one of the most honest dealers and a big admirer of yours. According to what he told me you reassured him about some objects he showed you and he is most grateful for that."

She only smiled as a reply. Of course she had reassured Michael about some of his objects, but she had also dissuaded him from buying others that were stolen. She had never hidden her criticism of the cavalier attitude even at Chrosby's of dealing with doubtful objects, and D.H. had obviously been made aware of this as his next well-measured remark showed.

"It is not easy to steer a right course between the ethical duty to deal with legal objects only and our duty to assist museums and honourable collectors to buy and preserve them," D.H. sighed, as if he spent much time thinking about this dilemma.

"I wholeheartedly agree," said Dina, "and that's why my job at Chrosby's is so fascinating."

D.H. was apparently satisfied, and at any rate Dina's charm never failed to work. The rest of the lunch passed pleasantly, and in the end they parted as good friends with the usual empty platitude - 'we should repeat that'.

Back in her office Dina applied for a short holiday break to travel to Cairo. She had never done this in the past when she travelled for a few days. But her lunch with D.H. had made her acutely aware of the potential dangers when you do not comply fully with your job contract.

## Cairo

For the past few hours it had been dark outside with only a few reading lamps lit in the passenger compartment of the British Airways plane. She had finally booked the flight from London to return to her mother country after a long absence. Unfortunately, no seats were available in business class, so she had reserved an economy seat. She was travelling home to attend her father's *arbaeen*, the traditional memorial for the dead. *Arbaeen*, which means forty, *i.e.* forty days after the interment, is the Egyptian version of a wake, with only soft drinks and unsweetened coffee on offer, however. It is an age-old custom in Egypt for Muslims and non-Muslims alike and even modernists like Dina have to celebrate it. She had announced her visit to her family, but without giving precise information as to which date and by which airline. She had also booked into an hotel in Zamalek, not wanting to stay in her late father's *imara*. She did not want to spoil her first evening or a leisurely breakfast that she needed to put herself in a good mood by meeting too early her relatives or her demented mother. It would have been too distressing. In any case her stay promised to be unpleasant, with all the inevitable talk about inheritance and family problems. Better to relax first and confront the family later.

Before squeezing herself into a seat next to an obese lady, she had a pleasant surprise. The stewardess offered her an upgrade to a seat in business-class in a low voice—apparently in order not to arouse any jealousy amongst other economy passengers.

Dina wondered about this unexpected privilege, but wisely enough did not comment on the sudden availability of a business-class vacancy. Perhaps her status as a Silver Member of the British Airways Executive Club, earned by her frequent travel, had caused the upgrade.

Her new neighbour, moreover, was not obese. A courteous middle-aged Egyptian, who even helped her to stow her hand luggage into the upper locker.

After departure he occupied himself with his laptop, while she studied the in-flight magazine with its glossy pages full of reports about international tourist sites, including an article on the Lake

District in England as a patriotic concession to the United Kingdom. The usual touristy praise made her sleepy. She prepared herself for a nap, when all of a sudden her neighbour turned to her.

"Sorry, to intrude, but I could not help noticing your interest in reading that article on the Lake District."

He spoke English with only a slight Egyptian accent. His voice was very pleasant. Manly, but also melodious. Neither a shrill clarinet voice nor a deep double-bass one. Dina was very sensitive to human voices and always classified them in the category of musical instruments. His was a saxophone voice. It prompted her to take a better look at her neighbour, although normally she was averse to being addressed by strangers.

He was middle-aged with curly hair and greying temples, of stocky built and wearing a jacket that looked too cheap for a business-class passenger. Only his intense brown eyes, which matched his voice, made him more interesting than his general looks. Dina responded with a banality about the beauty of the Lake District—just enough to keep their conversation going.

"I have been there recently," he said, "and what I liked most is the lack of crowds. In our country you can no longer escape them—in Luxor or at the pyramids you think you are in China now with all these Chinese around, and elsewhere you have millions of people squeezed into cities that were made for hundreds of thousands."

He had correctly guessed that Dina was Egyptian. He was extremely observant, because without the now ubiquitous head scarf, her slim figure and her lack of accent she could not necessarily be identified as one. An Egyptian who hated crowds—quite an unusual character, she thought.

"Have you been visiting England as a tourist?" she asked.

"Well, at least partly."

He looked at something on his laptop. After a while he seemed satisfied with his search, but still said nothing. After a seemingly interminable silence during which he occasionally looked at her, he smiled. She felt uncomfortable by his indiscreet stares and decided to pretend to go to sleep. But then something unexpected happened.

"I think I know who you are. You must be Dina Trevelyan—correct?"

...

"What? What did you say? You know my name?"

She was utterly surprised. She had never met him before, and when the stewardess escorted her to her seat she had not called her by name. Nor did she belong to the class of celebrities, who appear on TV or newspapers.

"Yes, I am pretty sure. But can you confirm my guess?"

"Well, I was called Dina Trevelyan in my previous life. I am Dina Ghalib now. But how did you know?"

He showed her his laptop. Prominently on the screen was a photograph of her illustrating an Arabic newspaper article entitled 'The scandal of the stolen treasures of Egypt.'

"You have probably not seen this yet. This article was posted on the Internet very recently. You can imagine my surprise when the lady praised for her campaign to protect Egyptian antiquities from corrupt custodians came to sit next to me."

She knew about the article of course. Mahmoud al-Allamy had attacked again and had sent her a link to their webpage. Dina was none too happy about it, however. She had only asked him to follow up the matter with the restitution committee, not to go public too early. There was no need to antagonize people before they had the chance to settle everything peacefully and discreetly.

What a coincidence that her new neighbour had it on his laptop!

...

The stewardess came at the right moment to offer them drinks. Dina had a tea because she knew from previous experience that airline coffee is undrinkable. Her neighbour wanted a coke. Both busied themselves with their drinks, making sure to place the cups precisely in the shallow recesses on the folding tables that the aircraft designers had created to prevent drinks spilling over.

Dina was glad for the interruption. There was something strange in this encounter and her usual awareness suddenly became more acute. Was the unexpected upgrade to business class mere coincidence or something more sinister?

Jürgen's warning came to her mind.

"You will make enemies, possibly even dangerous enemies. With a lot of money at stake, you'd better be careful," he had told her.

She had prepared herself to remain as unobtrusive as possible in Egypt, following up the matter discreetly with the restitution department, meeting Mahmoud al-Allamy in private; and otherwise just getting the inheritance problems behind her. She would not even tell her family anything about these thefts of Egyptian heritage that were the main, yet undeclared purpose of her visit. Now even before arriving at Cairo airport this mysterious neighbour confronted her with the news that he knew all about her mission.

Or was she simply paranoid, and there was nothing mysterious or, even worse, menacing in him?

"You seem to know a lot about me already," she said smiling, while he was drinking his coke with obvious relish, "but tell me something about yourself. What makes you so interested in Islamic art and the theft of Islamic art? That article you showed me is not anything that a normal internet browser would stumble upon by chance. Have you googled to find it?"

Her still anonymous neighbour laughed.

"I expected that question from a lady like you."

Did he only mean 'lady' as a polite term for her as a woman, or did he also know that officially she had been 'Lady Trevelyan'? While she was pondering this new riddle, he took a box from his jacket with his business cards. It was a simple cardboard box, not a silver container appropriate for a passenger travelling business. The card he presented to her read:

Ahmed Selim
Lawyer
Delta Research Association

Added to this, a PO Box in Cairo/ARE and two telephone numbers of a mobile and a landline.

That was all. Nothing more, no other details about his specialty in law nor a street address of either home or office.

Dina studied this slim information for a while.

"Well, Ahmed. I can call you Ahmed I suppose. And please call me Dina. What kind of lawyer are you then? And what does Delta Research stand for? The few lawyers I know are always proud to list their professional expertise in fashionable legal subjects like copyright-, company- or tax-law. What is your specialty then?"

Ahmed grinned.

"Dina—if I may take the liberty of calling you by your first name as well—you are amazing. You do me quite an honour by suspecting an understatement here. But I am in fact someone you might call an all-round lawyer. My day-to-day business is totally unfashionable standard cases of family law and inheritance law with a few cases of penal law thrown in, allowing me to defend some minor and unfortunately only a few major criminals in court. And to answer your next question: the Delta Research Association is a think-tank for the Egyptian government, which I was invited to join, partly due to my good law degrees, but mainly because I have an influential cousin in the Ministry of Justice. All that gives me respect but does not pay much. Are you satisfied now?"

It explained a lot, but not everything. Ahmed spoke impeccable English and was interested in Islamic art and art thefts, which was certainly uncommon in Egyptian all-round lawyers as he had called himself. Moreover, she asked herself how such a humble man with cheap clothes managed to travel business class.

As if he had guessed that question, he gave her the answer.

"Recently I have managed to keep a corrupt official out of jail, where he really belonged," he said smiling. "He wanted to thank me by sponsoring a short vacation in England including business class travel."

"At least a decent way to use corrupt money for a legitimate purpose," Dina could not help remarking. "But let me ask you something else: your Delta Research Association researches what exactly?"

"Whatever the government needs a so-called independent expert opinion for," he said. "Anything—from assessing the chances of an Egyptian initiative in UNESCO to a comparison of the British MOT with the German TÜV, when they want to increase the safety standards for Egyptian cars."

"Normally they make their decision before consulting us," he added laughing. "But it sounds better to have it approved by what is called independent counsel."

There was no point in insisting further. More questions would make her look overly suspicious and give him an importance that he probably did not deserve anyway. She still wanted to know, however, what made him download the newspaper article about herself.

As casually as she could manage, she asked him with an apologetic smile:

"I am satisfied. But tell me what made a lawyer dealing with family matters and mostly unimportant law offenders interested in that article?"

He remained unperturbed.

"Well, I always save the latest editions of that particular newspaper on my laptop. They have a lot of news, sometimes sheer gossip, but often reports about cases of corruption where my assistance could be required later. Their agenda is generally that of an opposition newspaper, but never openly, only under the veil of fighting corruption. But you certainly know that already, having used their services yourself. When I saw you sitting next to me I remembered having seen your picture there."

He yawned as a sure sign that his interest in continuing their conversation had waned, adding in a sleepy voice and without even looking at her:

"One of my few talents is remembering what people look like in reality, having seen their picture once. And do not quote my sarcastic remark about our government, because I would deny everything and sue you for libel."

He closed his laptop, reclined his seat and closed his eyes.

As everyone on board had gone or pretended to sleep, she did the same. She did not know for how long she slept, but when she woke up she saw lights on the ground below indicating they were approaching Cairo.

The instructions for fastening their seat belts and raising the backs of their seats came on, with the usual greetings from the crew thanking them for flying British Airways and "we look forward to seeing you again on board of British Airways."

Her neighbour turned to her and with a friendly expression in his intense brown eyes told her that he had a car waiting for him at the airport.

"If you like I can give you a ride to the address where you are staying. If it is a hotel in town it would be easy for my driver to find it or are you staying with your family?"

"No," she laughed, "definitely not with my family. I have booked into the Marriott Hotel in Zamalek, but no need for you to bother. I will take an airport taxi, so no need to wait for our turn at immigration or the delivery of suitcases. Thanks a lot all the same."

"It's your decision, of course. It was a real pleasure talking to you," he said. "I hope we will meet again."

"Anyway you have my business card in case you need help with any problems your family might cause you," he added laughing. "Or getting you out of prison if needed. Well, my apologies for that last remark. My friends always tell me not to indulge in my tendency to be too witty."

"No need for apologies," Dina said, "I should also apologize for having embarrassed you with my interrogation."

...

She did not know if she had made a mistake by mentioning the name of her hotel.

'My God, Dina, you are not so important after all,' she told herself.

She proceeded to immigration. Only once did she exchange a smile with her neighbour, who was waiting in the line behind her. When she collected her suitcase she did not seen him; perhaps he only carried hand luggage and had no need to wait for a suitcase on the carousel.

She booked an airport limousine from a special counter in order to secure a trustworthy driver and was looking forward to relaxing in her hotel room.

The long way from the airport took much less time than on her previous visits to Cairo. In the past she had driven through congested traffic in the suburb of Heliopolis with its attractive buildings dating from Cairo's golden days, when Baron Empain, a Belgian railroad baron, had created this modern extension of Cairo at the beginning of the 20th century. Despite the congestion, this had made travelling along the airport road much more agreeable than in other towns, where travellers have to drive through drab and even squalid suburbs.

But increasing traffic and congestion had changed everything. There was now an uninterrupted network of flyovers, where cars could drive without crossing other streets and without being stopped by red lights. It was a second, upper level of roads that facilitated circulation, with any reminiscence of urban Heliopolis relegated to the unseen bottom level below. In fact, the new airport road was only an extension of flight routes, not much different from a helicopter commuting between an airport and a helipad on her hotel roof.

Dina was glad to avoid the congestion but also sad. One more sign that the Cairo, where she had grown up and that she still loved for its historical heritage in spite of the crowds and squalor, had changed forever.

'This is what has become of a town, where the Mamluks once produced lamps to give a dim light to mysterious halls in mosques,' she mused. Her enthusiasm for traditional life and art was definitely out of place in a city with millions of cars driving along concrete flyovers.

Her driver interrupted her thoughts, as if he had guessed her sentimental reflections.

"You see how much easier it is now for us airport drivers. I could see your surprise at the new flyovers. They could have saved our livelihood, you must know. Formerly I could travel to and from the airport only once a day, now I can do it several times— that is if I find clients waiting for transport. Unfortunately there are so few now."

"I see," said Dina.

She knew from past experience that engaging in a conversation with Egyptian taxi drivers was not to be recommended for a seasoned traveller. Familiarity, answering questions about herself, her origin and her plans in Cairo inevitably led in the end to demands for an additional tip to compensate the drivers for their losses due to inflation, high petrol and meat prices and raising their many children for a better life.

He made one more attempt, but only met with her stony silence and gave up.

Arriving at the hotel, she nevertheless gave him an extra tip and was rewarded by a thankful smile. He was certainly a poor man trying to make a decent livelihood and deserved something extra, but she did not want to be pestered by the usual *baksheesh* requests. *Baksheesh* was one thing that would forever be part of Egyptian life and one that she did not miss at all.

Her breakfast the next morning lasted longer than usual. The food- and coffee-intake was not the main purpose this time. Avoiding for as long as possible the meeting with her siblings, discussing how to deal with their late father's estate and how to cope with her demented mother, the inevitable reproaches for her prolonged absence and lack of interest in her family were the real reason, why she lingered on, drinking more coffee than was good for her. The staff had already started to remove the breakfast servings and were clearly impatient for her to leave as nearly everyone else had.

Just as she resigned herself to finally phone her family, a waitress came and announced a visitor.

She looked up and saw Mahmoud al-Allamy, her journalist friend, approaching with a broad grin. He was the only person she had given her dates to and the name of her hotel. His pride at having landed one more coup against his usual targets was enough to make him show up so early during her breakfast.

"Hi Dina, *habibty*. So glad to see you. Let me show you something that will make your day," he said, and even before sitting down he took a newspaper from his pocket.

"Mahmoud, where are your manners? Let me welcome you first and let me offer you a coffee, if the impatient waiters still agree to serve you one," she replied, feigning indifference. "What you want to show me can come later."

"Anyway I know already what it is," she added after coffee was brought. 'You have sent its link to me yourself, if you remember. 'The scandal of the stolen treasures of Egypt', an article written by the eminent journalist Mahmoud al-Allamy. In fact, I would have preferred a more informal follow-up at this stage. We do not need any trouble if the matter can be solved discreetly."

He looked surprised and a bit disappointed by her reaction.

"They just ignore you unless you wield the big hammer. Anyway I did not accuse anyone in particular. Without naming any names I just mentioned that these antiquities must have been smuggled out of Egypt."

"I contacted the restitution department after I published the article," he added. "In fact I only met someone manning their office because the department was closed after the Arab Spring and has not reopened since. That man knew of your report, however, and promised it would be answered in due course. According to him all our claims are completely unfounded. After his reaction I hope you agree that we have to put the screws on."

"I hope he gave you the reason for his opinion?"

"He did," said Mahmoud. "Can you guess?"

It was a challenge, and Dina tried to imagine, what they could have found wrong in her report. After some time, while Mahmoud studied with some amusement her reactions, she came up with an idea.

"The only reason that comes to my mind would be that all items I mentioned as stolen were copies of the originals that had never left Egypt."

"Bravo, Dina," he said, clapping his hands in admiration. "That's what the man said in fact. According to him the originals are still safely kept in Egypt, except the chessboard that he even declared to be a totally new forgery."

Mahmoud was right with his scepticism. The people in charge of preserving antiquities simply denied that anything illegal had happened. She and Mahmoud were like the police arriving at a burglary scene, only to be told by the owner that no break-in had occurred and nothing was missing!

"These bastards," exclaimed Dina. "And who were the experts who gave them this opinion?"

"I have no idea," replied Mahmoud, "he only mentioned a committee."

"Of course, a committee always comes in handy if you need to give credentials to something stupid." Similar to the task of Ahmed's Delta Research Association: obediently proposing decisions already made before and by others.

"So what should we do next?" asked Mahmoud. "Request another inventory with you being present?"

"No, we do nothing of the sort," said Dina. "At most they will come up with another select committee of whom at least one or more will express the same opinion as before. More probable is even that they refuse one more examination as an insult to the integrity of their experts. Either you follow up this time with a more specific article with all details of the thefts included, or we write to President Sisi himself. But give me some time to think about the best course of action."

"By the way, I cannot but admire them for their barefaced lies," Dina added as a further comment.

"Why?" asked Mahmoud.

"It's a bit complicated," she said, "and not really important."

"Just try me," he replied laughing, "I am not as dim-witted as I look."

"They pretend to have the originals of the glass lamp and the wooden panel, while our items are only copies. It's an easy excuse: Mamluk lamps have frequently been copied before and a bad copy of a wooden panel could have been easily made from a photograph. They would never fool a real expert, of course, but cannot be dismissed off-hand, which helps to stall everything. Do you follow me so far?"

Mahmoud nodded.

"If they had used the same lie with regard to the chessboard, they would have betrayed themselves, however. No one knew anything about such a chessboard before and therefore pretending to have the original of an unknown and unrecorded object would have given them away. Therefore it had to be a completely new forgery. You see, Mahmoud, they are corrupt, but not stupid."

"Dina, you should change profession and become a detective."

She changed the subject and told him about her travelling companion and his online-copy.

Mahmoud's face darkened.

"So you happened to be upgraded to business-class, where you happened to be seated beside a man who happened to have my article that appeared two weeks ago on his laptop and who also happened to recognize you from your photograph in the article. Quite a lot of coincidences there."

"Now come on, Mahmoud. What do you want to insinuate by your remark?"

He shook his head slightly and pressed his lips together as a sign that she should be more suspicious of her British Airways neighbour.

"My article, which I stand by and for which I congratulate myself, has already caused me some trouble at its manuscript stage when I presented it to the editor for approval, and it could cause you some trouble as well. Don't forget that I am attacking officials for corruption and collectors for theft—mind you, none of them mentioned by name yet. What they fear most is losing that anonymity, and they will do everything to prevent that."

"I am impressed, Mahmoud, by your role in such a dangerous game," she said mockingly, while trying to avert the glances of the now clearly impatient waiters, who had resorted to putting the chairs on the now empty tables, while their own remained an islet amidst all the commotion around them.

"But I cannot see how all this is connected with my neighbour on the plane," she continued. She had of course her own paranoia to deal with, but preferred to remain level-headed while responding to Mahmoud's part in this dark drama.

"Well, you should know two facts. Our newspaper does not make any profit in spite of our large and still increasing readership. We are financed by a superrich prince-cum-oligarch from one of the Gulf states, who does not need his newspaper to make money, but he does want to get his political message across. I can only guess from talking to my colleagues in the political department what his particular political message is—most of the time Islamist and at some other times anti-Islamist as well. It all depends on what is currently in the minds of these arrogant *khalijis*. I am fortunate to be only their scandal or gossip reporter, so I can leave politics aside."

Quite ungratefully to his employer he was talking about 'gulfies', the slightly deprecatory term for the Gulf Arabs used by other Arabs envious of their recent riches.

"They often attack those who share their fundamentalist beliefs, when they happen to belong to another sect. Hard to define these days what our rich Arab brothers want to achieve in reality. But you can be sure—and this is my second fact—that all of them have their allies in a country like ours with her ruling class now compensating by making money for the loss of political clout in the Arab world after Nasser's death. Our rich brothers have their own agents in our country and could well have booked your neighbour's flight on British Airways and have you upgraded to business class after establishing your flight details."

"But what for? We had an interesting conversation about your article—that was all. Why all that trouble and all those extra costs?"

"To know more about you, where you are staying in Cairo for example, or identify you for a distant observer that you are his right target for further observation or something worse—whatever. And why all that, you may ask? Well, I have an idea that comes to my mind: I heard that our benevolent owner is also an art-lover like many other cash rich people are. He is perhaps none too pleased with you, or with me for that matter, after he read my article. Perhaps he even bought one of items that you and I describe as stolen. All that is only a guess, and I could be wrong of course."

Dina thought it over for some time. Could her idealistic crusade that had only just started have made her a target for dark powers? Or was everything Mahmoud said only a conspiracy theory, one of many rampant in the Middle East?

"Conspiracies, wherever you look," she laughed, a somewhat artificial laugh.

Mahmoud remained serious.

"In my job I have to realize that apparent coincidence quite often hides skilful planning or conspiracies, even if you, like many other naive people, seem to dismiss them as pure fantasies. You are in London dealing with a different kind of people than I do. Being a journalist in Cairo as a critic of the ruling class is more dangerous than your job—believe me. A mistake here can make you disappear or be tortured. All that you read in your newspapers, but never experience yourself. So don't dismiss my conspiracy theory off-hand."

"Can we ask you to continue your conversation elsewhere, please? We have to prepare the tables for lunch. I am very sorry."

The interjection startled both of them and they looked at the waiter, who had suddenly appeared with an apologetic smile on his black Nubian face.

It was a relief to have their sombre talk interrupted, and they thanked him profusely. Not knowing why these strange customers were thanking him, the Nubian retreated.

"We should celebrate your article—not indulge in gloomy stuff like this," said Dina, leading the way to the exit. "If you don't mind I want to invite you to a dinner. Let us say in a couple of days. In the meantime, I will have to face a real conspiracy," Dina said laughing. "I am on my way to meet my family, and they are very good at conspiring, even against me."

Mahmoud nodded appreciatively.

"Before you choose a restaurant, can I make a suggestion?"

"Of course, I am no longer acquainted with the gastronomic scene in Cairo."

"I hope you like Felfela, my favourite restaurant. It is quite near to my office."

"Felfela—the *ful* and *falafil* eatery? Are you serious, or do you just want to save my expenses? Come on, I can still afford a dinner in a real restaurant. Or have you lately become the only vegan in this country?"

Mahmoud grinned.

"I am certainly not a vegan, but I have meat only at home, which my wife gets from a trusted butcher. You have been away for far too long to know what cheap stuff they serve now in restaurants. There I prefer to eat *ful*, because we want to use our mouths also for talking, not only for chewing desperately on some piece of well-done steak or kebab from dubious animals."

Dina would have preferred Café Riche in the same neighbourhood, Naguib Mahfouz's favourite meeting place, where he had held court with his admirers long before he was awarded the Noble Prize. Dina liked the place because the owner tended to keep his literary and political café tourist-free by pretending that it was booked-out, whenever he saw foot-weary tourists approaching.

Dina and Mahmoud would be accepted even by the snobbish owner. Yet Café Riche was not famous amongst Cairo's chattering classes for its rather poor food but for rubbing shoulders with literati and journalists, who were certainly not the right company for talking about Mahmoud's daring article.

"So we shall meet at Felfela. Let's say in three days' time, on Thursday at 7.00 pm. Agreed?"

It was agreed, but the dinner would not take place.

"Welcome, welcome—so nice to see you again, Dina darling! We really missed you."

Her cousin Mona had opened the door with a large smile on her pretty face, after Dina had finally rung the bell to Maguid's flat. It was an enthusiastic welcome as custom dictated. Only missing was a *zaghrata,* the ululation Egyptian women traditionally use as a sign of extreme joy, which would have been totally inappropriate during *arbaeen,* however.

"Yes, I am also very glad to see you," said Dina.

The Ghalib building stood in Dokki, a still fashionable quarter on the Western bank of the Nile. Dokki had retained a certain urban charm, not marred by cheap concrete buildings crammed with as many flats as possible. One could walk there along the Nile, have an evening out in one of the many floating restaurants moored on the river, where foreign businessmen used to be invited to 'typical' Egyptian dinners accompanied by 'typical' and very loud belly dance shows performed by Russian dancers with good bodies and less good belly-dance skills.

The ten flats on five floors were large with high ceilings and very comfortable except for the late-night noise from the belly-dance shows that their father had wisely excluded by installing double glazing.

Dina had grown up there and still cherished her memories of a privileged childhood, while her father had been alive and her mother had not yet descended into increasing dementia. Her parents had often taken her out, driving along their street leading to the pyramids at Gizeh, where at a very early age she developed her love for Egyptian antiquities.

Mona leading her to Maguid's flat meant that everyone had assembled there to celebrate *arbaeen.* In many ways she resembled her elder cousin Dina. Both were brunette with the same stylish coiffure, although recent artificial colouring had changed Dina's hair into chestnut and Mona's hair into blonde, considered chic by Egyptian film stars. Dina, who followed a regime, was the slimmer one and more serious, while Mona's fuller figure and more sensual lips were witness to her healthy appetite for life's pleasures.

A lot of people were there—her brother Maguid with his wife and their two teenage children—a boy and a girl, and coming from the US her other brother Yusuf (or Joseph as he was called there), her cousins Mona and Halim with his wife and two teenage daughters and one elder son, in addition to quite a few others, most of whom she had never seen before.

A Coptic priest with his black turban had also shown up to add his prayers to the solemn occasion. All were seated on sofas and chairs arranged along the walls, and were balancing plates with sweets and coffee—unsweetened as custom dictated for this occasion—or tea cups on their laps. Her mother was not present. She was probably sitting alone with her young carer in their father's flat on the upper floor, brooding in her usual silence and possibly not even aware that her husband had died forty days earlier.

Dina's entry had interrupted the conversation, with everyone greeting her with the warmth due to the deceased's only daughter.

Her brothers' and her cousins' children were showing genuine interest in their relative, who lived in such an exciting city as London. She had not seen them for some time, during which they had grown too much to remember her and for her to remember them.

Her cousin Halim, the tourist manager, sprang up first and kissed her on both cheeks. He smelled heavily of cigarettes.

"So you managed to come, in spite of your heavy work load in London," he said. Typically for him, he managed to mix his show of joy with a reproach for not having visited earlier. "*Ahlan wa sahlan,* Welcome, welcome, my dear cousin!"

Dina thanked him and looked at Maguid, her favourite amongst her estranged siblings, who had also risen to greet her. Maguid was the youngest and smartest of them, more elegant and better looking in a rugged way, unlike his chubby relatives. Maguid had made a career in the army, where he had even advanced to the rank of Lieutenant-Colonel, the rank that Gamal Abd al-Nasser had at the time of the revolution. It was unusual for a Copt to volunteer for an army dominated by Muslims and had caused many raised eyebrows in their family at the start of his career, but his undeniable success had stifled all criticism, even making their father moderately proud of him. Dina had always liked him more than the others, partly for his good looks and also because he always seemed to be more sincere, lacking his other brother's and his cousins' hypocrisy.

Maguid looked at her admiringly.

"You have become even more beautiful than when I last saw you," he said, "your marriage to Alistair must have really done you good."

Dina burst out laughing.

"My marriage, you say? Well, I will tell you more about that in private. But let me first greet Yusuf, our American doctor, who I spot there if I am not mistaken."

She had not seen her eldest brother for a very long time and barely recognized him. They had been living apart for ages—he in the US, and she in the UK—never visiting each other, nor had they met during their occasional visits to Egypt, always at different dates. Her father had chosen him to continue the family tradition by becoming a medical doctor. After attending university in Cairo he was sent to the US for specializing in neurology, but had chosen psychiatry instead and was working as a psychiatrist in the US now. He had always managed to hide this change of profession from his father for whom psychiatrists were only charlatans. Moneywise it had still been a good choice in psychiatry-obsessed America, but privately it was really stressful for him to pretend to be a neurologist to his father, for whom he, like everyone else, lived in awe. Fortunately, their father did not like travelling and never saw Yusuf's surgery with its ominous sign of a psychiatrist. Yusuf was married to an American lady. Dina had never met and only seen her in photographs, where she looked typically American. They had two grown-up children. As a result, her brother was more of an American than an Egyptian now.

He was more corpulent than when they had last met and his hair was completely white, which was to be expected in a man of his age. But there were more troubling signs indicating that he was unwell. There were deep rings under the eyes, the corners of his mouth turned down, which made him look like a grumpy old man, and he had difficulty in getting up to greet his sister. He looked quite different from the optimistic and strong student she had seen last.

"Dina, I am so glad to see you after such a long time. I would have wished to meet you at a happier occasion, but such is life."

His voice was a bit quavering, not exactly the voice of a psychiatrist instilling confidence in his troubled patients. To Dina's satisfaction there was no trace of an American accent, unlike that of many compatriots living in the US even for a shorter period.

"Thank you, Yusuf. Later you have to tell me more about your life in America. But I do not want to disturb everyone now by my late-coming. We can talk later."

Dina waved a general greeting at her sisters-in-law and the other visitors. Only the Coptic priest, who had also stood up after placing his nearly empty plate of sweets aside, received the salutation due to him.

"*Abuna,* it is an honour that you have graced us with your presence."

*Abuna* smiled a priestly smile and after a short while opened his breviary and started a prayer, in which those who remembered the words joined in.

Half an hour of meaningless and well-minded conversation followed, but after that non-family members left with more greetings, well-wishing and condolences for the loss of such a great man. *Arbaeen* was over.

She used the opportunity to see her mother in the parental apartment on the top floor, but soon gave up after giving her a kiss on her forehead without any response. Her mother's carer, a young village girl, had been reading aloud rather hesitatingly from a newspaper to her charge. The article she had chosen to read to Dina's poor mother was about President Sisi having received a delegation of governors from Upper Egypt to discuss the recent problems affecting cotton production. It was absurd and made Dina sad. She looked incredulously at the girl and asked her why she bothered to read this banal stuff aloud.

"But, Madame Dina, don't you see?" said the girl with a timid smile. "Your mother likes being read to. She understands more than you think, and it is my duty to entertain her."

Dina was nearly moved to tears and apologized.

"Of course, you are right. Go on with your reading then," she said, placing a kiss on the girl's soft cheek and left to return to her siblings downstairs.

The Ghalibs, alone now, were waiting for her. There was an uneasy silence at first, which was soon broken by her nieces and nephews, who began asking their English aunt all sorts of questions— from Lady Di and British politics down to British food, of which they had heard horror stories. Dina found to her own surprise that she liked their questions and their unaffected curiosity, although she had always pretended to be rather irritated by children. Their presence made a welcome change to the stiff atmosphere of *arbaeen*, and their enthusiasm to meet their aunt contrasted refreshingly with the jaded attitude of her other relatives.

It was obvious that these were impatient to talk about something more serious, and Dina braced herself for whatever was expected from her.

It was Maguid who opened the subject that was on everybody's mind.

"Dina, we seriously have to think what to do with this building now that father has died. You must be aware that it is worth millions now, millions of dollars I mean, and all of us could do with that money. We have unanimously agreed to sell it; we only need your approval now."

So, that was it then. The end of the Ghalib property, possibly the end of the Ghalib community. Dina had expected something like this, but was still shocked.

"All of us need the money, you said? Well, I do not, thank you very much. I doubt also that our brother Yusuf needs more money, with his surgery in the US, where medical doctors earn a lot, as everyone knows."

She was looking at Yusuf for approval, but he did not comment.

"Do you then need more money, Maguid? What do you need it for—to buy a new home elsewhere, after you lose your big flat in this house? I doubt that your share in the sale will allow you to find a new property even remotely equivalent to what you have here."

Maguid's wife wanted to say something, but he cut her short.

"Fawziya, leave that to me. This is a matter that concerns only us, the children of our late father," he said, not in an unfriendly way, but in a manner that left no doubt that she should shut up. Fawziya shot a hostile glance at Dina, as if her sister-in-law was responsible for Maguid's remark.

"Not only do we need the money, but also Halim does, whom we have to help to make up for his recent losses. The last terrorist attacks brought tourism down. He had bought a flat when the sun was shining, but he is barely able now to pay the mortgage rates. Am I right, Halim?"

Halim nodded, looking downtrodden like his wife, who wisely refrained from joining in.

"Yet I suppose that apart from the building, our father has left enough to cater for all your needs?" asked Dina.

"Unfortunately not," said Maguid. "His treatment and our mother's long illness cost a lot of money in spite of other doctors offering their service for free to a former colleague. Besides that, our father did not want to make many sacrifices in his lifestyle, even after retirement, when he had no income. No—unfortunately there is not much left, and one day we would all have been needed to help support our parents."

"But apart from all that, we are facing something more serious now," he added. "I have been wanting to talk to you about this for some time. Did you have a chance to look at our neighbourhood before coming in here?"

"No, not really," said Dina. "It looks decent enough to me."

Maguid laughed.

"Yes, we cannot complain. It is very decent and even too secure and I will tell you why. Facing us on the river side is a heavily guarded building with soldiers on sentinel duty twenty-four hours a day. It is the home of one of my superiors, an officer of a much higher rank than mine. I cannot tell you more about him, but the general plans to have our building included in a high-security cordon to block out possible snipers or terrorists. Our

building, which could easily serve as a base from which to shoot
or throw grenades at his one, is designated to be the home for
more top brass, who need protection. There is a spirit of paranoia
now, understandable enough if you ask me after Mubarak's down-
fall, the Arab Spring and our Muslim brethren being keen on
taking revenge. Still the military do not want to expropriate us,
not least because of me," Maguid added, "a step they could easily
take under the present regime, and they are offering us a good
price. So now you have the full picture."

Everyone was looking at her waiting for her reaction. It was
obvious that all of them had been aware of these plans and had
been briefed by Maguid. But how did he know about the general's
plans?

"How did you know about this idea?" asked Dina, "has this
general approached you already and how much do they offer?"

"You know or you might not know that I am the head of the
housing division in the National Service Products Organisation,
the civilian outfit of the army."

He smiled.

"A typical Coptic job, of course," he said. "Somehow they do
not believe in our talent as warriors, but rather as administra-
tors—yes, that's where we have been best since the times of the
Pharaohs. And that's why I was informed about these plans, even
before father died."

The rest of the family had never been comfortable with a son
who had chosen a military career instead of becoming a doctor, an
entrepreneur or a bureaucrat, all of them decent professions for a
Copt. Yet Lieutenant-Colonel Maguid still had his place in the sec-
tarian Muslim-Christian division of work, because he was a pen-
cil-pusher instead of commanding in the trenches. Dina nearly
liked him for that and his characteristic irony missing in her other
brother and in her cousin Halim.

She had never suspected though, how serious the simple
matter of their inheritance had become.

"To reply also to your remark about buying a new flat for
myself," Maguid added, "I have the promise of the general that I
can continue to live here. You see, I am being quite open with you.

All of us will receive a lot of money, and Yusuf and I intend to help Halim and to find a decent home for our mother also; anyway she does have her own share in the inheritance and will not be left out. Of course you are welcome to join us in doing so, because, as you said, you are not in need of money. On the other hand, not only Yusuf but also you don't need an flat in Cairo, so everyone is a winner."

"The promise of your general, you said?" Dina smiled ironically. "If he later reneges on his promise, what can you do? Anyway, that is not my business. You are certainly wrong, however, by assuming that I do not need a flat in Cairo. It's quite the opposite. Since my divorce from Alistair, I intend in future to divide my time between London in the summer and Cairo in the winter! British pensioners do it all the time between their homes in Britain and Spain, and I will do the same."

Maguid tried to save the situation by the proven method of postponing a decision for later, when Dina would come to her senses.

"I beg you to think everything over. You might find during your stay that Cairo is no longer the pleasant city you remember. But please, don't wait too long. I will have to decide what to do before you leave. By the way, the general has offered one million US-Dollars, which is a lot in view of their strong position, because the possible threat of expropriation is an important bargaining chip. He and I know that the building is worth much more, of course, and if we make it easy for the army I could certainly convince them to double their offer. However, you must give me your definite reply before your departure."

They had dinner brought in truc neo-Egyptian style from a near-by pizzeria, during which the main subject of conversation was Dina's divorce. Maguid's wife and Dina's cousin Mona had a lot to say about a subject where their opinions were permitted. Halim's wife had no opinion, which Dina took as a sign that in her view to be divorced was not so bad after all. Mona was particularly knowledgeable, being twice divorced and the Ghalib's own version of Zsa-Zsa Gabor, as her cousins used to call her. The actress's famous quote 'I never hated a man enough to give him his diamonds back' had also earned Mona her reputation. Mona had managed to be married (and subsequently divorced) to two expatriates, one British and the other Italian, whose divorce settlements had left her enough to live in style, even though her efforts to become a famous novelist had never gone very far.

Dina was tired and soon retreated to her own flat below that of her parents. It was too late to return to her hotel now, and she wanted to inspect her Cairo pied-à-terre. It was clammy as any home not used for long time, and she opened the windows in order to breathe fresh air. The belly dance shows on the river were in full swing. Right across from their building she saw the sentinel boxes with soldiers guarding their neighbour's house, the anonymous general, who was threatening their future in their own home. The soldiers, smoking cigarettes while leaning on their guard posts, looked harmless enough, except for their machine guns they had put down, ready to be wielded again, whenever a duty officer appeared. Dina tried to imagine what would happen if instead of an officer a gang of terrorists appeared to attack these defenders of a hated regime. They would certainly not give the guards sufficient time to pick up their weapons before gunning them down.

It felt uncannily sinister to be in what had become the unfamiliar surroundings of her childhood, while the menace that loomed over their inheritance could be seen nearby.

Dina had a lot to think about. What to do with their mother? She did not know much about dementia, certainly less than their mother's young carer, but to move her from her flat, where she had lived with her husband for so many years, seemed cruel and could possibly cause her so much distress that it might trigger her premature demise. What to do with the other tenants? The apartments that were not occupied by the Ghalibs were rented out. What was her own legal situation? Was her approval to sell the flat needed or could she be outvoted by the other heirs? How serious was the threat mentioned by Maguid? As an insider to army affairs he should know, but on the other hand he could have his own agenda for gaining a promotion by pleasing his superiors. He had already been promised his own flat back, when their building was allotted to privileged army officers. And finally, what would be her own share after the sale of the building?

She knew a lot about stolen art and the protocols set to recover it, but next to nothing about Egyptian inheritance law.

Dina sighed. She needed expert advice, but from whom? It would not be wise to ask her family to recommend a lawyer, that was certain. Lawyers tend to take the side of people engaging them, when they differ from those consulting them. She could not be sure of an unbiased opinion in this instance.

Before going to bed she looked into her wallet to check if she needed to change more money. There was a business card amongst the cash. It was her mysterious neighbour on the plane's card, the all-round lawyer, as he had described himself, with inheritance law included in his practice expertise.

She decided to contact him in spite of her misgivings about his possible involvement in the art theft matter. He was certainly intelligent and could help her. And she could also learn more about him and his agenda under the guise of her brief on inheritance law.

"I am glad that you called, Madame Dina. I had already intended to phone you myself."

He had answered her call immediately, after she rang him during another lengthy breakfast session. No secretary, no switchboard—just Mr Ahmed Selim, the non-descript lawyer himself. Did he possess an office at all or was he conducting his business from home or from a desk in the Delta Research Association?

"Why?"

A short silence.

"You can certainly be blunt. Let us say that our conversation on the plane made me eager to see you again."

"Well Ahmed, I am flattered, if all you are interested in is conversation. I am however more interested in tapping your expertise in inheritance matters. That is one of your subjects, if I remember correctly. My family is causing me problems after our father's recent demise. Could you help me, please? For a reasonable fee, of course."

"Any time, Madame Dina. Always at your service."

She almost sensed him grinning over the phone.

"Could I meet you then in your office today?"

She already knew the answer.

"No need to bother. I shall come to your hotel, whenever it is convenient."

He had no office, that had become blatantly clear by now, probably only a desk in the mysterious Delta Research Association, where he could not invite visitors.

"Let us say at 5.00 pm then."

To spend only half a day of free time in Cairo in a meaningful way had never been easy, and even less so in recent years. Traffic congestion reduced the time that could be spent visiting museums, the old city or the pyramids so much that it was not worth the trouble, unless you had a full day at your disposal. On the other hand, staying in the hotel waiting for Ahmed Selim was not ideal either. Watching TV, reading newspapers or trying to have a siesta was all she could do. She could have avoided this ennui by inviting her lawyer to come round immediately. He did not seem to have other pressing engagements anyway and could certainly have come earlier. But she did not wish to give him an impression of urgency, which weakens your negotiating position, as she knew from her own business. Art sellers in urgent need of money were always at a disadvantage, when they dealt with traders, auction houses or other collectors.

Dina decided to have a stroll along the Nile, walk towards the Ritz Carlton, the former Nile Hilton on the opposite bank of the river, have a *shisha* at their terrace café as she had done so often before and return late for her appointment. To ensure that Ahmed would wait for her return she told the receptionist of her plan, although she was certain that Ahmed would wait anyway.

"Be a bit careful, Madame Dina. Recently there were some attempts to rob tourists just outside our hotel. Men in police uniforms pretend to check their papers and then abduct them in their car, dumping them somewhere after stealing money, credit cards, even passports. Security in this country is not as before, unfortunately."

Stepping out of her hotel she saw through the polluted haze of modern Cairo across the river on the eastern shore the familiar landmarks—the Ramses Hilton hotel, the Ritz Carlton hotel, the Arab League building and that of the National Democratic Party, Mubarak's fig leaf for his dictatorial regime. At this distance it still looked ok, although it had been scorched to a charred ruin during the Arab Spring.

A *felouka* with its distinctive lateen sail had left its mooring in front of the Ritz Carlton hotel with tourists on board for a Nile tour. The dark and fast flowing waters of the river in the foreground and the *felouka*, the traditional sailing boat, represented the eternal Egypt. But was it really eternal? Dina, hesitating, not sure if she really wanted to go on a long walk now, remembered the famous words of the Greek philosopher Heraclitus: that you can never step into the same river twice. The waters change and so do we. So much had changed recently, and so had she. Even to reach the Qasr-el-Nil bridge on foot had become much more difficult than before for pedestrians who had to climb stairs to reach a ramp that started at some distance from the river to allow for the continuous and unimpeded flow of cars crossing it. She was older and tired more easily. Eventually she decided to remain in her comfortable hotel awaiting her appointment with Ahmed Selim.

There was even a *shisha* service in their garden café, where she sat for the next few hours contentedly smoking apple-flavoured *shisha* tobacco together with drinks—starting with tea and ending with several whiskies, reading newspapers and working on her laptop.

"Oh, there you are already," she greeted her visitor, who interrupted her lazy afternoon. She looked at her watch. It was 5.00 p.m. Her idea to keep him waiting for her had certainly not worked.

Ahmed sat down, ordered a coffee with a curious glance at her whisky-tumbler, and said:

"At your service, Madame Dina, what can I do for you?"

She told him about her family and about Maguid's request to agree to the sale of their family's building, but omitting the army's intention to acquire it for their own use.

"Do I really have to agree? I still want to keep my flat and stay there, whenever I want."

Ahmed looked at her with his intense brown eyes. In spite of his cheap clothing and his common features she found him suddenly quite attractive. He exuded an energy and a vigour that somehow belied his description of himself as a lawyer of no importance.

"Are you the owner of the flat, or do you just live there, when you are in Cairo?"

"I just live there without owning anything in the building, just as all the other family members. My father, who owned the whole building, had wanted to give a flat to me in ownership before I married and moved to London. He wanted to secure my position in case I came back, if something in the marriage went wrong. But the others were not happy with this privilege, so my father never followed up on this idea."

She laughed

"My father was always suspicious of pretenders, particularly foreign ones. He had heard too many stories about English soldiers proposing to Egyptian girls to get them into bed, although they had wives waiting for them in England. Now I realise that he had another motive—he exaggerated the danger of foreign predators just to keep me at home."

What on earth had made her tell all this to a complete stranger? She had never been so spontaneous or even incautious before. Strange what a separation from a long term bedfellow had done to her. There was no doubt that the cheaply dressed Ahmed had charisma. Was she really attracted to him?

She decided to be more reserved in future, as she had been on the plane.

He had apparently not noticed her rather impetuous confession.

"Unless a judge decides otherwise they cannot force you to sell your share in the building. You can be sure that this is enough to stop their plans. Our courts are not known for their speedy dispensation of justice."

Ahmed lent back, smiling. A bit too smugly for Dina's taste.

She reached for her whisky glass that was empty, but she needed some time to think. After pretending to drink she asked:

"And what is my share?"

Ahmed took a mobile phone from his pocket.

"Thanks to modern technology I have this app with all the information needed. You told me that apart from his widow your father is survived by you and your two brothers. Give me a few seconds."

He clicked several times on his miraculous app and came up with the result in no time.

"In percentage terms it's 12.5 percent for your mother, 17.5 percent for you, and double your share, *i.e.* 35 percent, for each of your two brothers."

"What? My brothers' share is double of mine? You must be mistaken. All of us are Copts, we are not Muslims and the Sharia with its discrimination against women certainly does not apply to us."

She laughed, "you only have Muslim clients apparently—so you'd better get another app from the Coptic patriarchate."

His smug smile was still there.

"No Dina, not I but you are mistaken. You have lived too long abroad to know about Egyptian law. Copts like Muslims are still ruled by the Sharia in inheritance matters in spite of their efforts to change that. Moreover, according to Islamic law the individual portions of heirs cannot be altered by a last will, if your father even made one."

"He did not as far as I know. He only took our promise to let our mother live in her flat as long as she lives."

"Well," said Ahmed, "that is more a question of morals than of law. His wish alone has no legal consequence, and even a formal last will can only stipulate bequests to outsiders and not to one of the legal heirs. Of course, you can always agree amongst yourselves to respect your father's wish or to distribute the estate equally amongst sons and daughter. But in my experience that is rarely done even in the Coptic community when dealing with a valuable estate like yours. Brothers have their own and that of their family's interest in mind first. Your own brothers will not be different and will be quite happy with the Sharia rules."

"Bloody...," she nearly made a shocking remark about Islamic law, but stopped herself in time. Ahmed was a Muslim after all.

"Yes, you might think it's unfair, but in our society men still provide for their women."

The conversation had become too delicate for further argument.

He continued.

"How much is your building worth? Without having seen it— about two million US-dollars perhaps?"

A strange coincidence, for this was the exact value Maguid had mentioned. Had he guessed that figure with the knowledge that there were ten flats as she had just told him, or had he seen the building himself or had he even talked to Maguid? Nothing could be excluded when Ahmed was involved.

"I cannot give you a precise estimate without seeing the building myself. How many flats are there?"

"Ten, on five floors."

"With ten flats and assuming a total value of two million US dollars your share would be around 350,000 US dollars. Still not bad if you ask me."

He had arrived at that figure without even using a calculator.

"Of course the value of the building is only guesswork. In case of a sale it could differ widely from that. It would probably be even unsellable, if you insist on retaining your flat or if any tenant has to be forced to move out. Potential buyers always prefer an undisputed vacant property."

Dina had more or less made her decision already, but this calculation by the amazing Ahmed made her think twice. She wanted to have a pied-à-terre in Cairo, and since her separation from Alistair even played with the idea of moving back definitely. A share amounting to USD 350,000.00 could not be neglected either of course.

On the other hand, all the money talk was pure guesswork, as Ahmed had indicated. Added to this, money received in Egyptian Pounds had to be exchanged into British Pounds, and with the expected amount it would not be too easy. She did not need the money anyway and certainly did not want to go to the trouble of buying another property in Egypt, which would probably cost considerably more. She wanted her own family flat, with all her childhood memories attached to it, and that was final.

Felfela was crowded with the usual mix of young tourists and Egyptian families accompanied by their children. The restaurant, which specialised in all kinds of *ful* dishes and *falafel*, had for a long time been a popular fixture in Cairo's gastronomic scene and sported at the entrance newspaper articles with photographs of prominent customers, of whom Jimmy Carter was definitely the most prominent one. The food was delicious if you liked the staple dishes of traditional and simple Egyptian cuisine and it had, more-over, one advantage over similar eateries, and that was Stella beer! No concession to sour-faced fundamentalists here, and Dina was certain it would remain so after the Muslim brothers had been brutally evicted from power by the almighty military.

She had arrived in good time for her dinner with Mahmoud, but he had not shown up yet. Normally he was punctual and even the usual traffic jams could not be used as an excuse, as his office was nearby. But, investigative journalists such as him could always be delayed by something important, so there was no need to worry.

Dina did not want to order anything before his arrival and just had a peppermint tea.

After half an hour's waiting and after she had finished her second tea she started to worry and phoned him on her mobile. No answer! She left a message, trying to hide her impatience.

Another fifteen minutes later she knew that something must have happened.

His office would probably know more, but she had not both-ered to note the address on her mobile.

Besides, she was hungry, and could not sit there for any longer simply ordering more peppermint teas.

She ordered an array of dishes with names like *iskandarany* or *shakshouka*, together with a bottle of ice-cold Stella beer. Normally it would have been a delight to indulge her love of these dishes she had known since childhood. Yet thinking of what might have happened to Mahmoud soon made her lose her appetite.

She left her meal unfinished after a last attempt to locate Mahmoud by asking the waiter if he knew by any chance the address of his newspaper. Her question resulted in the usual

Egyptian overflow of help for 'Madame', also volunteered by other waiters and even by one of the customers who joined in, but with no useful information. When the customer tried to engage her in a conversation about the newspaper's politics, she left in a hurry.

The hotel receptionist knew the address. Mahmoud had told Dina that his office was near Felfela in downtown Cairo, but to her surprise his newspaper headquarters was far away, in one of the new suburbs that formed a ring around Cairo like the few petals of a withered flower. It was in 6th-October City, near the desert road to Alexandria, which was named after the start of the last war with Israel in 1973, considered a victory by both sides. The choice was probably prompted by lower property prices and a more secluded location, all of which was important for a courageous opposition newspaper that according to Mahmoud struggled to survive under an increasingly oppressive regime.

She left without a reply and directed a taxi to 6th-October City in order to learn more about Mahmoud's whereabouts.

Her visit remained inconclusive. After being sent around a few times she finally met someone who knew more about Mahmoud than just his name.

"He rarely comes here, because he works from home," this friendly staff member told her.

Well, well, apparently Mahmoud had not wanted to admit that he had no office but worked from his laptop at the kitchen table.

She tried Mahmoud's number again hoping for a reply this time.

After a while a quavering female voice answered.

"Who is it?"

"I am a friend of Mahmoud's, and yesterday we agreed to meet at Felfela this evening. Could I talk to him, please, because he did not show up?"

"Are you Madame Dina?" the same voice asked.

"Yes, indeed I am, so he has not forgotten after all. You must be his wife, right?" Mahmoud had mentioned once that he was married, but Dina had never met his wife.

She heard sudden sobbing coming over the phone line.

"So you don't know yet? Mahmoud was arrested last night."

More uncontrollable sobbing followed.

"What? Arrested for what?"

Dina was shocked. To read about repression and arbitrary arrests was something completely different from experiencing it so close to home. That this was an arrest without any legal justification was obvious. Mahmoud was a man of the pen and not one of action, and apart from writing about corruption was not involved in politics. He liked to attack injustice—a bit naively perhaps—where he could find it, but he had never been an activist himself, trying to change the world by more forceful means. Not even drug dealing or rape, which form the usual accusations when nothing else will stick, could be associated with him.

There were of course many other victims of the heavy handed military rule, which was, however, still welcomed by many after the chaos experienced during the short reign of the Muslim brothers. Yet all these cases remained rather abstract, when discussing Middle Eastern politics over a glass of wine. Mahmoud, the enthusiastic crusader against the cancer of corruption, was a friend, and not a nameless victim, and it was her friend, who had been taken away from his home to ...yes, to where in fact?

"Where is he now? In a police station or a prison? I want to see him as soon as is possible."

"I don't know! No one has told me anything. They just carried him away and only told me to wait and shut up!"

The poor woman cried loudly now.

"I would like to see you, if you agree," said Dina. "Just give me your address and I will come round as soon as is possible."

The flat in Huda Sharawi street was very close to Felfela, as Mahmoud had described his 'office'.

It was a normal lower-middle class flat as could be expected. Dina guessed that Mahmoud or his wife had inherited the contract from a parent. A continuous tenancy from Nasser's time was protected against rent increases, which made land developers eager to get rid of these unprofitable tenants. Mahmoud had once told her that the building was owned by the Ministry of Waqfs, who had already tried to persuade them to relinquish their tenancy so their building could be sold to a land developer. It had prompted him to write a scathing article about the housing situation in neo-capitalist Egypt.

Mahmoud's wife, a rather plump woman in her thirties, led the way to a living room whose walls were completely covered with bookshelves. A quick look revealed the owner's main interests—history and politics—which proved that Mahmoud could never have made a career in Egyptian politics.

After the customary Turkish coffee was served, Saniya proceeded to tell Dina the whole story.

Her husband had recently received warnings from undisclosed agencies passed on to him by an acquaintance whom she did not know. He had told Mahmoud that it was unpatriotic to always concentrate on the negative side of things happening in Egypt and that it would only help the country's enemies. He should soften his tone—or else!

Well, they did not say 'or else', but it was understood.

"But my Mahmoud has always been stubborn, with me, his editors, the neighbours and God knows who else. He told me that his last article was dealing with thefts committed by bribed officials and that he had problems obtaining his editors' approval for it. Apparently it was about a case you had told him about."

Dina nodded. There was something of a reproach in Saniya's expression.

"He did not want to disappoint you and as usual he ignored me."

Saniya had averted her eyes. It was clear that she resented Dina for being somehow responsible for Mahmoud's arrest.

Dina felt guilty, although she doubted that Mahmoud was in trouble because of her. He had only accused anonymous corrupt officials of theft, without even mentioning any names. They could safely ignore it or at most threaten him with libel suits. But his arrest meant that the police or other elements had unknown reasons for being afraid of him.

Upon leaving, she promised Saniya to find out, where they were keeping Mahmoud.

Yet before learning more about Mahmoud's whereabouts, she encountered a major setback herself. More serious than she could ever have imagined.

When she reached her hotel late that evening and before she could even enter the lobby, a young woman wearing the usual headscarf approached her. She had apparently been waiting outside for Dina and asked her if she was Ms Ghalib.

"Yes, I am," said Dina with a smile.

The woman immediately grabbed Dina's handbag and winked at some men, who were loitering in the shadows, quietly smoking cigarettes.

Suddenly Dina was seized from behind by what felt like at least ten strong arms, a smelly hand covered her mouth with a broad sticky tape and a hood was put over her head. Someone tied her hands tightly with a flexible yet strong plastic band. All this was expedited quickly and efficiently as if her abductors were well practiced in this.

Her last view was that of the woman looking impassively at her while still holding her unopened handbag. The unseen assailants bundled her and threw her into what felt like a metal box.

Even if someone else had witnessed this incident—and Dina had not seen anyone—there was only a slight chance of an alarm being raised. The latest upheavals in Egypt made everyone prefer to look away instead of interfering.

She soon became aware that she was in a car or a pick-up van. When she thrashed around; all her frantic movements only resulted in impotent bangs on the vehicle's floor and its sides.

Then there was the sound of a revving engine being turned on and the boot, or wherever else she was lying, started to vibrate slightly to a rhythm dictated by the movements of the car driving away.

Dina was so stunned that at first she did not realize what had just happened. Parts of her body started to ache from the brutal push into the car and from lying on a bare, metal floor unprotected by anything soft. Worst of all she was having breathing problems under the hood and what seemed to be a blanket thrown over her, probably to conceal her human shape from view. With her hands closely tied she was unable to tear off her hood. In order not to suffocate she tried to breathe as flatly as possible. The complete darkness under the hood prevented any orientation as to where she was and where she was heading.

Now fully aware of her desperate situation, Dina followed the instinctive and basic commands of her body that demanded as much comfort available under the circumstances. Lying on her side she stretched herself as far as possible and even touched something that felt like a tool bag, which she managed to use as a cushion for her head.

She remained still for a while after all that exertion and tried to think and concentrate on her situation. She had been kidnapped, arrested, taken away or abducted—whatever terms best described the activity of these men driving her away. They could be policemen, security agents or simply criminals, if such a distinction was even possible in her case.

The most obvious solution to regain her freedom was to ask for help on her mobile. The men had been in such a hurry that they had not searched her before throwing her into the car. There had been no need for it though. With her taped mouth she could not speak anyway, and the impassive looking woman at the hotel entrance still had Dina's mobile in the handbag.

Realizing that she was completely helpless hit her hard. It was a cold fear that crept into her veins, the fear of anyone facing unknown horrors or even death. She had never experienced fear before. Dina had always led a protected life, first in the care of her father and later by Alistair. The sensation of real and overwhelming fear was new to her, and it made her incapable of thinking clearly.

Being an avowed agnostic she could not even pray. The continuous waves of fear and increasing claustrophobia made her almost faint while lying motionless in her narrow prison.

The car continued, now more smoothly without the shock of sudden braking. They must have reached an empty road, away from the stop-and-start Cairo traffic.

These observations made her forget her fear momentarily. To analyze the reason for leaving Cairo worked similarly to focusing on Islamic art objects in order to be distracted from Alistair's betrayal. The comparison made her nearly laugh; at least it opened her mind for clearer thoughts once more.

She remembered the receptionist in the hotel mentioning gangs, often disguised as policemen or even being policemen themselves, who kidnapped unwary tourists to rob them of their belongings and to dump them later in a desolate spot outside of Cairo.

These could not have been real policemen, however, in spite of all the rumours accusing the police of criminal activities. The worst days of the break-down in public security were over, when the police were themselves sabotaging the Mursi government by creating disorder. Now they had reverted to their usual activities, including sometimes excessive use of force to clamp down on any act considered to be a violation of public, or better, political, security.

There was moreover one clear indication that they had not targeted her for money. They had bundled her away only after making sure that she was Dina Ghalib, not someone else. If the plan had been to rob anyone wealthy, such as other guests arriving with Louis Vuitton suitcases and crocodile leather handbags, they certainly had had many opportunities for that prior to her late night return.

To know more about her abductors she tried to listen to what they were saying. They were very careful, however, and did not talk except for a few monosyllabic directions given to the driver from someone sitting close to her—probably on the back seat.

Slowly cold fear crept in again. If they did not want ready cash, were they doing it for ransom money, keeping her indefinitely in a rotten hole, until she died of thirst or millions were paid? Or did they simply want to kill her?

Her crusade for the return of stolen antiquities could not be a reason for murder or could it? She knew too little about the criminal side of the modern antiquities market, although her friend Rietberg had told her not so long ago that it was second only to the drug trade that certainly had its own share of killings.

The car moved further along the empty road, heading for a destination where she would finally know her fate.

Suddenly the vibrations stopped and after a short while also the engine noises ceased. The car had come to a halt. Dina heard the doors slamming, when her abductors stepped out of the car. She waited for the back door to be opened, yet nothing happened.

She was thirsty by now, and her longing for ice-cold water or an ice-cold beer was as strong as her mounting panic at the thought of never being found again.

After what seemed an interminable time, the back door was opened. She was helped out of the car—surprisingly without any more roughness—and her hood and shackles were removed. She stood shaking in front of three masked men. She felt so relieved that she nearly thanked them for releasing her from her prison in the boot. All wore black balaclavas, which made them look fearsome, but which was less threatening than if they had shown their faces. Undoubtedly they did not want to be recognized later, and Dina took it as a sign that they did not intend to kill her.

One of her legs was numb after the long ride in her uncomfortable position, and she had to support herself by leaning against the car.

Its license plate and even its make on the back door were covered as well. Dina's heart leapt with joy. It was another reason not to fear for her life anymore.

The place was deserted and the ground was flat and rather rough. Only a few lights somewhere on the horizon indicated that they were not on the moon, but on earth with human settlements. The surrounding darkness was only lit by the myriads of stars adorning the unpolluted desert sky. The air was fresh and the complete silence was uplifting after the noise and the vibrations of the car.

Then one of her kidnappers spoke in a muffled voice under his balaclava.

"Now, listen carefully, Madame Dina. We have been ordered to give you a lesson. It is the first, but it will also be the last one. You are a not an Egyptian anymore and you have no right as a foreigner to insult Egyptians by telling them they are criminals. I think you understand what I am talking about. We will let you go now and you can walk to where you see the lights and seek help for your return to Cairo. You are lucky this time—next time it will be quite different! It would be the best for you if you forgot about Egypt in future."

He then climbed into the back of the car after a short salute from the other two, who jumped into the front seats.

With that they drove away. She saw the dust trailing behind their car for a long time, before they finally disappeared.

Dina was very relieved, but also very tired and sore and needed a rest. She wondered if she should stay there and wait for the sun to rise, when she could be spotted by a passing car and seek help. The idea was not unrealistic, because she saw tyre marks that did not belong to her captors' car. Yet the only way to rest would have been to lie or sit uncomfortably on the ground, while freezing in the cold night air.

She took a deep breath and started to walk towards the lights on the horizon. It proved to be quite a difficult terrain, as she stumbled several times on unseen stones.

But in spite of all her fatigue she kept trudging along. It was amazing how resilient human nature can be in extreme circumstances. The walk lasted interminably, until she approached what seemed to be a large village or even a town.

She soon realised where she was. Her kidnappers had dumped her near Wadi Natroun, the site of formerly isolated Coptic monasteries halfway to Alexandria, and now a quite populous town. The first person Dina met in the early morning hours was the driver of a small van with a load of onions. He nodded knowingly after she stopped and told him that criminals had abducted and robbed her.

"This has happened before," he said and sighed: "what has become of this world!" It was a remark she had often heard from people lamenting the fate of humanity in general, and of Egypt in particular.

The world-weary driver took her to the door of the imposing Amba Macarios monastery, where she was greeted by a friendly monk, who seemed only mildly surprised by his dishevelled visitor ringing the door bell at an unseemly hour.

Her story of an abduction by criminals met with no surprise here either and prompted the monk to give her 400 EGP to pay for the bus ride back to Cairo and the taxi to her hotel.

He wore traditional dress with a close fitting cap adorned with crosses and a long black *abbeya,* but he looked more modern and was definitely younger than the few poor and mostly uneducated monks, who had populated the monasteries in Nasser's time.

He declined her offer to return the money.

"We have become quite wealthy recently with our home-grown crops and can afford it," he said smilingly. "Just make a contribution to your own church. I can see you are probably a Copt yourself."

"It's true. But how can you see that?"

The monk laughed: "No *higab*, sister! You do not wear a head scarf as all Muslim women do nowadays."

"You are in good company, by the way," he added smiling. "In the 1930s a very famous writer crashed his plane near-by and was rescued by a Bedouin, as you were by our onion man."

"I know of only one writer who owned a plane at that time—Antoine de Saint-Exupérie," said Dina drawing on her education at the Lycée Français.

"Bravo, sister. It was him and our desert here was even an inspiration for his *Little Prince*. Unfortunately, it was only the prelude to another crash, when he died."

A Coptic monk who had heard of Saint-Exupérie—the new religious wave had brought some progress after all!

The dreadful experience of the last few hours had ended with a lesson in French literature that Dina had heard before. She had read the *Little Prince* and also had learned at school about the last part—Saint-Exupérie's fatal crash. Yet she did not see the writing on the wall— rescue from one misadventure does not protect the victim from a second fatal one!

Dina walked through the lobby of her hotel. She needed sanctuary from her anonymous attackers. The manager to whom she wanted to complain about her treatment from the abductors would certainly deny all knowledge of it and only blame her for being imprudent by returning alone late at night without someone protecting her. Could she trust anyone in this country now?

Instead she simply asked the receptionist for her key. Before anything else she wanted a hot shower, a triple whisky from the minibar and a long rest.

The receptionist exclaimed with a very friendly smile: "oh, Madame Dina, we are so glad to have you back. We tried to contact you in your room, but it seems you were away the whole night. I have a pleasant surprise for you, just wait a second."

He disappeared into the office behind his desk for a few seconds, and when he came back, he held something in his hand.

Dina's handbag!

"Someone found it just outside of the hotel and handed it in to us."

Dina could not believe her eyes. It was considerate of her abductors not to add theft to kidnapping.

She rummaged through the bag and found everything there, including both her wallet and her mobile phone.

"Thanks a lot, I have missed it already, and I even had to borrow money to pay for my taxi."

And adding just for fun:

"Could I have the finder's name, please? I would like to give him a reward."

"No, she did not leave her name. But she gave me a short message for you."

The receptionist did not continue. He seemed quite embarrassed.

"And what was that message?"

"Sorry, Madame Dina, but I am only the messenger. The lady requested me to tell you 'khalass!'. That word only, although she repeated it once more."

"So they want me to stop? Stop what?" asked Dina the totally perplexed receptionist, who had no answer either

She had a long, warm and utterly relaxing shower, then downed a triple whisky followed by a single one, because there were only four mini-bottles in the bar. She tried to analyze what had happened to her, while lying slightly drunk on the bed's soft mattress of her bed and not on a car floor hurting her body.

The abduction remained a complete mystery that defied any rational explanation, First of all, she could not imagine what had provoked such a drastic measure taken by the security services against her, even if in Egypt the understanding of the rule of law was quite different from that in Europe. She had denounced the theft or embezzlement of Islamic art treasures by anonymous functionaries of the regime—but so what? Egyptian newspapers—even those of the state press— regularly published tales of corruption, without their journalists facing persecution. What made her antiquities so special, that not only was she brutally abducted but also Mahmoud was put in prison, because both incidents were without any doubt related?

Then her even more mysterious release, the return of her handbag and her mobile and the strange message accompanying it?

The effects of fatigue, the hot shower and the whiskies set in slowly. Dina drifted into a long sleep with nightmares about being locked in a windowless dark room.

The bright light outside and the noises of an hotel awakening chased her gloomy thoughts away. She was alive and well, and that was all that mattered now.

Her next thoughts were about Mahmoud, her faithful ally, who was rotting in some prison. She tried to convince herself that she was not responsible for his article that had landed him in trouble, one that she never intended him to write—at least not at this stage. Yet somehow she had caused it, her picture was prominently displayed and without her talk of corruption he would not have published it. Moreover, she had promised his wife she would find him, without even knowing how.

The strong breakfast coffee revived her completely. She had to do something—but what?

In the middle of her thoughts Dina saw a waitress approaching with the message that she had a phone call. Someone to talk to was exactly what she needed now. She only hoped it was not one of her family, but Ahmed, the efficient and enigmatic lawyer, who moreover seemed to be interested in her.

It was Ahmed!

Impatiently she interrupted his introductory remarks on the phone and requested him to meet her in the lobby as soon as possible, which he did as promptly as could be expected from a lawyer without an office.

They had a very long talk, only interrupted by having to move to another place, when someone came to sit beside them.

Dina had decided to tell Ahmed everything—from her visit to Mahmoud`s wife, the abduction, her release and the strange messages accompanying it. She also told him about her crusade to repatriate Islamic antiquities to Egypt, which could explain both Mahmoud's arrest and her abduction, although she could not imagine why. Originally she had planned to ask once more for his advice in her inheritance matter, but that could wait now.

Ahmed listened attentively with his intelligent eyes fixed on her. When she had finished, he tried to console her by patting her leg. His hand rested on her thighs a bit too long perhaps, but she did not mind. After all she needed sympathy and also she found him quite attractive.

"I suppose you need some assistance now, but I cannot think of anything I can do," he said after a while. "Your kidnappers behaved completely out of character. We know the Mukhabarat are thugs, like all security services in our country—well, possibly also in others. Yet besides the brutal abduction itself all what followed seemed to be only a part of psychological warfare. They released you after a few hours with only a warning. That is somehow too considerate for the normal Mukhabarat, so who were they in fact, I wonder?"

"They even returned my handbag and my mobile."

"That does not smell of the Mukhabarat at all." His face had darkened, as if there was worse than the Mukhabarat." Mobile phones with all your contacts registered are usually of great value to them. Probably they made a copy of your directory. I will have to be careful in future using my phone."

"Sorry," said Dina. What else could she say? Her campaign had only caused trouble up to now, not the success she had expected.

Being abducted by a secret service who robbed her handbag and her mobile phone and later returned everything as a sign of good-will? It made no sense. She and her friends had become the target of a very anonymous group, who did not like something she had done, whose aim was to give her a warning, but not to harm her. What she definitely needed now was help.

She had an idea, how to get Ahmed on her side without having him suspected to meddle in security matters.

"For my inheritance problem I will need a lawyer after my return to London. Let's arrange that now, and no one—not even the Mukhabarat—will suspect that we discussed and will discuss anything else. Inheritance cases are part of your activity anyway. They would not waste their time by tapping your phone then."

Ahmed laughed.

"Not wasting their time is the least of their concerns. Anything can be of value to the professional snoopers and time does not count for them, because no one holds them accountable. Yet—you are probably right. Your idea will certainly remove me from their limelight."

"We will do it by the book then: a power of attorney plus an agreement on your honorarium—all that to be documented to make it official."

"I have one more request though," she continued. "I promised Mahmoud's wife to find her husband, a bit too hastily perhaps. Can you possibly help? No need even to mention anything about Mahmoud's campaign. You would just be a lawyer engaged to find an innocent husband arrested for unknown reasons and possibly have him released. Of course, you must have a mandate from his wife, not from me, although I will take charge of your fees for that as well."

Ahmed thought it over for a while.

"Well, I do have contacts in prisons—to inmates as well as to directors. I could do you the favour, of course, and you know why I will do it?"

"Why?" she asked, wary he would say something embarrassing.

"Because I admire women with a warlike spirit."

She blushed, something she had not done for long time.

The train to Alexandria had left Ramses Station with Dina on board. She was looking forward to seeing what had become of her family's former summer resort and to visiting the Bibliotheca Alexandrina. A quiet and relaxing break from her stressful days in Cairo—at least that's what she had planned.

Unfortunately, she had a companion. Her cousin Mona was nattering along without even taking any notice of Dina's need to rest and most of all her need for silence. Mona had immediately proposed joining her, when she mentioned her plan during a short visit to her family. She had not intended to contact them again right now, but then decided to show her presence in case news of her abduction had reached them. No one seemed to know anything about it though, and she did not mention it either. To make them aware of her problems was the last thing she wanted to do. They would immediately use her misadventure to demonstrate how dangerous Cairo had become and that it was only in her best interests to liquidate anything she held in the city, including of course her share of the family home.

"I saw a documentary on TV about the Bibliotheca Alexandrina recently, and I could be helpful in explaining everything about it," Mona said, which made Dina fear the worst.

The train was passing through Cairo's drab northern suburbs and Mona's explanations were in full swing. From the Ptolemies and their original Bibliotheca Alexandrina in late antiquity, via Julius Caesar, Marc Antony and Cleopatra and the Arabs down to Suzanne Mubarak, the now disgraced sponsor of the modern Bibliotheca—Mona had memorized everything. She was not stupid, only half-educated and a nuisance. Dina's efforts to cut her short by telling her that she already knew all about that were quite useless.

"Of course, you are the intellectual of our family and you know more than the rest of us," Mona admitted, which did not prevent her from continuing with her Bibliotheca-lesson.

Dina resignedly closed her eyes and cursed herself for allowing her cousin to join her on what was intended to be a relaxing excursion after her recent ordeal.

The train rattled along, the seats were comfortable and Dina started to doze off with casual polite interjections like 'is that so?'

or 'that's very interesting'. Outside nothing reminded her of the green fields speckled with the white egrets she had seen in her youth. It was all built up now, mostly cheap looking buildings with unfinished upper stories marked by steel rods pointing forlornly into the sky. They had been put up in the general building frenzy and were waiting for the owners to acquire the additional funds needed for completion. This was the ubiquitous sign that the new Egypt, now overpopulated with 80 million people, was no longer the leisurely Egypt of the past, when travellers came to enjoy exotic sights and cure their lung diseases in the still unpolluted dry air.

They approached Tanta now, halfway to Alexandria, when a lull in Mona's talking offered some respite from their one-sided conversation.

Suddenly Dina had an idea how she should sap her companion for more useful information.

"Tell me, Mona," she said, "what is it that makes my brothers so eager to sell? Our building is a good investment besides being our home. So why sell it? It doesn't make any sense to me."

Mona's face brightened up. Dina's disinterest in her Bibliotheca-saga had been all too obvious, even though she was trying hard to impress her intellectual cousin. What was required now was gossip, and Mona had always been very good at it. With her seemingly innocuous question Dina had opened a reservoir of information with its floods inundating her from the seat beside her. It lasted until they approached Lake Mariout just outside Alexandria.

## Gossip on Maguid:

He was now the unofficial head of the Ghalib family, despite being the youngest one. The eldest, Yusuf, lived abroad and did not count. Their cousin Halim had trouble making ends meet, was none too bright and did not count either, rather like Mona who did not for other reasons, mainly for being a woman. Maguid's employment in the army—although initially regarded with scepticism and disapproval by their father—had paid off well. Perhaps in the beginning he had been a quota-Copt in that traditionally

Muslim institution, but he knew how to make friends there, mainly influential ones. His most influential friend was the very general with the ambition to acquire the Ghalib building. "You know what I am even thinking?" asked Mona with a knowing grin on her pretty face. "I think that all this was originally Maguid's idea! Together with his chum in the army he concocted a plan to make money on the side by having the army pay for the building, including his own commission, and by granting him a grace-and-favour flat there, probably his present one, on favourable terms, or even for nothing."

"Grace-and-favour flat? What on earth do you mean by that?"

"Don't forget that my first marriage was to an English diplomat, who told me all about the feudal customs in your country. A grace-and-favour home is one of the perks granted to your nobility, when they retire."

Dina was suitably impressed.

"If that is true, why don't the other two not protest against his scheme?"

"It is not easy to challenge Maguid. You have seen yourself how he cut his wife short, when she wanted to interfere. Not that she didn't deserve it. Besides, your brother Yusuf and my brother Halim have their own interests in selling, although for different reasons."

Dina began to look at Mona very differently now. In that pretty head of hers—devoid of all the ballast of conventional education—she had developed special talents for which even Dina envied her. With her capacity for observation and psychological insight she would certainly have been aware of Alistair's betrayal much earlier than herself.

### Gossip on Halim:

Halim had done well in the tourist trade, while it was booming. He was employed by an important tourist agency; had negotiated with foreign partners to bring in tourists, was mostly travelling in business class thanks to special conditions granted by Egypt Air because his customers were regularly booked on the national carrier. The salary was good and used to be supplemented by annual bonuses. But the recent adverse news on Egypt, such as: repeated terror attacks against the police, against foreign tourists and the Coptic minority; reports of horrendous accidents on planes, buses and trains due to negligence; and the general Middle-East-malaise had led to a fall in tourist numbers. The agencies had had to downsize. "I think that they even sacked him a short while ago, although he does not admit it." Mona seemed genuinely saddened by the reverse of his luck. "After all that he had done for them! I think that he is trying to set up his own agency, and he might even be successful. He has formed a network of foreign partners for his employer, who call him Mr. Pyramids, and with some sweet talking he may have them switch their business over to him. Some of his present colleagues might also join him, before they get the sack themselves. But for start he needs ready money or a wealthy partner."

"You seem to know a lot about his plans," said Dina, "although he never mentioned them to you, as far as I understand."

"No, he did not, why would he? I am only his dumb sister. But I have seen quite a few of his colleagues, whom he has never invited before, coming to his flat, where they stay for hours. And there is something else that has struck me as being of interest. Recently he and Maguid have secretive talks together, which they always break up, when they see me coming. Knowing Maguid, it must be something concerning the army. Now, what do you make of that?"

"If I can guess correctly what's on your mind—no, Mona! You must be wrong."

"No, I don't think I am! Our army's main purpose is not to fight the enemy, at least not foreign enemies. It is to make money! They are engaged in all kinds of business, even though you might not be aware of that. Yet I have never heard of them being in the tourist trade. Why not try to gain a foothold in a field that is promising in the long run against all present odds? Your well connected brother Maguid together with his equally well connected cousin Halim, and Maguid's influential general as a third partner.

Makes sense, doesn't it? Now you can certainly understand why both of them want to sell. They want to have the start-up money in order to make much more later, and all of that by pleasing the army that is in control of everything."

They had changed roles: Dina, the sophisticated and cosmopolitan member of the Ghalib family, receiving lessons from the half-educated Mona, whose only contact with the outside world had been hapless and divorced foreign husbands.

"Mona, I think I misjudged you. You do have a sharp mind."

"Never mind, I am used to being misjudged, most of all by my *khawaga* husbands."

She laughed happily

"Well, to complete this interesting survey—what do you think of Yusuf?" asked Dina.

## Gossip on Yusuf:

He had been abroad too long for Mona to know much about him. Before his present visit he had come only once to Cairo with his wife and stayed a few days in the flat reserved for him before making the usual tour to Upper Egypt. "Poor man, married to this woman! She is afraid of everything here," said Mona." Imagine— she won't eat anything before she has washed it herself, and she doesn't use tap water for that—only bottled water. I wonder what she does in restaurants, except take over the kitchen herself. She only went outside, when Yusuf accompanied her; she was probably afraid of being raped by a savage Arab."

"Only even savage Arabs would prefer a camel to this skinny lady for doing something like that," Mona continued, laughing.

Dina started to like her. It was not only her pretty face, but also her uninhibited spirit that made her quite remarkable.

"And of course—no smoking! A cigarette is regarded as more dangerous than a smoking gun in the US, and poor Yusuf had even been smoking a pipe before his marriage. He has been in America long enough, however, to stop smoking forever. All the others, including me, were glad when they left and we could return to our bad habits."

"He looked somehow sad to me, when I saw him during *arbaeen*," remarked Dina.

"I would get depressed myself if I were married to that bitch! But in answer to your question about the sale of the building – of course, he is in favour. What can he do with property in a country that has become alien to him and that frightens his wife? Money is always better, although he probably does not need it."

"We did not talk about you," said Dina, "you seem to be an interesting person yourself."

Mona smiled.

"My dear cousin, you have managed to extract a lot of information from me, without giving anything in return. But never mind, I like talking about myself."

It was mostly about her husbands (the first British, the second Italian), how she met them (working as a secretary in both embassies at the right time), what they did (the Brit a diplomat; the Italian a businessman), how they were (the Brit nice, romantic, full of subtle humour; the Italian nice, more macho-like and full of more coarse humour), why they separated (the Brit becoming a bore and a philanderer; the Italian becoming a brute) and what they left her (the Brit money; the Italian a flat he had bought her in Cairo).

She also had something to say about her present life, *i.e.* her present love life.

"I am deeply in love once more," she confessed, "but this time marriage is going to be more difficult."

"Why? Is he still married?"

"No, he did not even have a girlfriend before, which makes him particularly charming in his inexperienced ways. Anyway I have enough experience for both of us."

She grinned.

"But he is another diplomat, and this time from the Gulf. So he is a Muslim, besides being a member of the ruling family there. We could of course marry legally, but in order to be accepted by his family and also to be entitled to his inheritance I would have to convert to Islam first.

"And that's what I am not willing to do."

She sighed with an unusual show of resignation. "I am not a devout Christian myself, as you can imagine. But in spite of that and even though I am neither interested in politics nor in religion, I could never become a Muslim with an Islam like we have now. Besides, our family would shun me forever, and I could not bear that thought."

"So what do you do then?"

"What most people would do in our situation. We meet, we sleep together, he buys me presents, very expensive ones by the way,"—she flashed a large diamond ring of several carats—"and we enjoy life."

Dina's idea of a good life was rather more conservative, but she could not help thinking that Mona's lifestyle had also something to it.

"You will probably also want to hear what I think of the idea of selling the building, although I did not inherit anything from my uncle and I have no share in his estate. To put it bluntly: I simply do not care! Besides the one rented in your building I have my own flat, which I always use when I want to meet someone in private, and if they sell I will save the rent and stay in my own flat all the time."

"So why don't you stay there now?"

"I like company unlike you—even our family's company," said Mona.

They were approaching Alexandria railway station now and on leaving the train took a taxi to the Bibliotheca Alexandrina, the original purpose for Dina's excursion. She had learned much more from Mona's gossip, however, than by visiting the library with its imposing building and less imposing book holdings. After a nostalgic lunch at the venerable Hotel Cecil they took the train back to Cairo.

The main result of their trip was that against all expectations the two very different women had become friends. Dina even told Mona a little about her work and her latest endeavours to repatriate Egyptian antiquities. Mona's knowledge about that seemed to be limited to the bust of Nefertiti—"where is it now—in Paris or London?" she asked—but she listened with interest, because it reminded her of something she had heard from her new lover, the *khaliji* diplomat.

"Jasim—that's his name— once complained to me that one of his uncles pesters him all the time to buy antiquities in Egypt and to smuggle them out of the country by diplomatic courier. Unfortunately, his uncle holds a high position in the emirate and Jasim cannot ignore him. He insists, however, that he has never managed to buy anything that was not a fake. I am saying this, because I do not want him to become one of your targets."

"I will forget what you told me," laughed Dina. "I certainly do not want to start a fight against your lover."

She was still not sure if Mona would sometimes during another gossip session have something unkind to say about her as well, but that did not matter. What would really matter later, was the role that Mona's love life played in investigating Dina's sudden death!

She spent another night at the hotel instead of in her flat and woke up early the next morning with a pang of conscience. Her demented mother living above her flat and her scheming brothers were not the neighbours she was keen to see. And her new friend Mona intended to meet her *khaliji* lover that evening in her own flat.

Yet the sense of her guilt was not caused by avoiding her family. She had been enjoying herself, while Mahmoud was in prison—most certainly for the same reasons for which she had been abducted and for which she was responsible. But she was free, whereas she had as yet no information which prison he was languishing in and if he had suffered the usual welcome beating or not. In fact, she did not even know if he was still alive.

It was too early to contact anyone. At any rate she could not call Mahmoud's wife before having definite news about his whereabouts.

Taking breakfast before knowing what to do later is not very relaxing. Yet again Dina tried to delay any action for as long as possible by ordering more coffees than was good for her health. She read the day's newspapers that were hardly uplifting for her spirits either.

Finally there was nothing else to do but return to her room.

Reclining on her bed she switched on the TV to distract herself from her frustration.

In the midst of a vintage black-and-white film featuring the famous singer Farid al-Atrash accompanying a silly story with his schmaltzy songs the phone rang.

"There is a Mr Ahmed Selim here, who would like to see you," said the receptionist.

"Send him up, please."

Dina was overjoyed. She liked films with nostalgic reminders of her childhood, but Ahmed, hopefully with good news, was much more welcome now.

He carried a bouquet of roses that he pressed into her hands and said: "Congratulations, Dina. Mahmoud is free!"

Dina did not know what to say. Her eyes welled up, and she was on the edge of tears.

She hugged Ahmed and kissed him on both his cheeks. He was not well shaven, and it tickled her, but at this moment Ahmed appeared to her as a knight in shining armour having slain the dragon.

At first he seemed surprised by her reaction, but it did not take him long to understand that her hug was not only a sign of gratitude. Then something happened that she had not thought possible before.

Ahmed scooped her up, carried her to the bed while returning her kiss, this time on the mouth, and started to undress them both. The flowers fell to the ground, without either of them even noticing. All this happened so forcefully that she could not have resisted even if she had wanted to. But she did not want to—her sensuality that had been suppressed long before breaking up with Alistair resurged and she let herself go with an intensity she had not felt for a very long time.

Both rested in bed after what had been another adventure for her—for the first time a pleasant one. They did not talk much, which was all the better, and in spite of this newly created intimacy he had not lost his slightly ironic ways, which gave her a sense of security. She had never felt insecure before, even after Alistair's departure, but the recent events had given her a disturbing feeling that everything around her could crumble at any moment.

After a while she asked him a question that had been on her mind since they met on the airplane.

"May I ask you a question?"

He laughed.

"I am married, if that's what you want to know."

"No, Ahmed. I couldn't care less about your marital status," she said, a bit offended to have been taken for a sentimental—or worse—a moralistic woman. "What I want to know is if you have been somehow set up to me, to follow me or control me, whatever. I think after - how do I put it? - we have become more intimate, I am allowed to ask this question. Our first meeting and the newspaper article on your laptop were a little bit more than sheer coincidence, are they not?"

"They are not! "he said emphatically. "I have been aware of your suspicion since the beginning, but it was really only a coincidence."

"A very fortunate one in fact," he continued, giving her a hugging squeeze on the arm. "How do you imagine otherwise—which dark powers would have been able to let us sit together on a flight to Cairo that we both booked separately and without even knowing each other?"

"Well, I admit to having discussed that with Mahmoud, and he could imagine a certain scenario."

"Which brings us to Mahmoud with his other scenarios," said Ahmed, "the reason why I wanted to see you in the first place."

"I know," said Dina, "but unfortunately we seem to have been distracted."

Both laughed. But Ahmed became serious once again

"I found him in a prison cell at a police station, not in Tura or another of the more sinister penitentiaries or 'corrective institutions', as the Americans say in their hypocritical way. It was not even difficult to get him out. The first of my usually well informed sources I contacted told me where to find him. It only needed very gentle persuasion to have him released on bail that I could easily provide in view of the moderate amount. I almost had the feeling that they were only waiting for a reason to release him, which was strange. They did manage to scare him to death though by a threat that if he continued publishing libellous articles the next treatment would not be so lenient."

"Thank God all the same," said Dina, "I was already fearing the worst. I suppose he is back with his wife now?"

Ahmed turned towards her with his intense brown eyes unblinking.

"Yes, he is and if I were you I would wait some time before contacting him. Well, this reminds me of your own case. Both of you received a painful slap on the wrist with a stern warning to keep silent in future. Very frightening indeed, perhaps executed by some thugs from the Mukhabarat, but certainly ordered by more sophisticated authorities, who do not want to really harm you, unless you disobey their orders."

"But don't be mistaken," he continued, "next time they will harm you or Mahmoud for sure."

The harsh reality had come back after a totally pleasant interlude in Dina's life. Neither of them was in the mood to resume their erotic activities.

Yet when Ahmed got up to go to the bathroom, Dina started to giggle.

No man likes a woman do that after lovemaking, and Ahmed was no exception.

"What is so funny?" he asked.

She became embarrassed.

"Never mind, Ahmed," she said. "Never mind."

The worst thing to say in such a situation. He insisted on a reply, this time with clear signs of annoyance. There was no escape.

"You won't believe it," giggled Dina, "but this is the first time I have seen a circumcised one."

He gasped and broke out into loud laughter, greatly relieved. His sudden fear of being ridiculed in his manhood disappeared. So after that they fell upon each other for a second time.

Mahmoud was sitting on a sofa with his wife close beside him. Something in her attitude reminded Dina of a kidnapper she had seen in a film, who was hovering over his hostage on the phone, ready to slap down the receiver at any moment, when the hostage said too much.

Dina had gone to his place against Ahmed's advice. She could not leave Egypt before at least saying good-bye. The wife's less than friendly looks and Mahmoud's unusually timid expression made her almost regret her decision. Something had to be done though to get things right and to let them understand her own position.

"I am so glad that my friend Ahmed, whom I contacted as soon as I left you," she said, looking at Mahmoud's wife, "managed to get you out of prison so quickly," now looking at Mahmoud.

"Oh, it was you who engaged him," said Mahmoud, shooting a sideways glance at his wife. It was clear that she had not mentioned it nor was she prepared to say anything positive about Dina, in her mind the person most responsible for her husband's misfortune.

After a while Mahmoud opened up a bit, with his wife, still looking unfriendly, glued to him.

"They did not really treat me badly, just handled me roughly as could be expected," he said. So he got the same medium-rough treatment as she had.

"But they made it clear to me that there were things of greater importance than the disappearance of Fatimid antiquities, and that I had endangered matters of national security by my article. Have you any idea what they could have meant?"

It was asked in a tone of reproach.

"No," answered Dina, "I have not the slightest idea. I myself would never engage in Egyptian politics, nor would I have drawn you into such a dangerous game."

Mahmoud seemed to believe her, but not his wife, who even smiled sarcastically at Dina's reply.

Mahmoud ordered his wife to prepare Turkish coffee for all of them, a gesture that normal hospitality would have required before. His wife obeyed, shooting one more hostile glance at Dina.

"You must understand, Dina, that my idealism to fight corruption in every form that you well know is limited by the care I owe my family for our security and livelihood. And that will be in danger if I meddle with what they call matters of national security, *i.e.* almost everything as understood by our rulers," Mahmoud said.

"I suppose you know our famous saying 'if you see the lion's teeth, don't think he his smiling'," he added. "The lion's teeth have nibbled at me, but I do not want him to devour me. So no more Mamluk lamps, Fatimid chessboards or wooden panels for me—stolen, embezzled or destroyed, whatever."

At first Dina had intended to tell him of her own experience with the lion's teeth, but now decided to keep quiet. There was no need to frighten her beaten co-crusader or his wife more than the police—or whoever else—had already done.

They drank their coffee in silence.

With a last wish for their good fortune she left, to everyone's relief.

A "let us stay in touch" met with only a nod from Mahmoud.

She should have informed the embassy about her abduction. She had been a British citizen for a long time thanks to her marriage to Alistair, and unlike her surname she had not taken her original citizenship back after their divorce. Even a divorce did not justify exchanging a travel-friendly British passport for one that needed visas for nearly every country in the world.

But what could she tell the embassy? She had no proof of what had happened, and now she had reappeared unharmed, unrobbed and unraped. How could she accuse unidentified security people of having kidnapped her? What would they think of her? One more hysterical woman with a sunstroke perhaps? Any diplomatic or consular contact with the Egyptian authorities would not yield a result either. Even if they knew anything about her abduction—and that was far from certain—they would simply go into denial.

No, she would keep quiet now, and she was sure that Ahmed would have advised her to do so. As a lawyer living in this country he knew that it was not wise to antagonize the very people whose favour was needed occasionally.

To give up on her crusade of saving Egypt's national heritage from greed, was still a painful decision. Everything in her combative character revolted against conceding defeat. Yet, nothing could be done now in Egypt anyway, after Mahmoud had backed out and after she had received her own brutal warning.

The one thing that remained for her to do in Egypt was to face the challenge of her scheming siblings in their inheritance case.

If Dina's motives had been only rational, she would have given up here as well. Egypt had proven to be a dangerous country for her, her family meant nothing to her, and she had a comfortable and financially secure life in England with an interesting job. She would certainly not return soon and live even for a short period in polluted Cairo, while nourishing nostalgic memories in the neighbourhood of a resentful family. The only pleasant experience she had was with Ahmed, and that could not be easily repeated—he was a married man after all. Yet—who knew? Their affair could still continue, if they were still in the mood then—in London for example, but perhaps also in her Cairo flat.

She had been obstinate all her life, a trait in her that Alistair had often complained about. Most decisions—in fact mainly the banal ones—in their marital life had to be made according to her wishes and whims.

Whatever the arguments raised against it, she had decided to keep her apartment, and that was it!

All the frustration with her aborted antiquities campaign had made her all the more adamant that she would thwart her brothers' plans to sell the building, which also meant a lot of damage to the interests of the remaining tenants and most of all those of her poor mother.

She called Halim and asked for a family reunion.

The day before her departure she had another phone call in the morning.

"Mustafa Fezzani here. Am I talking to Madame Dina Trevelyan?"

"What was your name again?" asked Dina.

"Mustafa Fezzani. You know me from our university days."

His voice was sonorous and well measured, with a slight tone of annoyance at not being recognized immediately.

It was the same Mustafa, whose surname she had forgotten—her former classmate at the American University, who she had met—or better—who had met and buttonholed her during Radwan's reception in Damascus, some time ago.

The change from his former rather squeaky voice probably meant an advancement in his career. Dina was very good at interpreting such signs in a person.

"There is something important I would like to tell you. Could you come to meet me in my office this afternoon?"

Another signal of elevated status. He wanted to show off by holding court in his probably impressive office.

"Unfortunately I will be travelling tomorrow, and I do not have much time left," said Dina as sweetly as possible, "could you come here instead, after I have had my breakfast? Around 10 am or so?"

"Well, in that case I would need to cancel another appointment this morning," was the expected reply. "But it is important that I see you. I shall be with you between 10.30 and 11 am then."

At moments like this Dina's ever ready feminist resentments became acute. She was now looking forward to what this pompous and self-important ex-classmate had to say.

He arrived at 11.15, with the 15-minutes delay accorded to important ones, dressed in a formal suit and smiling benevolently. She met him in the lobby, not in her room, although there was no danger that anything that had happened with Ahmed could be repeated with Mustafa Fezzani.

First of all he obviously felt he had to convey his increased importance.

"You must know that I have been promoted to deputy director of the Antiquities Department in charge of international relations," he said. "And I wanted to meet you in that capacity and also as a friend."

"How did you know about my presence in Cairo and my hotel?" Dina wanted to know.

"Well, part of my new job is to be informed about everyone in our field," he said, smiling knowingly. "But I heard that you were in Cairo from Mahmoud al-Allamy, when he contacted me before publishing his unfortunate article about you and the missing Fatimid chessboard."

She had suspected something like that.

"So? What is it you want to tell me?"

His smile disappeared and he looked at her with a grave expression.

"I strongly advise you to stop all further activities concerning this matter. The artefacts that you describe as being stolen have become a matter of national security, and any further investigation might lead to very undesirable results."

"A strange piece of advice coming from someone involved in the preservation of national heritage," commented Dina.

Her opinion about Mustafa had changed, he was probably more important than she had thought; he was definitely also in alliance with the people who had been able to kidnap her and to arrest Mahmoud.

"And pray, dear Mustafa, what are these matters of national security?"

He smiled the smile that only the true bearers of secrets manage.

"I think you do realize that such matters are always secret and that I cannot talk about them. But please do take my advice seriously."

"I will certainly think about it, because you are not the first to give me this advice. Or to Mahmoud for that matter," she said, not really expecting a reply, which in fact never came.

They shook hands and he took his leave. Dina wondered if she had seen the teeth of a non-smiling lion once more.

Next on her list was her family. The family reunion she had requested took place in Maguid's flat. Only her two brothers and Halim were present, neither cousin Mona nor their wives. It was strictly inheritance business everyone wanted to discuss, without the need for interference from even close outsiders.

The atmosphere was tense from the outset. Her brothers had not been given any signal from their sister since her arrival that she would agree to a sale. Moreover, she had spent more time at her hotel as if she wanted to avoid them.

Maguid was perspicacious and sufficiently blunt to come to the point.

"Look, Dina, all of us here are aware that you prefer to stay in an expensive hotel and not in your own large and comfortable apartment, which would have cost you nothing. We are not interested in the reasons as to why you want to stay away from us—that is entirely your affair. But if that is so, why for God's sake don't you call it quits, take your share from the sale of the building and on occasional visits come as a foreign tourist enjoying your life in five-star hotels?"

"That is, if you ever want to come back!" he added. "That is exactly Yusuf's choice, who is in the same situation as you. What is the advantage of having property tying you up in Egypt, when you pass the rest of your life in America or England?"

He turned to Yusuf for approval.

Yusuf nodded in agreement, in his usual morose manner.

As to Halim, he seemed to have resigned himself to her lack of cooperation. He had met her in London recently and that inconclusive meeting must have made him aware that Dina had no intention pleasing her family. Their father was gone and their mother was demented, so the last link to her family was broken.

Maguid was right of course with his argument—rationally speaking.

Yet we are not steered by our brains alone, and Dina's sensitivities had been refreshed by her recent experience.

Only one day after Ahmed had left, she wanted to repeat her adventure, hop into bed with him and forget—for a short while at least—her campaign, matters of national security and her unpleasant family. One hidden reason for wanting to extend her affair was her unavowed competition with Birgit, the stupid blonde, in the female need for erotic attention, where Birgit had been the winner so far. Because erotic fulfilment cannot be had at a distance, Dina's flat in Cairo would be ideal for continuing her affair with Ahmed. They could meet there during extended holidays and after her retirement, if that was also what he wanted as a married man. And if not, she could always agree to sell the building later.

...

To tell Maguid about her most hidden motive was impossible. She could also not mention how disgusted she was about his plan to get more than his normal inheritance share by scheming with his general across the road.

"Apart from my interest in keeping my own flat," she said after a while, "a sale would be cruel to our mother. Like most demented people she must be very much attached to her familiar surroundings. It would also be unfair to the rest of our tenants."

It did not convince either of her brothers. Her mother could be looked after by the same carer and probably stay with Halim. They had discussed it already—Halim and his wife were willing to have her in exchange for a certain support from their cousins and by using inheritance share. The other tenants were mostly expatriates, who could easily find something else in Cairo.

"Yes, they are mostly expatriates, but not all of them," Dina had to say, "what about that elderly Egyptian couple living downstairs as protected tenants with their rent frozen from Nasser's time? They could never find anything else."

Arguments in favour of anyone not part of the family were useless from the outset; her brothers would not move an inch.

"Do not forget that you will have army people as your neighbours if we sell the building," tried Maguid for one last time. "Not exactly your idea of a quiet neighbourhood. And sell the building we will, we can simply outvote you."

"According to the law you cannot do that," replied Dina without having the slightest idea about the law, "and I would certainly use all legal means to prevent that. One thing I know about

Egyptian jurisprudence is that it takes a long time. Long enough to deter any potential buyer from offering a decent price for a building with someone stubborn like me, who does not want to move out."

She stood up, said a lukewarm farewell greeting and left.

She was not sure if trying to meet Ahmed before her return to London was a good idea. To impose herself, even discreetly, on someone who possibly saw her only as a pleasant bed-companion for a one-night-stand, was a horrifying thought. Her pride could be hurt, and her pride was very important to her. She decided not to contact him, hoping instead he would call.

And that's what he did! His voice sounded more urgent than she had even hoped. They agreed to meet for a farewell dinner. Both proposed nearly simultaneously her hotel restaurant as the venue, which was the obvious and most convenient choice for a possible later relocation to her bedroom.

The dinner was moderately good, and they talked a lot about everything, except about what was really on their minds.

"*Here is looking at you, kid,*" Ahmed said once and raised his glass.

"I am very impressed," Dina said. "You saw 'Casablanca'?"

Although he was decidedly modern, she would not have thought that 'Casablanca' was popular in Cairo.

"Oh, nothing special. I am a cinema buff after all."

Suddenly Dina started to giggle. She had giggled quite a lot during these past few days, more than she had for many years.

"Then let me also quote: *play it again, Sam*!"

He understood immediately and played it again in her room, where they stayed till early morning.

After driving her to the airport he topped it off with one more quotation.

Giving her a last kiss, he said:

"*I think that's the beginning of a beautiful friendship.*"

## London

Returning to London felt like a return to normality.

Cairo had been anything but that. The city of her youth with its relaxed and secure life had changed radically. Nothing seemed to be secure anymore, and there had only been a few moments of relaxation. The differences of her experience in both mega-cities was not completely in London's favour, however. Her affair with Ahmed had been a welcome change from her routine in London and romantically speaking a change even from nothing to a lot.

Dina was now facing a dilemma, which had troubled her for the last few hours as she had tried to sleep on the plane without success. Her zeal to save stolen Islamic antiquities could certainly put her into serious trouble, potentially into a life-threatening situation. The warnings she and Mahmoud had received in Cairo were ambiguous, but sufficiently serious not to be dismissed, even when back in England. International borders have never been an obstacle to kidnappings and killings, and she wanted also to feel secure, when she travelled to Egypt in future.

Zeal and caution seemed to be irreconcilable. Ahmed had advised her to end her crusade for her own sake, and he could judge the situation in Egypt much better than she could. Alistair and Rietberg would have certainly advised the same, if they were around.

Then her usual stubbornness conquered her concerns. If everyone caved in so easily we would never achieve anything, she mused—from returning an artwork to its lawful owner to a regime change! Her new heroes, the demonstrators on Tahrir Square faced with the risk of being shot or tortured, had persevered and managed to topple Mubarak finally. She had a less powerful enemy: the greedy antiquities mafia, who should not deter her either. Capitulation, which she had already contemplated, was certainly out of the question!

Anyway matters had been taken out of her hands already. Back in her London flat she found a message on her computer from a British art-magazine with a link to their website. The message itself was short, only expressing the hope that Dina would like the article and closing with: 'very much looking forward to your comments'.

Inside was an article about Dina with her portrait and on the cover the mysterious chessboard, whose picture she had obtained from Martin. She had given the magazine an interview about the stolen antiquities months before and had forgotten all about it. The magazine was published around the date of her return from Egypt. It was a special edition focusing on the sleazy side of the art market with the supposedly sexy title 'Fakes, Fences, Felony—the Black Art Market.'

The cover designer had added shimmering white knights and balaclava-clad black baddies as the chess set complementing the silver board with its ebony and ivory squares. It was all quite silly, but also ultra marketable.

However, the inside article was a serious piece of work with precise details about her proof for these thefts and her own comments about the collusion between thieves, corrupt officials and traders, giving the Fatimid wood panel, the Mamluk lamp and the rare Fatimid chessboard as typical evidence. The latter account was a résumé of the Aswan excavations under the leadership of a certain professor, who had done everything to hide the appropriation of this priceless object for himself and much later introduced it to the market.

Coincidentally an even better opportunity to get her message across presented itself at the same time. On her answering machine was a call from a reporter working for an Arab TV-station based in the Gulf. They had heard about Dina's praiseworthy efforts to save Islamic heritage and wanted to interview her at home. An interview broadcast in the whole Arabic-speaking world would be like dropping a bomb on the corrupted burcaucrats and the equally corrupt dealers and collectors. This opportunity could not be missed!

The TV-station was known for its pronounced Islamist tendencies, and for this reason was not particularly welcome in Sisi's Egypt. Another more cautious person would have refused to take yet another provocative action, but Dina had already crossed the Rubicon and was now eager to continue her attack and go ahead with another even more widely distributed interview.

As the TV-station had also a base in London, it was not long before they arrived at Dina's flat with an astonishing array of staff and equipment.

Several cameramen swarmed around preparing the cameras, one extra person had to arrange the painfully bright lights, the live shooting could be followed on two monitors, and a makeup girl put so much on Dina's face that she was reluctant to look in the mirror to see the camera-compatible but otherwise garish result, while the interviewer sat calmly in the midst of all this commotion with a glass of juice rehearsing with Dina the questions and answers.

It was very Hollywood and quite fun after her first butterflies had vanished.

The interview started with an overview of Dina's private background and her credentials as an expert in Islamic art.

Her private life was dealt with very quickly. Alistair was not even mentioned by name, but as 'my former husband'.

Her Islamic art studies and her long experience in the field working for Chrosby's led to the main subject: Islamic art threatened by theft and corruption, as had recently become apparent with the appalling fate of artefacts stolen from Egypt..

The interviewer became a little nervous as she rattled out the names of different dynasties. He was justly afraid that at this stage his audience would switch to another, less intellectual channel. Her history lesson into the Mamluk and the Fatimid dynasties that followed was certain to put off even more viewers, but had to be made in order to help everyone understand why she was so eager to fight for the preservation of these treasures.

She felt secure in herself and when recounting the whole story she did not mince her words.

At the end her interviewer asked her to sum up in a few words her investigations and the message she wanted to give to art lovers everywhere.

"The official guardians of Egypt's antiquities found only one lame excuse after I reported the thefts of the Mamluk lamp, the wooden panel and the chessboard," she said accusingly. "They pretended that only copies of the Mamluk glass lamp and the wooden panel were offered on the market, while the originals were safely stored in the museum reserves. Quite the opposite is true of course! What I am saying can be proven by an independent group of experts.

"The undeniable truth is that both were stolen from an Egyptian museum, as I have already established.

"The chessboard disappeared directly from an archaeological site in Aswan, not from a museum. As no similar example exists, they had to declare it a complete forgery, which is also a lie. Its authenticity has been proven by several tests including a metallurgical analysis of its silver frame," and summing it up: "People at a high level must have been involved in this scandal, because all the authorities concerned tried to stall and are still keeping a lid on everything. And let me add that apart from these indisputable cases there are certainly many others, where theft could be proven with some assistance from the authorities."

The interview was broadcast soon after, and made some people extremely angry.

She soon realised that amongst others, her employers did not appreciate her interview at all.

Soon enough the news of Dina's interview with the Gulf TV-station reached D.H., Chrosby's suave director and Dina's recent luncheon host. Someone close to him, who was interested in Middle Eastern affairs and knew enough Arabic to watch the Gulf-TV on cable or satellite, had informed him. That someone could only have been her own assistant, her previous one's replacement, who had quit after having her second child. The new one was a young ambitious Japanese graduate with an MA from SOAS. He was the son of a Japanese diplomat, who had represented his country in several Middle Eastern countries, and was himself born in Egypt, where he had spent his first years in school. His Arabic was excellent and from early on he had decided to make a career connected with the Middle East. He soon proved to be a real asset for Chrosby's, because he quickly acquainted himself with Islamic art, worked overtime and wrote most of the auction catalogue entries, leaving Dina with a much less onerous workload.

Studious assistants are always a mixed blessing, however—they tend to be ambitious with a desire to take over one day. Shinzo Fukuda was no different. He was always too reserved to show any undue ambition, but Dina felt uneasy with him all the same. He was very polite and most of the time quite tense, which made communication with him formal and not as spontaneous as Dina had been with his predecessor.

What made her situation really uncomfortable, was Fukuda's close relationship with D.H. D.H. had recently published a scholarly treatise about his favourite subject, the Japanese netsuke, quoting specialised literature written in Japanese. It was well known at Chrosby's that D.H.'s Japanese did not go much beyond the occasional 'sayonara'. It was also common knowledge that Fukuda had helped a lot, without being credited for his work except by a short and non-specified thank-you in the foreword. D.H. compensated Fukuda by supporting his career, starting with his assignment as Dina's assistant, and by inviting him to his regular dinner parties.

She knew that he had denounced her, when she received a warning from the directors. The letter said that she should have cleared her interview with the directors before going ahead, because she had been introduced as an employee of Chrosby's. The letter also stated that they would never have agreed to have Chrosby's described as a company mainly interested in the investigation of crimes associated with art. That characterisation could deter even legitimate clients.. The letter concluded with a stern reminder that something like this should never happen again.

After receiving this warning Dina seriously thought of quitting. Her situation at Chrosby's had become almost untenable. Apart from being unable to cooperate with Fukuda in future, let alone acting as his superior, her standing in the company was seriously compromised after that letter. The money she earned was the least of her concerns, because it was not much anyway. But to leave Chrosby's meant she would be cut off from the world of Islamic art and become a pensioner like Rietberg and that at a much younger age, because she was unlikely to find another auction house to employ her.

Within a short time she had lost both her father and her husband and was on the point of losing her job as well. She had never felt so desperate, not even at the hands of her kidnappers.

Dina postponed a decision about her job until another meeting with Rietberg, whose moral support she now needed more than ever. Perhaps he had a similar experience during his long career and could offer her some advice.

Yet her employers were not the only ones she had angered with her interview. Others, who were more dangerous, had become even more enraged.

Rietberg contacted her immediately after her return in the hope of getting her report of what happened in Egypt. However, she had wanted to settle down first, prepare for her important TV-interview and catch up with her work at Chrosby's. It suited Rietberg well too, because he was leaving immediately for a lecture tour in the US for a couple of weeks.

They agreed to meet after his return. On the phone she mentioned that she had some serious trouble in Egypt and more recently in London. Because he knew Dina as a level-headed person, these events had to be serious indeed and he became curious.

He suspected that they were related to the missing antiquities. Her diatribe against the players in that market made him want to know more. In his free time he searched the internet, and the more he learned about that jungle and the exorbitant amount of money involved, the more he took an interest in Dina's campaign and the more he became concerned for her.

The hospitality extended by his hosts, the American faculties, was generous, and he enjoyed mixing with colleagues and students as he had done in the past. From time to time he called Dina, who pretended that all was well. She did not sound very convincing; but as she did not want to elaborate on the phone, he was much looking forward to their next meeting.

When his phone rang on the day of his return—and it did not ring so often recently—he immediately answered the call with an eager, yet premature "Hi Dina."

It was not Dina. It was the police.

Rietberg put the receiver down—but he could not move. He just sat there—he couldn't recall if it was for a short or a long time. Even his brain felt frozen with only one thought remaining: Dina was dead! Dina had always been around, she had been a distant but ever present part of his life, for much longer than any other person, and now she had simply vanished. The thought that Dina could die had never once crossed his mind. She was always life itself with her charm, combativeness, sensuality and intelligence, and now she was dead. The police had given him the news in their normal matter-of-fact manner. No word of consolation, but of course they could not possibly know how close they had been.

Marie-Anne, who was sitting at her desk writing on her computer, sensed that something was wrong.

"What happened?" she asked. "Have you seen a ghost?"

Rietberg was still so stunned that he could barely answer.

Dina had been found during the night lying dead in a pool of blood in front of her building. The police had been called to the scene by a severely shocked passer-by who was nearly killed when Dina fell out of her window. They had found a list of persons to be contacted in case something happened to her in her wallet, and Rietberg was one of them.

Of course, nothing could be said yet as to the cause of death. The police only asked Rietberg to be available over the next few days, because they wanted to talk to him.

Marie-Anne did not ask for more details, knowing that he remained completely in the dark after the short call from the police. She tried to console him, hugging him and taking his hands. But she soon felt that he only wanted to be left alone. She forced a double straight whisky on him and left him brooding alone in their drawing room.

The next few days passed like a bad dream. Once he even tried, as if in a real dream, to convince himself that this was all just in his imagination. He had been able to do this in dreams before, which usually made him wake up with a feeling of relief that reality was so much better. This time reality could not have been worse.

He was now very much looking forward to being contacted by the police to learn more. Chrosby's, who had only just been informed, did not know anything more than he did.

Slowly speculation set in.

Suicide, the most obvious cause of falling out of a window, could be excluded. Or could it? Perhaps some of the serious events she had mentioned had literally driven her over the edge. Murder was equally improbable because Dina would never have let a murderer enter her flat. Or would she? There had, after all, been cases known of burglars forcing home owners to open the door with their own key.

It could not have been an acquaintance whom she readily admitted, because nobody she knew could possibly want to do her any harm. Or could they? Many—if not most—murders are committed by persons known to the victim.

To continue speculating like this would bring no result but be pure masochism.

He simply had to be patient until the police had the time to interrogate Dina's acquaintances.

The second day, after what seemed like an interminable wait, the phone rang. It was still not the police, but Alistair who had been on Dina's list as well.

Rietberg almost did not recognize his voice. He had always known and often disliked him for his poised, almost indifferent banker's manner. This time Alistair could barely speak coherently, when he asked Rietberg what had happened. At a certain moment he even seemed to be have been unable to speak due to sudden sobs. He promised to take the next plane from Stockholm and see Rietberg immediately to coordinate what was needed to be done.

It was bitter irony that both men with their never declared competition for Dina's attention would have to close ranks after her demise.

Things were moving fast now.

Two policemen showed up—an inspector and a sergeant. The inspector was a middle-aged man in civilian clothes, with no special feature except his eyes. They were blue, a bit watery as if he enjoyed a tipple or two, and had the cold expression of someone who had heard too many lies to look friendly. The uniformed sergeant was much younger with a rosy face and did not utter a word, just jotted down their statements. Both seemed slightly surprised by Alistair's presence as if they had not expected him so soon.

There was a moment of indecision, when they were obviously asking themselves if they should interrogate both men separately. Rietberg held no illusions that in their eyes they were both to be treated as possible suspects. Close acquaintances and former husbands always are.

Finally, the inspector decided to take their statements together.

Alistair, who had just flown in from Stockholm, was quickly eliminated as an immediate suspect, as was Rietberg a little later, after a moment of hesitation as well. Marie-Anne vouched for his presence during the night, and even the most suspicious policeman could not suspect this grey, old and non-athletic man of being able to push a healthy woman out of the window.

The obvious and standard questions they asked both men were: if Dina had suicidal tendencies; or if they knew of anyone wishing to hurt her.

Alistair shook his head.

"I don't think that our divorce could have been a reason for killing herself," he said. "She never gave me the impression that our separation caused her any anxieties or depression. Perhaps she started to regret it at a later stage, just as I did. But a motive to commit suicide? I don't believe it. And I do not know of any enemy either."

Rietberg was not so sure. The last impression he had of Dina was in fact that of a frustrated, perhaps even troubled, woman, who moreover must have made enemies through her campaign to save Islamic antiquities. But she never showed any signs of resignation or despair expected in someone who thinks of killing themself. As for a murder, a car accident in Cairo caused by an irate museum custodian accused of theft—perhaps, but not a well-planned murder in London.

"I agree with Alistair," Rietberg gave as his answer, "we can rule out suicide, and to my knowledge she had no real enemies either."

Fortunately, the police had their own methods to resolve the painful matter of identifying the body. Rietberg had seen films with a relative being led into a grim mortuary, where an indifferent assistant uncovered the face of the victim. He dreaded the idea of himself or Alistair being exposed to that ordeal. Instead, the police had a photograph of Dina with them where she looked peaceful enough for both men to have a brief look and confirm her identity without causing them too much distress.

As to the cause of Dina's death the police remained totally uncommitted.

"We will have to wait for the coroner's decision," they said and left.

After a moment's silence, when the police had left, Alistair started to cry. Rietberg, who had had his moments of crying before, looked very surprised at this man, who he had never suspected of warm feelings for anyone, including his own wife.

Between repeated uncontrollable sobs Alistair made a strange confession.

He had intended to leave Birgit and resume relations with Dina, and was only afraid of her reaction.

"Dina had been right all along," he said. "It was foolish of me to live with a much younger woman with not many interests in her life, except men and money. I always thought that Islamic art, Dina's pet subject, was boring, but only golf and a little banking gossip was much more so, not to speak of other matters that soon became boring with Birgit. You cannot imagine how much I was looking forward to living with Dina again for the rest of my life."

He wiped his eyes.

"Alas, it is too late now!"

In fact, everything was too late, after Dina had gone.

Marie-Anne who had served everyone drinks remained silent in her own discreet way. Now she said something very constructive.

"As the police were saying, we have first to wait for the coroner's verdict. If it is an open one, which is most likely in this mysterious case, I do not expect much from the police. Unless they can identify a suspect on the CCTV, I doubt that they will be able to find the murderer. They know nothing of her background and what has recently happened to her in Cairo. But you two could join forces to find the killer, because you know more about her than anyone else between the two of you. You have done some detective work before, and it would serve as a kind of consolation for her loss."

It was exactly what Rietberg had been thinking, but had not dared to say for fear of being accused of indulging in his detective hobby at Dina's expense.

"The police might find some clues on Dina's computer," he remarked.

"All the better then," replied Marie-Anne, "but if not, it will be your turn. I think both of you should travel to Egypt and retrace her steps there. You cannot expect the police to do that. My female intuition tells me that her murder—or even her suicide, although I don't believe it was one—is connected to what happened during her last trip to Egypt."

"I am a banker, but I believe in female intuition," agreed Alistair. "Dina has often demonstrated this to me."

To Rietberg's relief mentioning Dina did not make him cry again. He was now focusing on the task ahead.

Alistair refused Rietberg's proposal to stay with them in London, because he still had a key to Dina's apartment and as her executor and heir could move in as soon as the police had finished their investigation. In the meantime he would stay in his club.

"The first major row I had with Birgit was about inheritance," Alistair told them with a bitter smile. "When she learned that Dina and not herself would be my heir, she was livid. She accused me of not loving her enough and of a lack of loyalty. At that moment something in me snapped. This much younger woman was probably only after my money! Dina had already had her doubts that she would stay long with a much older man for anything else. And when Birgit began having affairs with other— needless to say much younger—men I knew that I had been an old fool all along."

At least Rietberg could be sure that Marie-Anne did not stay with him for the same reason, because he had nothing to leave, except a heavily mortgaged flat. Yet although he had a tendency to make inappropriate comments for wit's sake, he preferred not to mention that this time. It would have been utterly frivolous and certainly not be considered witty by either Alistair or Marie-Anne.

As expected, the coroner issued an open verdict, meaning that nothing definite could be said as to the cause of death. The ball was back in the police court, with only meagre evidence to make something out of the mysterious case of Dina's sudden death.

Then something remarkable happened. An English tabloid published an article on its front page entitled 'Another Egyptian Balcony Murder?' The article started with the few facts known of Dina's death and then continued by recalling similar deaths of prominent Egyptians in London and Cairo who had also fallen from balconies. Dina was the only one with a foreign passport, but belonged in that list because she was Egyptian born and was a former citizen; she was also a well-known personality as a 'famous art scholar', as they described her taking a few liberties.

They cited so many cases that they could hardly all be coincidental. The tabloid was surprisingly well informed, with its article probably based on research by the police themselves and leaked to the newspaper by an insider. The list of balcony murders was impressive, even creating the myth of a balcony phantom in Egypt:

- The most prominent victim was Ashraf Marwan, son-in-law of president Nasser, security advisor and former chairman of the multinational Arab Organization of Industrialization, the holding company of Egyptian military factories. In 2007 he fell from a window of his apartment on the fifth floor of a building in Carlton Place, London.

- Thirty years before another arms dealer, Ali Shafik, secretary in the office of the former Egyptian vice president Abdel Hakim Amer, a presidential rival, was also brutally murdered in his London apartment.
- Perhaps the most spectacular example was that of Egyptian film star Souad Hosni in 2001. The 58-year-old actress, once known as the "Cinderella of Egyptian cinema", plunged to her death from the balcony of her apartment in London
- Mimi Shakeeb, another Egyptian actress, 'fell' from her balcony in Cairo in May 1983.
- In the mid-1970s, the Egyptian ambassador to Britain, General Leithy Nassif also fell to his death from a balcony in London.
- During the Arab Spring in early 2011 Sally Zahran, a pro-democracy activist, was killed by falling from a balcony in Cairo.
- The latest known case was Bassem Sabry, another activist, who 'slipped' from a balcony of his 10th floor flat in Cairo.

All these cases had a common factor apart from the cause of death, known in dictionaries as 'defenestration': they were never solved. Not one of them! Many rumours circulated—the most popular being that the Mukhabarat, the Egyptian secret service, was behind the murders, although in Ashraf Marwan's case another usual suspect, the Israeli Mossad, was a better guess. Ashraf Marwan had worked as a double agent for Egypt and Israel and according to the official Egyptian version he used the trust the Israelis had in him to mislead them about the Egyptian attack that started the Yom Kippur war in 1973.

Souad Hosni's threat to publish her memoirs with damning details about prominent politicians she had slept with, reinforced the idea that defenestration was the favourite method of the Mukhabarat, just as a poisoned umbrella was for the Bulgarians, while the similarity to the rumours about the death of Marylyn Monroe was additional fascinating stuff for the conspiracy theoreticians.

Yet no one was ever accused of or even implicated in these murders.

It was Alistair, an avid newspaper reader, who had spotted the tabloid, and he immediately contacted Rietberg.

"As I have been saying all along," said Rietberg, never shy to repeat what he had said before, "it is wrong to belittle everything mysterious as an unfounded conspiracy theory. Conspiracies do happen."

"The chief problem is only how to distinguish between absurd speculation and real conspiracies though," said Alistair.

"I wonder, why this article was published," mused Rietberg. "If the police are behind it—as they could well be—did they want to convey a certain message to the public concerning Dina's death?"

"I can imagine which message," answered Alistair scornfully. "It states that all Egyptian balcony murders are insoluble *per se*. Too many wogs or foreign politicians are involved. It's an internal Egyptian affair after all and not of concern to Her Majesty's police force. So why lose time and resources by investigating such a crime? I bet that we will not hear from our police again."

Alistair was proved correct. He gained access to Dina's flat and her belongings a couple of weeks later, but still much earlier than could have been expected in the case of a thorough investigation. There was no sign of further activities by the police.

Once, while discussing the case with Marie-Anne, Rietberg shocked her with a theory involving Alistair of all people. It had to happen. While the law says that everyone is presumed innocent until proven guilty, Rietberg's experience with cheating students had told him otherwise.

."I always thought that the police were overly suspicious. So why did they not interrogate Alistair more thoroughly? He had a clear motive—if he wanted to leave Birgit and return to London, he needed Dina's flat as his home, and he could not be sure that Dina would agree. Then he had the means to enter her flat at any moment—the key, don't forget that. Perhaps all his grief over her death was just for show. After his bad experience with Birgit—if we believe his story— he may have become disillusioned about all women, and perhaps he hated Dina enough to throw her out of the window."

"Jürgen, you have a sick mind," said Marie-Anne. "How can you ever imagine anything like that? Besides he was not even in London; he flew in from Stockholm after the murder."

"Well, we have only his word for it."

"I think that you underestimate the police. They must have checked his flight details."

"Perhaps they did, perhaps they did not. No need to go out of their way for only another Egyptian balcony murder."

"Nonsense," said Marie-Anne, "I will not listen to any more of your sick theories."

There was nothing to indicate that something horrific had happened behind the door. There were no traces of official seals or crime scene tapes preventing access to the premises. If there had been, the police must have removed everything. Alistair was standing there, hesitating a while before he put his key into the keyhole to open the door. His heart was beating faster than usual. Entering Dina's flat was like intruding on her privacy, even though she was dead now.

At that moment the door of a neighbouring flat opened, and a distinguished looking man stared at Alistair.

"Who are you?" he asked. "This has been a crime scene! I am the victim's neighbour and I feel I have the right to ask."

His tone was not aggressive, but he spoke with the firm voice of someone with natural authority. Alistair decided to answer, instead of ignoring him.

"You don't know, who I am," he said, "but I know who you are. You are Mr McCauley, the barrister—correct?"

The man looked utterly surprised and a little suspicious.

"How do you know me? I don't recall having met you before."

"You have not in fact. I am the ex-husband of the lady to whom this flat belongs or rather belonged," he explained. "Before I bought it for her a couple of years ago, I made some enquiries about the location and her neighbours. That's how."

"A barrister seemed to be respectable enough to me to be her neighbour," he added with a smile.

"Ah, that explains it. I am sorry for having been impolite. Please accept my condolences," said Mr McCauley. He had become quite friendly, perhaps flattered to be called 'respectable'.

"Why don't you come in then? I cannot tell you what happened here the other night, but as Mrs Ghalib's husband you might be interested to hear the little that I do know."

Alistair, who was on the verge of telling him that her name was Lady Trevelyan, stopped short. He had almost forgotten that she had adopted her maiden name since their divorce.

McCauley told Alistair that the day before she died he had come out of his door in the morning, when he saw Dina heading towards the lift with a man.

"It looked as though they had spent the previous night together," he said, and adding with an apologetic smile, "sorry for that remark, but I never saw you both together before."

"We were divorced," said Alistair curtly.

"Not only that, but everything else with Dina—we were on a first names basis—convinced me that she did not commit suicide. She was simply not the type, as you will know better than I do. I do suspect that this man was somehow involved in her death, probably the murderer even. There had never been anyone visiting her before as far as I know, apart from a German colleague, who came from time to time to visit her, but it was not him."

"You did not see her coming back later in the day in the company of this man or anyone else?"

"No, I did not. And to make it quite clear. I am not one for spying on my neighbours, my observation was purely coincidental."

"Of course, of course," said Alistair. "Did you tell this to the police?"

"Of course, I did, and they wanted me to describe him. Unfortunately, I was unable to do that, except the usual 'of medium height', etc. He wore an overcoat, a scarf and a hat— quite normal in this cold and not meant to hide his exterior, but it covered him enough to make any identification impossible. I cannot even tell you if he looked British or foreign, just that he was white."

"What was his hat like? Fancy or an old-fashioned fedora? The reason I am asking is that normal hats have gone out of fashion these days, so that could help to identify him."

"It was a normal hat, as everyone wore in the past."

"That's peculiar," said Alistair. "But please tell me: did you have the impression that he knew her well?"

"The police asked me the same question," said Mr McCauley. "It could be or could not be. Passing a night together—even in separate rooms—points to a certain degree of intimacy in my opinion, don't you think?"

McCauley smiled apologetically again for this remark to a divorced husband.

"He was standing behind her and followed her into the lift. As he never turned around I did not see his face, nor did I want to join them in our narrow lift. They did not exchange any words, however; not even in the lift, from where I would have heard them, while I waited for my turn. I got the impression that they were not exactly on friendly terms."

"Well, let's hope that the CCTV will help with the identification."

"I do not want to disappoint you," said McCauley. "But with my experience as someone dealing with the law for all of his life I know that even the clearest pictures on CCTV—and most of them are grainy—only help if the person is already known to the police. A complete stranger remains a complete stranger."

"Unless the police publish his photo on a poster."

"Oh, my God," laughed McCauley. "Sorry for laughing, but to be honoured by a 'wanted poster' these days you must have killed hundreds, not just one."

Roaming around in her flat made him feel uncomfortable, but he had to do it. If he wanted to search for clues, he had to start here.

Everything looked tidy as to be expected in her flat. No signs of a struggle and everything, was apparently in the right place. Whoever the killer or killers were, they had done a neat job, as the police had done, who had left no more traces than a bit of powder used for taking fingerprints on a solitary used glass sitting on the kitchen table. Dina must have forgotten to put it into the dishwasher. It contained traces of milk that had turned sour since—a strange *memento mori*, which upset Alistair more than anything else in her flat. The fingerprints must have been Dina's, otherwise the police would in the meantime have taken the glass away as evidence.

During his search he could not find her mobile phone, despite his efforts and in spite of going through all her clothes, nor could he find her computer. Both were probably still with the police. He needed to know her contacts in Egypt before setting out on his fact-finding mission. He made a mental note to claim them from the police.

Fortunately, he found some business cards with Egyptian addresses in her wallet. The question was why neither it nor any of her jewellery she had kept in a drawer in her bedside cabinet were stolen. It would have been in a normal burglary, but also in a murder committed for other reasons in order to make it appear as such. Could the murderer have wanted to demonstrate that he or they had other motives or were they just eager to leave the crime scene as quickly as possible?

It was also remarkable that all the windows were closed. This was the ultimate proof that she did not leap out of the window voluntarily, unless the windows had been closed by the police, which was possible. One more question to ask the police.. She had been pushed by someone who was neither sufficiently shrewd nor cared enough to make it look like a suicide. The killer or killers had perhaps not wanted anyone looking up after her fall to spot the only open window in the building, which would have facilitated their detection before they had the time to vanish.

The last item for his methodical search was the answering machine. It no longer blinked because the police had certainly listened to the tape. There were twelve calls, all of them registered after Dina's death. Most of them were of no interest to Alistair and only concerned catalogue entries or administrative matters to be dealt with on her return. After a lengthy and tedious session of eavesdropping on calls that were meant for Dina's ears alone, he listened to the last one made by a caller, who spoke in Arabic.

It was a man's voice, a deep and melodious sounding voice. Alistair, who after his studies at the spy academy in Shemlan, up in the mountains of Lebanon, always pretended to know Arabic could not understand everything that the man was talking about. Yet what he did understand was enough to make him feel uncomfortable. There was something intimate, something intense in it as if the man had a special relationship with Dina. Alistair did not like the thought, but what he termed in his mind as 'special' had a clear erotic connotation.

He decided not to ask for Rietberg's help to translate. Although it was he who had betrayed Dina he could not bear the thought of Dina enjoying herself in someone else's bed and least of all to share these doubts with Rietberg.

In any case, he thought he knew the identity of the caller already. One of the business cards Dina kept in her wallet was from a lawyer called Ahmed Selim in Cairo. That did of course not prove that he was the mysterious caller with millions of other Ahmeds around, but it was a credible possibility.

To have the address of an Egyptian lawyer, who knew Dina, was certainly helpful for their future investigations in Egypt. Their plan was to look for clues to her murder, but Alistair hoped, without admitting the rather morbid thought to himself, to reap also some information about her recent love life.

He decided to stay in her flat while in London. There were certainly more calls or emails to be expected from people who were still unaware of her fate. He had an obligation to inform her friends, and he could possibly learn more about her recent activities also.

It was still uncomfortable for him to move into her home, where everything reminded him of her, including the discreet smell of bed sheets, but nothing of a male presence. He had not imagined how difficult it would be for him to clear her clothes and underwear from cupboards to make room for his own, or to replace all the female bathroom trinkets with his shaving brush and his razor. These mundane tasks made him feel very lonely.

He had to occupy himself with something useful. After phoning around for some time he managed to contact the inspector who had interviewed him. As he had presumed, the windows of her flat were already closed when the police arrived and they were still keeping her computer and her mobile phone until they finished studying the hard disk and her phone directory for any clues.

"You will get both back, as soon as we have been through everything, including the deleted files. Yet, I am afraid to say that with the slim evidence that we have, our investigations will be very difficult," the officer told him. "Because of the closed windows we can at least eliminate suicide as the cause of her death."

'Difficult investigations!' thought Alistair. 'Why didn't he say that they have given up already?'

"Perhaps you can help us by informing her family in Cairo," the inspector continued. "As you know, we found your name on a list she kept in her wallet of persons to be contacted in an emergency. There was also one with a telephone number in Cairo, someone called Nesim Ghalib, obviously a relative. But although we have tried several times, no one ever picks up the phone."

"I can tell you why," said Alistair, "Nesim Ghalib was her father who died recently, and the only other person who could be reached at that number is her demented mother, who never answers the phone. You can leave the whole matter with me, though. I will contact her brothers. But let me ask you one thing: is there anything on the CCTV? I suppose there is one?"

"Nothing conclusive there either," answered the inspector. "It's a large building with many people exiting and entering throughout the day. All we could find concerning your wife was that she left her flat in the morning before she died in the company of a man; she returned alone in the evening. We would of course like to talk to this man, because he could perhaps give us a clue, but nobody in the police has recognized him nor do we have his picture on our files."

"What did he look like?"

"Very difficult to say as well. He was wearing an overcoat, a scarf and also a hat, which makes any identification almost impossible. The record on the CCTV tape is moreover very short, because both left the video range quickly, and it is of a low quality. We can only hope that one day we come across a picture of someone who looks and walks in a similar manner and who is known to us. If you think you can help, you are free to come and look at the tape of course."

"No," said Alistair, "I don't think I can help. I have been living in Sweden since our separation, and even before that we had very few friends in common. But why don't you show the tape to Chrosby's where she worked? Dina knew a lot of art collectors and could have met this one at home. Someone else at Chrosby's, perhaps her secretary, could help with the identification."

After a short pause the inspector said: "That's a good idea."

It was obvious that he was not pleased at Alistair's suggestion. The police never like outsiders giving them ideas, especially when it is a reasonable one.

For the next few weeks Alistair was occupied with all the administrative problems following the death of a relative, including cremation, probate and organizing a memorial service. Strictly speaking, he was no longer a relative after their divorce. But even as a divorcee he was still her closest connection in the eyes of everyone else, and he was also her sole heir, just as she would have been his. Alistair had insisted on drafting reciprocal wills after their divorce. Nothing else would have been fair in view of their many, mostly happy years together.

Organizing her memorial service was a real challenge without access to her computer or mobile, where she stored the names and addresses of her many friends and contacts. Chrosby's could, of course, help with the names of her professional colleagues and clients, and Rietberg managed to find a few acquaintances, who should also be contacted. In the end they had assembled a large number of mourners, but there were definitely others who would probably take offence at being left out.

One thing both Alistair and Rietberg were certain of, however, because Dina had frequently made this point: no priest, whether Anglican or Coptic! The ceremony was therefore devoted only to remembering her lifelong fascination with studying art and cultural heritage preservation for coming generations. Rietberg was the obvious choice for making this eulogy. The lighter touch, also customary in memorial services, was provided by Alistair praising her talents as a hostess and cook. In the end it was the saddest moment of the funeral.

After the funeral Alistair and Rietberg resumed their plans for their fact finding mission to Cairo, both with some trepidation as neither saw the other as an ideal fellow traveller.

"I don't know if it is such a good idea to travel together with Alistair," said Rietberg to Marie-Anne. "We have nothing in common except our grief for Dina, and I am not even sure if his grief is sincere."

"Oh, come off it or stop talking to me."

He had interrupted her, when she was preparing a paper for a conference on the treatment of colon cancer. He knew that she did not want to be disturbed by someone more interested in the fate of dynasties than in the fate of colons. But their need to make a final decision on their travel plans for Egypt was somewhat more pressing now.

"What shall we talk about while we are together for a week or more except about Dina?" he asked. "I am not interested in him, nor is he in me. Besides, I have never been in his company without Dina also being around. All this could be pretty awkward."

"I made this suggestion with both of you present, and you both agreed," answered Marie-Anne with a frown. "Besides you cannot prevent him from going to Egypt alone and if both of you are travelling separately it will be even more awkward than anything else. Knowing you, I don't think you will be able stay at home either."

It was spoken with authority and it was convincing.

"OK then," said Rietberg. "*Roma locuta est, causa finita est.*"

As a medical doctor Marie-Anne had enough Latin to understand. She laughed and forgot her annoyance at being interrupted.

Rietberg and Alistair had their first difference of opinion, when talking about booking their flights and hotel.

Alistair, who after his retirement had only travelled to Egypt once with Dina, recalled having organized this trip with the help of her cousin Halim, who worked for a tourist agency.

"He had promised us specially discounted rates—a five-star hotel and business class included. What he provided was business class on teetotal Egypt Air and a stay in a four-star hotel. We could have found better rates elsewhere. Because Dina did not like my comments, I kept quiet then. But I decided never to entrust this cousin of hers again with the task of organizing any travel to or in Egypt."

Rietberg objected immediately. Marie-Anne tried to stop him criticizing Alistair, but Rietberg, who had never lost his blunt German ways, could not be stopped.

"I beg to differ, Alistair," he said. He thought it was the appropriate discreet English way of saying 'no'. "On the contrary, involving Dina's cousin is ideal for our investigations. By doing this it will give us an introduction to her family that we have to contact in any case. They might even give us advice as to how to gain more information elsewhere. By booking through him we will also secure his good-will. That's if he is still in the tourist business."

Alistair was not used to being contradicted, and he showed it. Rietberg's arguments were convincing however, and when Marie-Anne served as their arbiter he agreed and was happy to go along with this idea.

Alistair managed to find Halim's office number on his mobile phone, only to be told that he no longer worked for the agency. A call to his private number, which they gave Alistair, was successful however.

Alistair had not informed any one in Dina's family yet and prepared himself to break the sad news of Dina's death before talking of organizing their trip.

"Of course I remember you," said Halim, after Alistair had introduced himself. "How is Dina?"

"Unfortunately I have very bad news—Dina is dead."

The nearly audible gasp at the other end of the line was a clear sign that this news came as a total surprise. For a while no one spoke.

Then Halim said:

"Please accept my condolences for the loss of your wife and my beloved cousin. But when and how did she die?"

"I will tell you more in Cairo," Alistair said. "I intend to come to Egypt together with a friend of ours to learn more about her recent visit and discover if anything can possibly explain why she died. I wonder if you could assist us in organizing our travel arrangements as you did before so admirably," said Alistair with all the hypocrisy he could muster. Rietberg and Marie-Anne looked at him with admiration.

Even if Halim had been made redundant Alistair was sure that he would accept this commission. There was always the possibility of taking his cut by referring them to his former agency or another one. Alistair had lived in Egypt for long enough to know that a business opportunity was never refused, whatever the odds.

<u>Cairo</u>

After their four-hour flight—of course with Egypt Air—during which they both pretended to sleep for most of the time to avoid any conversation. They were greeted at the airport by Halim carrying a sign with their names on it.

He performed the usual tourist guide ritual, repeating 'welcome to Egypt, welcome, welcome'. In the circumstances he lacked his usual welcoming grin and inserted a few suitable expressions of condolence instead; but he seemed happy enough to have tourists again and help assist them through passport control and customs, a task that was not overly demanding anyway.

"Dina fell out of window, yet no one knows why yet. All this cannot be covered in a few words. Now we are both too tired, but we will give you a fuller picture later, when we meet with your entire family," said Alistair, when Halim wanted to know details.

Rietberg could understand now why Alistair was not very keen to see him or the rest of her family, but they had not come for pleasure. They needed Halim's services to take them to Dina's flat in Cairo and possibly help them to start their investigations. This last arrangement had caused another dispute earlier between Rietberg and Alistair; the latter wanted to stay in a decent hotel. He had been traumatized by moving into Dina's flat in London. He refused to use the Cairo one as suggested by Halim.

"No, Jürgen," he said, "you cannot ask me to do this. First of all, I resent that he offered this arrangement as a favour, as if I had no right to move in by myself as Dina's sole heir. Moreover, that flat was Dina's before she knew me, and I could not stand the idea of seeing more of her personal belongings. Imagine what looking at her childhood toys would do to me." He almost cried. "Besides, we would be in almost permanent contact with her family, who she never liked for very good reasons. An hour at most a day with the Ghalibs is enough, and after that I will need a stiff whisky at the hotel bar."

Rietberg, who tended to be misanthropic at the best of times, sympathized with Alistair. Yet, although he understood Alistair's Ghalib-phobia he had to disagree once again. Halim could interpret a refusal of his offer to stay in Dina's flat as a sign of arrogance on their part, while they needed his good-will and his introductions to the rest of the family. Staying with them, as a family member, could make the difference between being given a limited input as opposed to more intimate and more discreet opinions, in other words more useful information.

And then the ultimate argument:

"You may own Dina's share in the building as you were saying, and at the moment this might not be so important to you. Don't give her family the impression however that you don't care about that. You should even try to have the deed transferred to your name during our stay."

Alistair had to agree once more, but Rietberg decided to let him win the next argument, because he was keen to rub along with prickly Alistair in future. As a history professor he had learned some lessons from the golden age of diplomacy. Winning without the opponent loosing face was done best by adopting a falsely dissident view, and then allow the opponent to win you over to your own idea.

Halim's car took them directly to the Ghalib building in Dokki. He drove himself—an obvious sign that it was his own car and not that of an agency who would use a limousine with a chauffeur. Rietberg had from the beginning decided to keep his eyes open for any signals to help their background search. The first observation he made was that Halim was probably not very successful in his career or had even been made redundant.

As most flights from Europe arrive late in Cairo, it was past midnight, and they immediately went to Dina's flat. It had seldom been lived in over the past years and did not contain the toys or any similar memorabilia from her childhood, because she had always hated sentimentality and had given or thrown everything away long ago.

Moving in for a few days posed another more practical problem, *i.e.* where both men could sleep. Fortunately, there were two separate bedrooms. Sleeping together in one even large bed would have been an unbearable thought. Sharing a bathroom was bad enough, but manageable for discreet partners, and both of them were undoubtedly discreet.

"Good night. Tomorrow morning you have to tell us more about what happened," said Halim, "and after that we shall plan your stay in Cairo."

"I hope not," said Alistair, after he had shut the door.

They were all there, when Alistair and Rietberg descended the few steps to Halim's flat: Halim; his sister Mona; and Dina's brothers Maguid and Yusuf. Fawzia, Maguid's wife had not come, probably because her husband feared her pert remarks. Halim's wife, about whom nothing could be said except that she was unobtrusive, had prepared a full Egyptian breakfast and then disappeared. They were treated to *ful,* boiled eggs, salad onions, white cheese and pickled *turshi* with flat *baladi* bread. There was tea, bottled water and—rather incongruously—Pepsi Cola.

Diving into this copious breakfast helped to bridge the uneasiness both sides felt about one another. The Ghalibs were probably wondering what the real aim for Alistair's visit was, especially as he had brought Rietberg along, about whom they knew nothing.

Of course, Dina's death was the only topic of their talk.

Alistair took it upon himself to inform them. He could tell them little except for the facts themselves. Her fall from a window could have been caused by accident, suicide or murder, but nothing concrete was known as yet, even by the police, as far he could tell.

Maguid became quite agitated at the mention of a suicide.

"I cannot believe that Dina killed herself," he said vehemently. "During her stay here she was her usual self and she has never shown any suicidal tendencies. It has to be an accident or worse even, murder!."

Was he so deeply religious? Rietberg found no other explanation for Maguid's remark. To commit suicide is a deadly sin according to Christian belief—but being a murder victim was not, however. Murders could even create saintly martyrs. Was Maguid so fanatical in his beliefs that he preferred to remember his sister as a murder victim and not as a sinning suicide?

"That might be, but we cannot rule out suicide," he corrected Maguid. "Lately I had noted signs of frustration, even bitterness in her. Better to wait for the police investigation's results than to speculate."

Maguid did not reply at first, but then asked him, slightly irritated:

"May I ask you if the purpose of your visit is to find out anything about her death?"

Before Rietberg could reply, Alistair proved once more his talent at hypocrisy.

"That is certainly one purpose, but not the main one. My main reason is to present my condolences to you as her family," he said with an expression to indicate he was hurt by Maguid's misunderstanding.

Maguid and Mona still looked sceptical. What was really behind their visitors' interests in Dina's stay in Egypt? Nothing of whatever she did in Cairo could be relevant to explain a suicide or a murder in London. Or could it? Both, however, were sufficiently discreet not to press the matter further.

Halim tried once more to promote his business.

"What about starting your stay with a trip to the pyramids of Gizeh and Saqqara?" he asked. "I have arranged for a car with a trustworthy driver to take you there. If you know how to ride you could even ride from Gizeh, where they have horses to rent, to the pyramid of Maidum."

Alistair, who could scarcely hide his opinion about Halim's services, answered bluntly.

"Both Jürgen and I have lived in Egypt for many years and know every stone of the pyramids. While we are here, we would prefer to have your help in retracing Dina's steps on her last visit. I wonder if you know the main reason as to why she was here."

"Of course, it was to attend *arbaeen* in memory of our father," said Halim. "When I saw her in London last she promised me that she would come."

"That was one reason, but not the main one," Rietberg remarked. "I had had long discussions with Dina in London about a scandal involving the smuggling of Islamic antiquities out of the country, and she was here to follow-up a report she had made to the Egyptian restitution department, which is in charge of that."

"You are right," Mona chimed in, although she rarely had anything to say in family gatherings. "She told me about it during our trip to Alexandria."

"Why didn't you tell us?" asked Halim with a frown.

"Because no one asked me."

Rietberg looked at Maguid, who did not comment. His expression was inscrutable, as if he knew. As the most informed of the brothers he could have read Mahmoud's article. In that case not admitting it could have a reason that seemed a bit farfetched, even to the ever suspicious Rietberg. Perhaps Maguid knew about her crusade and the risks involved and used this knowledge to persuade her to give up everything in Cairo.

Alistair, whose mind was occupied with other things, turned to Maguid.

"There is also something else: how long would it take to have the ownership of Dina's share transferred to me?"

All the Ghalibs looked at one another.

Finally, Maguid answered.

"I am afraid to have to disappoint you," he said. "The building belongs to us alone now, because we as her family inherited it."

"You must be joking," said Alistair, a bit too bluntly, "I am her sole heir by her last will and testament. I can only hope that after her loss we don't make everything worse with inheritance disputes."

Maguid tried to defuse the situation by a conciliatory remark.

"You can always stay in her flat. Of course, for only as long as we own the building."

Alistair was unable to hide his anger any longer.

"Thank you for reminding me of that point. In fact, we all own the building, and that includes me!"

Rietberg was yawning repeatedly, as he always did when something embarrassed him. He was embarrassed for Alistair, because he was wrong and Maguid was right. Rietberg had made a mistake when he had agreed at first that Alistair inherited Dina's share. His own research into Egyptian Islamic trusts had taught him that inheritance of landed property in Egypt was always ruled by the local law, as it was in every other country. As a British banker Alistair should have known that as well, even with a limited legal education. Rietberg's efforts to prevent Alistair from losing the dispute were in vain, however. Alistair was not in the mood to heed Rietberg's discreet hints to shut up.

Yusuf, who usually played a more passive role in conversations, now came to Maguid's defence.

"We do not want to antagonize you, Alistair," he said, "but land property in Egypt is inherited according to Egyptian law. That rule is no different in other countries, including England, by the way. Our law in these matters is the Sharia, which is, unfortunately, still applied regardless of the religion of the parties concerned. According to Islamic law Dina's last will can still provide a share for non-heirs like you are after your divorce, but for one-third of her estate at most. Surely what she left in London is worth much more than her share in this building, so her last will has no effect on her property here. As a divorced husband you are not a residuary beneficiary either, so her original family inherit all her Egyptian possessions."

Rietberg and Alistair listened with scarcely hidden surprise to this detailed report on Egyptian and Islamic law delivered by an American psychiatrist.

Before Alistair could say anything stupid or offensive, Rietberg stepped in.

"Yusuf is right," he said. "I happen to know a little about Sharia rules myself, I can confirm that everything he has said is correct. My advice to all of you is: let us forget about this relatively unimportant matter and concentrate on retracing her steps during her last stay in Cairo, as a tribute to her memory."

Alistair knew that he was defeated and kept silent. It was obvious though that his feelings for Dina's family had not improved.

Rietberg knew that from now on only he and not Alistair could expect any help from Dina's family, if at all. The little goodwill they had for Dina's widower had evaporated due to Alistair's arrogance. During the discussion the brothers had obviously formed a common front against Alistair.

Dina's cousin Mona witnessed the dispute with no more than an amused smile. She was not an heir, and moreover the dispute offered good gossip material.

When they were alone, Alistair was still grumbling.

"Even if I was wrong, as you were saying," he said, "I wonder how this American shrink Yusuf is so well informed about the law in Egypt and even in other countries, as he said. Did you hear when he told me that I am not a residuary beneficiary! Where has he got that term from? They must have consulted a lawyer, as if her inheritance was of prime concern for them."

"Perhaps her death was not totally unwelcome," he added.

Rietberg was shocked. He tended to be suspicious himself, but this went too far.

"Alistair, please control yourself. You have not the slightest reason to have any doubts about her family. Besides, you will have given them a similar impression about yourself by opening the subject of her inheritance so soon - even though I myself had recommended it. Dina's murder must have a very different explanation. Remember that it was you who brought my attention to the article about the balcony murders - perhaps Dina's case belongs in that category. I have heard Dina talking *in extenso* about her crusade against corrupt officials, and I even warned her of the consequences. Don't let us lose time by chasing her innocent brothers, who only happen to be unpleasant."

Now he had done it again, persuaded Alistair to come around to his point of view. although this time it should finally have been the other way round.

Alistair had two contact numbers to start with, which he had found on business cards in Dina's wallet. It was not much, but with her mobile phone still held by the police it was all he had.

The first belonged to Ahmed Selim, the lawyer with the melodious bedside voice.

The second one was that of a certain Mahmoud el-Allamy, a journalist on an Egyptian newspaper. Here Rietberg could help with the identification. During his lengthy sessions with Dina she had called him her closest ally in her campaign to save Islamic antiquities from theft; his role had been to follow up her report about the missing artefacts to the Egyptian restitution department. He was probably the best informed person about her recent activities in Egypt. Rietberg wanted to contact him immediately.

Alistair thought not so. For reasons Rietberg could not understand he seemed more keen to meet Ahmed Selim. This was an opportunity to let Alistair win an argument, so Alistair phoned the lawyer first. In the end it proved to be a good decision.

As had been the case with Dina, Ahmed answered the phone immediately.

There was a little pause after Alistair introduced himself as Dina's ex-husband.

"Yes, what can I do for you?" he asked, "and how is Mrs Ghalib?"

Alistair looked at Rietberg and signalled to him Ahmed obviously did not know what had happened yet.

"I have very bad news, Dina died under mysterious circumstances."

"What?" Ahmed seemed to be deeply shocked. "What happened? When she left Egypt she seemed to be in perfectly good health."

"Her death had nothing to do with her health. Perhaps you can tell me more about a possible reason," Alistair said. "I found your business card in her wallet, so I suppose that you met her during her stay in Egypt."

"Yes, we did meet, several times in fact. She had some problems with her family after her father's recent demise and wanted my legal advice in an inheritance matter."

Several times for inheritance meetings? Was everything in Egypt about money alone, or had there been something else between them?

"Look, Mr Selim, I, as well as one of her closest friends who is with me, would like to know more about this. Could we meet perhaps?"

"Of course," said Ahmed. "There is also something else that could interest you."

They met in the lobby of the Marriott Hotel. Ahmed had proposed the venue because he had his meetings with Dina there, as he said. In the lobby only, or in her room? Alistair wondered. He could hardly avoid another gaffe.

It was to be a lengthy session, because Ahmed had a lot to tell them.

"Her family had put a lot of pressure on her, because they want to sell their father's building in Dokki, where she had been brought up."

"That's where we are staying now," said Rietberg.

"Not for long, I assure you. Now that Mrs Ghalib is no longer an obstacle, the building will change hands soon."

All of them had ordered whiskies, which helped to overcome the initial tension. Two of them had slept with Dina, one of whom, Alistair, rightly suspected the other one, Ahmed, to have done so as well, while the latter knew of course that Alistair as her husband would have done so. The only unsuccessful lover was Rietberg, which did not prevent Alistair from being jealous of him as Dina's intimate partner in scholarly matters. It was certainly a psychologically overloaded meeting.

After a while Ahmed asked Alistair:

"Has Dina made a last will, and who did she nominate as her heir?"

"I am the sole heir according to her last will," said Alistair, "but her family and also my friend Rietberg here told me that it does not entitle me to a share of her estate in Egypt, if that's what you want to ask."

"That is true if your inheritance abroad exceeds one third of her estate, which is probably the case," confirmed Ahmed.

Yet soon the news he gave them about the threats to which Dina had been subjected overshadowed everything else.

Alistair and Rietberg listened with increasing horror to Ahmed's report of her abduction and the arrest of her ally Mahmoud al-Allamy.

"Unbelievable," Alistair said finally, "Poor Dina, how she had to suffer."

"During our time in Egypt, many years ago, nothing like that could have happened," commented Rietberg.

"No, Sir," disagreed Ahmed, "it did happen all the time to us Egyptians, although not to privileged foreigners like yourselves. Now no one is really safe, especially if you act against what they call 'public security'. You must have heard about the Italian student, who was tortured to death after foolishly carrying out some research on Egyptian trade unions."

"Yes, I read about it," said Rietberg, "but were they not criminals who did this? I remember that the police found his belongings with a criminal gang."

"Who were all killed in the raid and could not tell anyone that the evidence was planted. Very convenient, don't you think?"

They drank their whiskies in silence. The first steps in their fact finding mission to Egypt had found more contaminated dirt than Alistair and Rietberg had ever suspected.

"I still have some problems in seeing a connection between what happened to Dina here and her antiquities campaign," said Rietberg after a while. "Even assuming she had accused specific persons of theft or corruption—and she had not as far as I know—it is inconceivable that even an undemocratic regime would revert to such drastic measures in that case. Ministers have been continually accused of corruption and nothing serious has happened. When I lived here the brother of President Sadat himself was attacked in the Egyptian media for his illegal dealings, even in the state-owned press, and the only one prosecuted was the man himself."

Ahmed smiled.

"While all our leaders were dictators, there are still differences between them. What one tolerated, the other would not. But let's leave politics aside for the moment. Dina had engaged me to negotiate Mahmoud al-Allamy's release from prison. You might know about him—the journalist who wrote an article based on Dina's accusations. We should try to meet him to gain a clearer picture. He is very scared now since his arrest, which happened around the time of Dina's abduction. As his lawyer, to whom he owes his liberty, I can probably arrange a meeting with him."

Their wait for Ahmed's call to confirm their proposed meeting with Mahmoud gave them an opportunity to meet old friends they still had in Cairo. Alistair went off to see some bankers he had known and who were still in the land of the living. Most of all he was looking forward to a game of golf at a new golf course in Qattamiya to the south of Cairo, which he wanted to test for a change from his old favourite course in the shadow of the pyramids. He was a bit apologetic when he announced his plan to Rietberg.

"It might appear frivolous under the circumstances," he said, "but Dina herself would have wished me to play a game that made us pass many happy hours together."

Of course. It is general consensus that the dead always want the survivors to have some fun during the mourning period. Rietberg could not therefore find anything untoward in Alistair's idea. Knowing Dina's opinion of golf Alistair was wrong in one respect, however. The many hours they had spent together at the golf course were certainly happy for Alistair but less so for Dina.

Rietberg himself planned to go to the land registry archive behind the High Court building, where he had passed his own happy hours studying Ottoman trust documents during his sabbatical as a young professor. He wanted to find Ustadh Farag, the then director of the archive, who had become a close friend, probably the only one he ever had in Cairo. He had little hope of learning what had become of him after more than thirty years though. Ustadh Farag would certainly be long retired, or perhaps even passed on.

For nostalgia's sake he walked along the same streets as before, from the Garden City House, where he had been staying, via Qasr el-Nil street to Fouad Street where the archive was. It had always amused him that this main street was still generally known by the name of Fouad, the Egyptian king who died some seventy years ago, and not by its official name, 23rd July Street, so-called in commemoration of the officers' coup in 1952. As an historian Rietberg did not understand why Nasser chose such a convoluted name which had no chance of gaining popular acceptance. Nasser Street instead of Fouad Street would have sounded pretentious, but would certainly have fared much better as a name.

In downtown Cairo nothing had changed much on the outside, the splendid buildings dating to the royal period were still standing and continued to look slightly neglected, as before. The truly ugly new buildings were constructed elsewhere, so Cairo's centre had not lost its faded charm. The traffic congestion was worse, the taxis had a different colour and almost all women now covered their heads with the *hijab*—but that was more or less the only visible difference to the city that he had known in the past.

When Rietberg arrived at the land registry, they would not grant him admission. A permit to use the archive had always been required, but now security was even tighter. With little expectation of success, he asked at the entrance if anyone knew where he could find their old director, Ustadh Farag Abaza.

"Yes, he is here. Just walk up the stairs and you will see him when you enter the archive; he's at his usual place," was the utterly surprising reply. The man guarding the entrance had become much more friendly now. Someone who knew Ustadh Farag had to be treated with respect.

Rietberg—although never the sportive one—sprinted up the stairs.

Indeed, there he was, Ustadh Farag, greyer, more corpulent and more wrinkled, but with his cheap suit and his striped tie very much the familiar and always helpful bureaucrat, who had spent his whole life guarding the old documents.

Both men nearly cried at their meeting again after so many years. To escape from the indiscreet stares of other users they continued their talk about old times in a near-by café. Ustadh Farag had decided recently to spend his ample free time by writing a detailed index with short annotations about each document to facilitate the work of scholars—"scholars like you," he added with a smile. When Rietberg mentioned that his present interest was stolen antiquities, Ustadh Farag proceeded to tell him a story about such an incident during his directorship that had caused him much distress.

Several so-called *waqf* deeds establishing trusts between the 16th to 19th centuries had disappeared from the archive and were never found.

"I was even suspected of helping the unknown thieves, but in the end was exonerated. However, my small salary was reduced for twelve months as a punishment for what was called negligence on my part. It was later discovered that the thief must have made copies after studying the documents a first time and at a second time returned these copies and kept the originals."

"Do you know who he or she was?"

"Yes, that was the easiest part, because you know from your own experience that we keep a logbook of our users, together with a list of the loaned documents."

"So was he or she arrested?"

Ustadh Farag had a resigned smile.

"When all this was discovered he had already left the country. He was a foreigner, a distinguished professor, no less!"

At least the gender issue was clarified now, which was not a bad result in politically correct times.

"Our—or rather my—mistake was to instinctively trust the *khawaga,* more than my fellow countrymen in spite of all the looting of Egyptian antiquities by foreigners in the past, not least by bona fide scholars."

Rietberg was captivated by Ustadh Farag's sad tale. It was a useful addition to Dina's complaints about Egyptian venality, which was about money—but there was also a Western form of venality, this one concerned with antiquities.

Rietberg and Ustadh Farag chatted for a long time, reminiscing over shared memories, and parted knowing that they would never meet again.

One thing they did not touch upon was politics. Rietberg had hoped to gain Ustadh Farag's opinion about the latest upheavals in Egyptian politics. He was a devout Muslim, as revealed by his *zabiba,* or prayer bump, the brown spot on his forehead created by procrastinations during prayer. Rietberg was keen to hear his views on the Muslim brothers and their leader Mursi, who was now in prison. But Ustadh Faraq blocked him. He did not want to touch on this subject, which Rietberg interpreted as fear. That was new; even in Mubarak's time the president was criticized or more often even ridiculed in private conversations. Something had changed for the worse in Egypt, which was ironic considering the Arab Spring had promised a brighter future.

On his way back to the Ghalib building he passed by some of his former favourite places. The bookshop on Soliman Pasha square (another surviving royalist name in spite of its republican renaming as 'Talaat Harb square') had been sanitized; no more books lying outside for easy browsing, now only accessible on shelves inside. The café on the terrace of the former Nile Hilton was still there, but had increased its prices to a level that could only be called obscene compared with those in other places. There was no more shisha on offer when he sat down for an expensive tea. Rietberg was not immune to the usual grumblings of the elderly— everything in their youth had been so much better!

When he arrived at the Ghalib building, he saw a huge Mercedes with a diplomatic licence plate drawing up in front of the entrance. A rear passenger door opened and out came Mona, Dina's cousin, with a bright flashing smile.

"What a coincidence," she said, "I am so glad to see you again."

Then the car drove away. Rietberg could just see the silhouette of a man sitting in the rear seat behind a chauffeur.

"Why don't you join me for a drink at my place? We had no time to talk before."

She was pretty and definitely more agreeable company than the rest of her family. Her unfortunately bleached hair was well-groomed and not covered and fell down freely framing her fine head, with its brown sparkling eyes and small dimples on her cheeks. She was immensely attractive, a playful alternative to the more serious Dina. Rietberg immediately accepted her invitation. It was also much better than having a conversation with Alistair in Dina's flat now.

In the lift, he inhaled her expensive perfume. Rietberg did not know much about women, but something indefinable in her ways seemed to signal that she had a very recent erotic experience. Rietberg guessed from the diplomatic Mercedes that she was probably sleeping with a diplomat.

Her flat was furnished in a girly way, lots of pink, lots of chintz and lots of souvenirs. Either she had travelled a lot or they had been given to her by friends or lovers. On a desk with little room for serious work she had arranged many photographs of various people, most of them grinning 'cheese' at the photographer. This was an interior chosen by either a naive girl at puberty or a post-puberty slightly frivolous woman, in Mona's case obviously the latter. Mona had apparently no intellectual interests: there were no books, just a huge TV-screen. All in all her personality was definitely a complete opposite to that of her cousin Dina, but very likeable in her own way.

After all the recent serious conversations Rietberg did not mind some banal chit-chat with Mona. It was unhealthy to think of Dina's death all the time.

While she prepared the drinks—unsurprisingly alcoholic ones—he studied the photographs on her desk. Most persons were unknown to him, apart from her, her cousin Maguid and her brother Halim, who had been united on a family photograph. In the middle was an elderly man—probably their late father—flanked by a sour looking woman and a man wearing a hat. A standard old-fashioned European fedora that was no longer worn anywhere, and certainly almost never in Egypt!.

It was probably taken before or after a sailing trip on the Nile by one of the touts offering this service at tourist spots. because there were several *felouka*s in the background at their mooring place near Qasr al-Nil bridge. The group did not look particularly happy, except Halim, whose job was to provide happiness to everyone on a tourist excursion.

"That looks funny," Rietberg said casually, "could that be Yusuf wearing a hat?"

Mona gave him a glass of malt whisky, probably part of a duty-free diplomatic consignment, and laughed.

"Yes, that's Yusuf and his wife you see in the middle together with my uncle, when they visited Egypt. Yusuf has always played the *khawaga* by wearing a hat and even calls himself Joseph now. He also used to smoke a pipe as another sign of being western. Unfortunately, his truly western wife forced him to quit smoking altogether. Poor Yusuf! In spite of all his efforts to become part of western society, he can never keep up with the fleeting changes of ideas and fashion there."

After serving herself an astonishingly large portion of whisky, unpolluted by either ice or soda, she added:

"Yusuf adopted a hat during his studies in the US when it was already coming out of fashion there. Yet old black-and-white gangster movies with mafia types shooting or sitting at a bar, always with their hats on, made a lasting impression on him."

"You must have seen many such movies yourself to know that."

"Oh, yes I have; I love them. In this particular case our good Joseph has not missed this fashion change by mistake, though. Once he confided in me that his wife, in a rare moment of adoration, told him that he looked like Humphrey Bogart wearing a hat."

She laughed once more.

"In my opinion he looks more like Stan Laurel, but never underestimate the vanity of men."

Her European diplomatic husbands cannot have had an easy life with this woman, Rietberg thought.

He could have made a contribution to the American hat fashion story by mentioning Edward Hopper's famous painting with two men sitting forlornly at a bar with their hats on. Yet by that he would only show off his erudition as a university professor, and Mona would not be able to resist making fun of him. He decided against indulging his professorial ways, rather reluctantly though.

He liked Mona's carefree way of talking. Unlike her relatives she saw the funny side of everything, and moreover she was obviously without a financial agenda, which was taken care of by others.

They talked a lot about Dina. Mona was fascinated with his story of how and when he had met her.

"Why didn't you marry her?" she asked. "Or were you satisfied by having sex with her only?"

Things had never been so easy for Rietberg, unfortunately. But how could he explain the difficulties a German professor would face if he had a relationship with a young Egyptian girl? Mona would never understand, because she had no complexes at all.

He quickly changed the subject to her own memories of Dina and her last stay in Egypt; but all the time he could not get that hat-wearing Joseph out of his mind. If Dina's brother had stayed in Egypt after the death of Ghalib senior, as he had understood from his conversation with the Ghalibs, he could not have been the one seen on the CCTV leaving the flat with her. Or could he?

He hesitated to ask more about him. Mona was anything but stupid and would quickly become aware of the unusual interest he had in her cousin.

"I suppose you were all present and well informed about what Dina was doing in Egypt, except attending *arbaeen*?" he asked as casually as he could. "Neither Alistair nor myself know anything concrete."

"Yes, we have all been here since *arbaeen* to settle the inheritance matter, except Yusuf, who had to travel to Amsterdam for a few days to attend a congress of psychiatrists. But Dina did not tell us whom she saw during her stay. She never seemed to like us anyway."

The last remark prompted her to talk of her trip to Alexandria with Dina, when they had become friends. That change in Dina's attitude to her seemed to have mattered a lot to Mona.

"You know, Jürgen—I hope that I can call you that," she said, becoming very serious all of a sudden, "to become the friend of that exceptional woman was very dear to me. I am quite happy with the way I am, but I am also aware that no one—including my lovers—ever takes me seriously. But Dina did, and I shall be always grateful to her."

When he left her, after another Laphroaig, he felt somehow rejuvenated; partly by her refreshing company, but most of all by the news about the man with the hat, who had travelled to Amsterdam during that period. It was quite probably a pure coincidence that someone like him was on the CCTV tape—hats were certainly out of fashion, but had not died out completely. But it was certainly worth looking into the matter more deeply. Amsterdam was too close to London to rule out further speculation.

When he entered Dina's flat Alistair was already there. He had cut short his visits to his banker friends so as not to miss a game on the new golf course at Qattamiya. He was obviously proud of his respectable score in spite of the handicap of rented clubs. His game had reminded him of a famous story that was told in the Cairo golfing community about the old course at the pyramids.

"You know there is a story about a British officer teeing up on top of the Cheops pyramid to shoot his drive directly onto the first green. Certainly an urban legend, but in those blessed times, before mass tourism, climbing the pyramids was still permitted, and his clubs would have been carried to the top by a sweating caddy. Not that I would have tried it myself even then."

A khaki-clad officer swinging his club on top of one of the great wonders of the world in an occupied country—no better symbol of colonialism than that!

Rietberg could now understand Dina. She had once told him that she always suspected her husband of being more interested in golf than in her or even in his own job.

He told Alistair about the man with the hat and his travels to Amsterdam, changing the subject from golf back to Dina.

"What?" exclaimed Alistair. "Could he be the same one who was seen with Dina? This could only be if, instead of attending the congress of psychiatrists in Amsterdam, or in addition to it, he went to London as well. In that case he must have lied about his travel to Europe, which would make him a suspect immediately, of course. It also surprises me that he is still here. The inheritance problems could be solved in his absence, after the brothers agreed amongst themselves to sell the building. He always gives me the impression of being unlucky with his life, or his wife, in America, or both, and therefore is in no hurry to return home."

"Speculating or having impressions is not the same as being sure," replied Rietberg.

"How can we make sure then?" asked Alistair. "Asking questions sounds like a police investigation, and we cannot possibly do that."

Rietberg agreed.

"What we can do, is request a copy of that photograph, or take another picture, or even better a video with Yusuf wearing a hat and show it to Dina's neighbour and the police, hoping they can identify him. We also have to know more about that congress of psychiatrists in Amsterdam."

Alistair laughed.

"It's 30 degrees Celsius outside, so how would you make Yusuf wear a hat?"

"He does not wear a hat against the cold, it's an acquired habit; he imagines he looks like Humphrey Bogart in his films. Mona told me that."

"Yusuf a Humphrey Bogart? Are you serious? But if you want, let us give it a try. We could invite the whole bloody family to a nice outing when a hat could be worn, perhaps a sailing trip on a *felouka*? I have done this often with guests from abroad to let them enjoy the magical side of Egypt. I only hope that the presence of Dina's brothers does not spoil my own pleasure."

"And you take a video with Yusuf stepping onto the *felouka* with his hat. A very good idea that. It could help the police to identify him as the man on the CCTV-tape," agreed Rietberg.

"There is one more thing I can do, when we are back in London," added Alistair, with growing enthusiasm for detective work. "We have to know more about Yusuf's situation in America, especially as he is apparently reluctant to return there. I happen to know the Chief Executive of a mortgage bank in Philadelphia, a former colleague of mine in the British Orient Bank. These mortgage people know everything about everyone in the United States or they can tap the right sources, because they have to make thorough checks before lending hundreds of thousands of dollars. He owes me, because I wrote a glowing report about him as a reference, when he applied for the job."

"A very good idea once more," said Rietberg, glad to be able to approve an initiative taken by Alistair finally.

The *felouka* trip was a mixed success from the touristic point of view, but a complete failure from the criminalist one. Almost all the Ghalibs joined the party, even their demented mother, who seemed to enjoy it. The only one not present was Yusuf.

Maguid apologized for him.

"He does not feel well and prefers to stay at home."

The other one not feeling well was Alistair, who had organized the excursion with the detested Ghalib-family and even had to pay for it, for the sole purpose of making a video on his mobile phone of Yusuf with his hat.

"Perhaps he is afraid of getting seasick," said Rietberg, but no one laughed.

Something was obviously not quite right with Yusuf, not only his hat, but also his inexplicably morose or sad demeanour. Besides, as was apparent from the beginning, he seemed to avoid Alistair's and Rietberg's company and never talked to them, except when he gave Alistair his astonishingly professional legal brief about Dina's inheritance.

Rietberg sensed something indefinably suspicious, and as always he trusted his instinct. "You have seen too many movies with police inspectors who solve their cases by trusting their miraculous instincts against all existing proof," Marie-Anne had once jokingly remarked.

The excursion lasted three hours, with the captain steering and sailing with the usual north wind while going upstream. It was truly romantic, but only after they reached the middle of the river beyond Rodha-island. A large number of radios, recorders and even portable TV-sets had become essential accessories at the mooring place where they were playing loud so-called music, flicking between rap and Abd al-Halim Hafiz, the 'Egyptian nightingale'. The infernal noise could still be heard at quite a distance, because sound travels far on the waters of the Nile.

But once they were out of reach they were back in the good old days with the simple pleasures of listening to the sound of water, the flapping sail and the creaking boat, drinking beer, eating sandwiches brought along by Mona, smoking and having a quiet conversation. Particularly moving was the moment when the poor demented mother started to sing a nearly inaudible song. The magic of the eternal river was back, and even Alistair started to enjoy the trip together with Dina's much disliked family.

Yet how would they obtain a photograph with Yusuf and his hat now?

Their next days were spent going out to do some sightseeing, independent of Halim's services.

Their excursions reconciled them with the uncomfortable megalopolis Cairo had become. But the touristic sites had not been neglected as other parts of the city and were still easily accessible, although only after considerable time spent in the seemingly permanent traffic jams.

What had entirely changed though was Maadi, the former leafy suburb in Cairo's south where Alistair and Dina had lived for many years. Alistair wanted to see their former ivy-covered villa, even enter it, if the present owners agreed to his nostalgic visit. Rietberg, who had often been invited there by Dina, immediately proposed to join him. He remembered their lazy afternoons together in the large garden, with whiskies brought by the Nubian servant, while the occasional braying of a donkey with its rider passing the garden punctuated their quiet conversations.

Looking forward to reliving the good old times spent in Dina's company they rented a taxi for the day and set out to drive along the broad corniche along the fast flowing waters of the Nile that looked as eternal as ever.

An unpleasant surprise greeted them when they turned left to enter Maadi. The suburb had changed beyond recognition. Former villas were nearly everywhere replaced by ugly concrete buildings, most of the lush gardens had disappeared in the process of de-gentrification, and to find the Trevelyan villa they had first to cross a new flyover spanning the railway line then double back while trying to explain to their driver, where they thought the villa was. After driving around for some time they arrived at their destination. In fact, it was only the street and the street-number that had not changed, everything else had. There was no villa anymore nor the large garden with its palm tree; now it was replaced by two four-storey buildings with satellite dishes defiling every balcony and old air-conditioning units gracing their walls.

"*Sic transit gloria mundi,*" said Rietberg, who liked to quote Latin proverbs. Alistair's first thought was to ask someone in the building about the fate of the former villa and its owner. He dropped the idea as soon as he saw a man coming out of the building. The contrast between his appearance and that of villa owners was too obvious to ask such a futile and perhaps provocative question.

After this misadventure they admitted to each other that they were truly grumpy old men, for whom everything in the past was better. Alistair was glad to return to the Dokki building, which seemed luxurious now in comparison with the hideous concrete structures that had replaced his villa.

On one occasion, when Rietberg returned to the Ghalib building carrying two bottles of Stella beer from a Coptic grocer, he met a man in the entry area, obviously an Egyptian tenant of one of the rented flats.

The other tenants were all expatriates—the Spanish press councillor, the Japanese Sumitomo representative and a teacher at the German school. Rietberg only knew the teacher who had invited him once for a drink in his flat. His living room was furnished mainly with the orientalist furniture in vogue with expatriates—a beautiful large copper vessel used traditionally to simmer *ful* to its required softness; the inevitable inlaid oriental stool; and a few uncomfortable chairs of so-called Islamic design. Their conversation was mostly about tourism in Egypt that the teacher and his wife had apparently completely covered, so they had a lot to say about lodging in the Siwa oasis and camel tours in the desert. It brought back memories of Germany, where tourism is the modern form of 'Wanderlust', yet a lot more popular. Rietberg left after a while with a deep sigh of relief.

The Egyptian, who Rietberg had seen and briefly greeted before with a small nod, addressed him in halting English:

"Please Sir, may I ask you a question?"

"Go ahead," answered Rietberg, in Arabic.

The man—quite old and cheaply dressed—seemed relieved that his limited language skills were not needed.

"So you speak Arabic. But you are not an Egyptian?"

"No," laughed Rietberg, "no one has ever taken me for anything else than a German."

The man was evidently encouraged by Rietberg's laugh and lost his shyness.

"Can I invite you for a cup of tea in my home? I prefer to ask my question there, in private, where no one can hear us."

"Of course, but I hope you do not mind that I carry my beer with me," said Rietberg. One never knew what pious Muslims might take offence at.

"No," said the man, who seemed completely relaxed now, "I am not one of those."—In short: not one of the Islamic fundamentalists.

His flat on the ground floor was as large as the other ones, but furnished much more cheaply than all the Ghalib homes. The only sign that he had obviously seen better days were a set of chairs in what was known as the 'Farouk Seize' style, the Egyptian version of 'Louis Seize' fashionable in the fifties and earlier. His wife, a woman of similar age with friendly eyes, looked surprised at the *khawaga* entering with her husband. They presented themselves as Abd al-Rahman and Khadiga.

Rietberg was offered the obligatory tea and the two old people started a polite and banal conversation, praising Rietberg's Arabic and asking if he was married and had children. Normally he would have followed the lengthy procedure, but he was more interested in knowing what the neighbour had to ask him so confidentially.

Abd al-Rahman immediately obliged by asking the question that was on his mind.

"I have seen you recently together with your friend, and I was wondering if you came to buy this building," he said, looking somewhat anxiously at Rietberg.

"No, definitely not," Rietberg answered laughing. "I do not have the money, and besides even if I bought it, I am not sure I would be granted a residence permit."

He thought that his answer would come as a relief to the old people, who were obviously worried about their situation after the building was sold.

In fact, it was the exact opposite. Abd al-Rahman and Khadiga looked deeply disappointed.

"What's the matter?" asked Rietberg, "you do not seem to have liked my reply."

"No, we had hoped for another answer," said Abd al-Rahman with a sigh, while his wife nearly started crying.

Then Abd al-Rahman explained. They had rented the apartment since the early seventies from Ghalib senior under a system of strict rent control. They could afford it even with his small salary as an employee of the Egyptian Railways. Because the rent could not be increased in spite of inflation, it now amounted to nearly nothing, which helped to compensate for the rising living costs elsewhere. Yet recently they had reason to fear that their quiet and cheap life in the Ghalib building would not last for much longer.

"The army has shown interest in buying the building," said Abd al-Rahman. "I know this because I overheard a conversation between an officer and Maguid Ghalib. Apparently they want it as an annex to the army residential building near-by. If that happens, we shall have to move out for sure. Neither the army will let us stay here, nor would we like to stay with a lot of army people."

While the Ghalibs received a decent income from the expatriates who rented their flats 'furnished', *i.e.* outside of rent control, with not much more than a few chairs as furniture, they received next to nothing from Rietberg's hosts with their unfurnished flat. It was a classic clash of interest, between landlord and tenant, and without a satisfactory solution in sight.

He knew about the intention of Dina's brothers to sell the building, of course, but had never realised that they were negotiating with the army.

"But can they throw you out? You are protected tenants after all."

Abd al-Rahman looked surprised.

"Protected tenants—you say? Not for the army! That's why we had hoped that someone else buys the building. You will understand now why we are disappointed by your answer."

"This is sad news indeed," said Rietberg. "I suppose it would not be easy for you to find another home at an affordable rent."

"Not easy, you said? It is impossible! My pension would not even cover half the rent of any new apartment, and our savings are too meagre for buying even a small one. Our only possibility is to move in with one of our children, who live in small flats themselves."

Khadiga started to weep silently.

It was all very depressing. Rietberg tried to find words to console the two elderly people, but only managed to say that it was still too early for them to despair.

"Perhaps the Ghalibs will not sell, if they do not come to an agreement with the army."

"*Inshaallah*," said Abd al-Rahman with resignation.

Rietberg took his beer bottles and left his hosts regretting that he was unable to console them. He decided to talk to Maguid about this.

The day before their return to England Maguid invited Alistair and Rietberg for a farewell dinner at his flat. He had not invited his brother or his cousins; only his wife Fawziya was there. She had prepared a tasty meal with chicken soup as starters and stuffed vine leaves for the main course. A bottle of red Chateau Grand Marquis from the Gianaclis vineyard and—as a concession to Rietberg, who did not like Egyptian wine—two bottles of Stella beer were prepared to accompany their food. Maguid had whisky, the favourite Egyptian dinner drink except for pious Muslims. Fawziya drank bottled water.

Rietberg was surprised that the rest of the Ghalib family did not attend. He did not ask why, but had his own interpretation for their absence: Maguid wanted to explain something in private.

Alistair had no intention of analyzing Maguid's intentions and asked him quite bluntly:

"Where are the others?"

"Well," answered Maguid smiling, "all of them are occupied with other things at the moment, but they will join us later for drinks."

After attacking his chicken soup he said:

"There is something I want to tell you to avoid bad feelings between us in future. I suppose that Dina has told you about our plans to sell the building after our father's death and that she was opposed to it?"

"She did in fact," lied Rietberg, who did not want to name Abd al-Rahman downstairs as his source. It was all new to Alistair, of course. He looked surprised but fortunately did not comment.

"Dina told me also that you want to sell to the army," Rietberg lied once more.

He tried not to look at Alistair, whose expression was now one big question mark.

"Yes, indeed," said Maguid. "So you already know the background. There are several reasons in favour of this sale, which Dina unfortunately did not want to understand. The price we can achieve is not only good, but also secure, because the army unlike other bidders has no financial problems."

Fawziya tried to support her husband's argument, but as usual a short look from him cut her short. She took a second helping of the vine leaves, while Maguid continued:

"There is another factor that I do not want to mention in front of the others. Yusuf needs money quite urgently. He refuses to tell us why, but it seems he is quite desperate. I think that he has gambling debts, because I have seen him going into the Ritz Carlton casino, where foreigners like him can play roulette. As a true gambler he was probably trying to recover his losses at a single stroke of luck. I do not have a high respect for gamblers, but he is our brother, after all."

"And why are you telling us all this?" asked Alistair.

Maguid answered, somehow entreatingly:

"Look Alistair, I am no fool. I know that yours and your friend Rietberg's opinion of our family is, like Dina's, not the best. But as I was saying before, I do not want you to leave Cairo without understanding our position as well. Apart from what I told you about Yusuf there is more. The army expressed their interest a long time ago, and I had to keep putting them off week after week when our father was still alive. If we wait for much longer I risk losing the support of the general in charge, and I have already seen the first signs of that happening. In view of his close relationship with the Minister of Defence, losing his favour could certainly damage my future career or even my present position as the head of the National Service Products Organization for the army. It may all sound egotistic to you, but our motives are certainly more rational than Dina's. Because of reasons she would or could not explain she refused to sell this property, which she did not even need. As in the past, she would scarcely have used it in the future anyway, if at all."

Before Rietberg could answer, Alistair nodded his agreement:

"Although I did not know all this, because my friend Rietberg here has never mentioned it before," he said, looking at Rietberg with a sign of reproach, "you are probably right. Dina was quite headstrong and stubborn, often just out of spite."

Maguid had a point. They could understand his reasons for selling the building. Still Rietberg was not convinced that Maguid

had told them everything. An army officer selling the family heir-
loom to the army? It smacked of corruption and the suspicion that
Maguid would get more from the deal than just the general's
support.

"You will still lose all your rental income when you sell,
however. I suppose that it is not so little, the amount you receive
from your tenants?"

Maguid laughed.

"My dear Professor Rietberg," he said, "I suppose that you
are not a landlord yourself. I will tell you what we receive from
our tenants—a decent rent from our three expatriates and next to
nothing from our dear Egyptian couple downstairs. All that is
offset by the lack of income between the time an expatriate moves
out and another moves in and by the damage that our tenants
cause in their flats, for example by our Spanish diplomat. The
señor forgot to turn the bathtub taps off, and the water leaked
down to the flat below. But we will not receive any compensation.
He refuses to pay and due to his diplomatic immunity we cannot
force him. This is in addition to the time and money I waste collecting rents, paying taxes and employing tradesmen for the
upkeep of the building. As to our Egyptian tenants downstairs, I
had asked them for a voluntary increase of the ridiculously low
amount they are paying thanks to socialist rent control, but they
refused. 'We know our rights' was their only answer! No, getting
cash for the building is much better, believe me."

Before Rietberg could raise more objections to a decision that
was none of his business after all, Halim, Yusuf and Mona came
in, returning from whatever they were doing—probably only
waiting for Maguid's appointment.

"Oh, I do love your vine leaves, Fawziya," exclaimed Mona,
"can I have some please?"

Mahmoud al-Allamy came to the Marriott Hotel, after he had
heard from Ahmed that Dina had died. At first he was so shocked
that he was reluctant to meet anyone. Ahmed finally convinced
him that as his lawyer he only wanted to talk about his arrest and
give him legal advice for the future. Mahmoud's paranoia and his
fear of being under surveillance made the originally planned

presence of Rietberg's and, most of all, Dina's husband's impossible. If both came to the meeting he would get up and leave immediately. He did not want anyone suspecting him of further activities in a case he had been drawn into by Dina.

He was more afraid of his wife than the police, and therefore proposed the hotel and not his home as the venue. As he admitted himself, his wife had made it quite clear that any links he had in the Dina affair had to be cut, and that included his lawyer, who had been engaged by Dina.

Ahmed was glad that it was only Mahmoud who showed up. In Mahmoud's flat his wife would not leave them alone for one minute and would constantly control their conversation, ready to intervene at any moment if Dina's name or Egyptian antiquities were mentioned.

'What has become of the courageous anti-corruption fighter', thought Ahmed, when he saw him entering the lobby making furtive glances all around as if he was trying to spot anyone looking like a secret policeman. Even in prison he had not looked so frightened. Constant hammering and reproaches by his bossy wife were the main reasons that Ahmed could think of.

As expected, it was a very hesitant start. Mahmoud was a pious Muslim and could not be tempted to lose some of his reserve with a stiff drink.

"Just Turkish coffee, please. A *mazbout*." He got his medium-sugared coffee, while Ahmed settled for a bloody Mary, hoping that Mahmoud would interpret it as the name of a special tomato juice.

At the start Mahmoud wanted to know the reason for Dina's death. In spite of his grudge that she had involved him in something dangerous, he still admired her and was proud of their friendship. He was deeply upset by the news of her death and wanted to know more. Yet Ahmed had decided to keep him in the dark, and mumbled something about a car accident. If he told him about her fall from a tenth floor, Mahmoud would have a heart attack. As a journalist he certainly knew about the balcony murders—for everyone in Egypt the preferred method of the Mukhabarat to eliminate public enemies. Hinting at such a murder would only increase his paranoia.

Ahmed intended to ask him about any contacts he had made before writing his article that could have been the cause of his arrest and of Dina's abduction, because his contacts might know more about Dina's death or even be implicated in her murder. He had to handle Mahmoud carefully though. Ahmed decided to play the card of a lawyer who could provide help in future only if he knew everything about his background..

"If someone sues you in the future for libel in your article, and that can always happen even after you have been released from prison, I as your lawyer have to know of anyone who you spoke to. To name them could help in such a case. It is always better than proclaiming your right as a journalist to protect your sources. I doubt very much, by the way, that this right is respected in our country. As you rightly said, your main duty now is to protect yourself and your family from further trouble."

Mahmoud was still hesitating.

"I owe you my liberty, but how can you be my lawyer? It can be only if I pay you an honorarium officially. Under the circumstances it is better that no one knows that is was in fact Dina, who paid it."

"Don't mention it," said Ahmed with a reassuring smile. "Dina left me a decent sum for covering all my fees concerning your case, but I shall always say that it was you who paid me."

Mahmoud was visibly relieved and opened up.

"Only never tell the real source of your fees to my wife who hates Dina. And if she asks how much I paid make it very moderate. Otherwise she won't believe you."

Both laughed at the thought of deceiving Mahmoud's jealous wife.

The result Ahmed gained from this cautious approach was the name and the telephone number of the only other person that Mahmoud had contacted for his article after his brief from Dina.

That person was Mustafa Fezzani, deputy director for international relations in the Ministry of Antiquities, Dina's former university classmate!

Mahmoud told Ahmed that the purpose of his visit to Mustafa Fezzani was to establish whether anything about the stolen objects had come to the knowledge of the authorities and if he could enlist Fezzani's support to trace them.

"I was surprised by his reaction however," said Mahmoud, who had lost much of his reserve. "He seemed to know about all or some of the pieces I mentioned, but instead of offering his support he warned me not to continue. He even mentioned that matters of national security were at stake and I as well as Dina should be more careful in future. As I have heard this crap about Egyptian solidarity and patriotism *vs.* foreign interference often before, I dismissed his advice and published my article nevertheless."

"That's very interesting," said Ahmed. "Have you any idea what he meant by national security?"

"No, none at all, but after my arrest I became convinced that he did not imagine it."

"Did you mention this to Madame Dina?"

"I intended to at first," replied Mahmoud, "but then decided against it. She was not happy with my article anyway. She told me she would have preferred trying more discreet means before going public. Of course, now with hindsight I know that both Fezzani with his warning and Dina with her caution were right."

"My next article will be about something totally different. A rigged tender to build a new school perhaps," he added laughing. "National security is only involved in what our children should learn, not in the safety of school buildings."

As everything in their Egyptian cat-and-mouse game had to be planned in advance in order to avoid irreparable mistakes, the three conspirators—Alistair, Rietberg and Ahmed agreed to meet once more to discuss their next steps. The first one was to contact Mustafa Fezzani, who could probably shed some light on the mysterious arrest of Mahmoud al-Allamy and the equally mysterious abduction of Dina.

As to the venue for their meeting, Ahmed proposed the Marriott Hotel once more.

"I would have liked to invite you for a change to the Automobile Club, where I am a member," he said regretfully. "It's never advisable though to discuss a confidential matter where you are well known. Your presence will raise questions as to who you are, and the waiters in that club have always been expert eavesdroppers since King Farouk's time, who was a regular customer himself."

Ahmed was certainly more important than they had thought before. Both Alistair and Rietberg knew about the important role the Automobile Club played in Egyptian politics. It dated from the time when automobiles were the privilege of only the happy and influential few, and the club tried to live up to its reputation by a restrictive selection of members, which meant that Ahmed was much more than he seemed.

They were lounging in their armchairs in the hotel lobby with some drinks, kept busy by reaching from time to time for their glasses that were put on a low table at an uncomfortable distance.

"What is the idea of low armchairs if you can only reach your glass with so much exercise?" Rietberg asked.

"Easy," said Alistair, "to stop you from falling asleep during a conversation!"

"Meaning a conversation with us?" Rietberg asked.

"To make our conversation more interesting for Mr Trevelyan let us discuss the best way to contact our deputy director for international relations," Ahmed said. "Would you like to hear my suggestions?"

They certainly wanted, so Ahmed continued:

"Our friend Rietberg here should not show up and the same is true for you, Alistair," he said. "Fezzani does not know Rietberg, and Dina's husband could make him suspicious as to the true reason why we want to contact him. Possibly he has not even been informed about Dina's death or the divorce, and while any male will understand a husband who tries to spy on his wife's activities he surely does not want to get involved in a marital dispute," he said. "But I am quite a well-known lawyer, who can always contact him to discuss a confidential matter. He will not refuse to see me, even to only satisfy his curiosity as to why I would like to."

This lesson in diplomacy was convincing. It was Ahmed's role to contact the deputy director of the Antiquities Department in charge of international relations.

Unfortunately, Mustafa Fezzani was in Paris on a mission to discuss a joint exhibition of the Egyptian Museum in Cairo with the Louvre. This was a most difficult undertaking because of the Louvre's justified fears that Egypt would not return items sent to Cairo, which although having been 'legally' obtained in the 19th century were considered stolen by current criteria. Fezzani's negotiations could therefore last for quite a long time and be further extended by some sightseeing in the *ville de lumières* making good use of his travel expenses.

Ahmed promised Alistair and Rietberg to keep them informed about his meeting with Mustafa Fezzani, in case it took place after their departure from Egypt.

Just as he started to heave himself from the deep armchair, Ahmed stopped.

"I almost forgot to tell you about my latest theory regarding Dina's abduction."

Alistair and Rietberg looked at him in surprise.

"So you know more about the motives of the Mukhabarat?" asked Rietberg.

Ahmed grinned.

"No, I don't, but in my opinion the secret services had nothing to do with it."

Reaching for their glasses they waited.

"I have thought over everything that Dina has told me. There are a few things which I had not attached much importance to initially, but which later struck me as relevant," Ahmed started.

"The first was about the car, in which she was abducted. After they hauled her out of its rear she could also see its front briefly, when they returned. The thing she remembered was that the car's licence plates and its make on the front and back were covered. When I asked her to try to remember more, she told me that its radiator grill looked quite peculiar with several equal vertical slots. She had never seen such a car and therefore remembered the shape. What can we conclude from this in your opinion?"

Alistair's and Rietberg's talents as amateur detectives were challenged. After a while Rietberg asked:

"Is there a particular car that is known for that kind of radiator grill?"

Alistair, who did not want to be left behind, said:

"They must have covered the car fearing it could point to the driver's identity, which is not the case for standard cars like Toyota, Honda etc. So which type of car was it?"

Ahmed clapped his hands.

"Together you are my equals, if I may say so in all modesty! You have asked the correct questions."

Rietberg and Alistair did not exactly like his patronising remark, even if he had meant it ironically. Curiosity won however and they listened to what Ahmed had to say.

"The answer to both questions is: it must have been a Jeep! The Jeep Cherokee has exactly that kind of distinctive grill, and is in fact produced in Egypt by the American-Arab Vehicles Company, a joint-venture of Chrysler's with the Arab Organization for Industrialization, the holding company for Egyptian military factories. I do not know of anyone in Egypt except the army driving this quite expensive vehicle with no practical use in the city. It is produced for their use and is their standard issue. Consequently, the make 'Jeep' would immediately point to the military, and therefore it was covered in addition to the licence plate."

"The only army connection we know of is Dina's brother Maguid and his dealings with his general. You do not want us to believe that he was behind all this, do you?" asked Rietberg.

"I'll come to that later, but let me first refer to something else Dina had seen. When the leading member of the gang climbed back into the car, the others gave him a kind of military salute. They were probably not supposed to do so, but it is understandable, when you are used to automatically saluting a superior. Of course, also policemen salute, but the normal police were certainly not involved in the abduction, and I have never heard of the Mukhabarat following any kind of etiquette. So this points once more to someone connected to the army as Dina's abductor."

"Their only motive I could imagine was to frighten Dina and encourage her to give up her flat and support Maguid's and the army's wishes. They could not care less about antiquities, that's for certain. Still a bit rough, don't you think?" asked Alistair.

"Soldiers never care about roughness! We have in fact to get used to the idea of different parties involved in everything that happened to Dina and her journalist at more or less the same time. Let me remind you that it is always difficult to say which part of government is harassing people and for what. During the Tahrir-revolution the army acted with so much restraint that soldiers manning the tanks were offered roses by the demonstrators, whereas the Ministry of Interior tried to save the old regime. Now it is almost the opposite. There are distinctions between the military, the Mukhabarat, the Central Security Forces and the normal police—bitter rivalries even. But which one of the powers that be, or to use a modern term, the 'deep state', was acting in Dina's ordeal I don't know. Not yet!"

Rietberg had always suspected Ahmed of having a hidden agenda, who should be regarded with circumspection in spite of his critical remarks. The reason for accusing the military for Dina's abduction, as he had done right now, could well have been to exonerate their habitual rivals in the security services of this, or worse, of her murder. Ahmed's next remark confirmed his suspicion.

"Maguid's role in all this is still not clear to me. As a quite high ranking officer and as Dina's brother he must have been involved or at least been informed. He seemed to have liked his sister, though, so why would he want to frighten her so brutally out of her wits? He or Yusuf must have had more urgent problems, which we don't know of as yet, to go so far. In fact, there is one more piece of evidence pointing to Maguid. Dina told me that the woman who stopped her at the hotel entrance asked her whether she was Ms Ghalib. Now everyone else, except her own family, knew her only as Ms Trevelyan, her former name. Even Mahmoud's article referred to her as Ms Trevelyan. So this is further proof that Maguid was involved. The whole operation had probably nothing to do with the army as such, but Maguid as a rather high ranking officer could have used some soldiers and the vehicle for his private affairs."

There it was—the probability that the crime was nothing more than a family affair. With all his critique of the highhanded government Ahmed had managed to shift the focus away from them to Dina's own family. His was a clever analysis, but it provoked more questions and the need for more drinks, which were ordered by Alistair and which provided the necessary pause for finding objections to Ahmed's theory.

"I still assume that Dina's abduction and Mahmoud's arrest, which happened more or less simultaneously, were made for the same reason and by the same people," said Rietberg. "In Mahmoud's case I cannot see any army connection nor Maguid's involvement, however, or do soldiers arrest civilians and shut them away in normal prisons in your country? That was a job done by the police or the Mukhabarat, not by the army."

"One more very clever remark," agreed Ahmed smiling condescendingly.

Rietberg decided to let it pass this time also, but one more similar comment would receive a suitable rebuke.

"As you admitted yourself, Mahmoud was certainly not arrested by the military police. But if Dina's kidnappers were people belonging to the army, as I presume, we can no longer cling to the idea of accusing one single party of being involved in everything, even if it happened at more or less the same time. There might be more than one agency with different motives. Dina was waging a war on two fronts, so that's not surprising."

"Now you have made a very clever remark," interjected Alistair in a deadpan voice.

Ahmed got the message and laughed.

"Certainly she lost her war, which was won by her adversaries, whoever they were—but who was it who struck the final blow?" he continued.

Something was still wrong with Ahmed's theory. Rietberg remembered his report of Dina's abduction, when they first met.

"Did her kidnappers not tell her to fight crime in Britain, but not in Egypt? She had never mentioned anything about her antiquities campaign to her family, however, except to Mona, and that was after the kidnapping. On the other hand, the sale of the building—Maguid's only interest—has nothing to do with crime and could not have been meant by that warning," he objected, "so neither he nor anyone in the army was involved."

For the first time Ahmed seemed to be at a loss for an answer. After a while he found one:

"Then Maguid must have been informed about her antiquities campaign early on and tried to shift any suspicion away from him to dark forces within the government. Perhaps he read Mahmoud's article in his scandal paper."

"Perhaps," replied Rietberg without much conviction. He felt tired all of a sudden, most of all by Ahmed's ambiguous argumentation. Their visit to Cairo had raised more questions than they could answer, and he wanted to get some sleep before boarding the plane early the next morning.

"We can sit here all evening and speculate, but we will reach no results," he said, barely suppressing a yawn. "I think we should leave it to Ahmed to find out more. He has the connections and all the time needed for further investigations in Egypt. So let's call it a day and wait in London for future reports from Cairo."

"*Inshaallah*," said Ahmed.

## London

After Rietberg's return from their fact-finding mission he gave Marie-Anne a full account of what had happened.

Marie-Anne tried to find a common thread in the disparate information.

For once she was not busy with medical papers and could concentrate on what she had to say.

"If I have understood your rambling report correctly, we have two different threads here," she said. "One is that ominous national security thing, the other her family relations and the army. Perhaps they are even linked. The common denominator could be Maguid, Dina's intelligent and well-connected brother."

Rietberg thought it over. They were having dinner together, which had been prepared by Marie-Anne. Her talents in the kitchen never matched those of Dina, but he could not even hint at it for fear of creating serious offence.

"Mm, this tastes delicious," he said and continued with all the hypocrisy needed from time to time in a marriage, "your talents to sum up my report match yours as a chef."

It encouraged Marie-Anne to go on.

"There are several loose ends there, however, which you and Alistair need to clarify."

"Yes, and you are the only person I know who can tie up one loose end."

"Me? I am a medical doctor, not a detective," protested Marie-Anne.

"So, I suppose you know other doctors, a psychiatrist perhaps?"

"Of course, I know one or two," said Marie-Anne. "But we don't need marriage counselling yet, or do we?"

He told her about Yusuf's absence from Cairo to attend the World Psychiatric Congress in Amsterdam.

"As I was saying, I have my suspicions. He is much too enigmatic for my taste. Your colleagues, the psychiatrists, will certainly know about that congress; they might even have attended it. Could you ask them about its date and if a colleague from Philadelphia called Yusuf or Joseph Ghalib really went there? I suppose it would not be too difficult to consult the list of attendees."

Marie-Anne hesitated and before answering played with her worry beads that she had recently acquired to serve as stress relief. She had too much work, while he could afford the luxury of reading books and playing the detective. He already wanted to apologize for burdening her with his request when she spoke.

"My psychiatrist friends might wonder why we want to know this. If I were them I would advise asking Yusuf himself. It would be even more difficult, if by any chance Yusuf is a patient of one of my colleagues. In that case he would not be allowed to say anything. It's not that rare to find that psychiatrists themselves are treated for neurotic disorders, you know."

"That does not astonish me at all," said Rietberg, "perhaps Freud should have lain down on his couch himself."

"Very witty," said Marie-Anne. "But I will do you this favour for Dina's sake."

"Marie-Anne, you are a treasure!"

As almost expected, no one called Yusuf or Joseph Ghalib had attended the congress that had taken place at approximately the date of Dina's murder. That was all that Marie-Anne's psychiatrist colleagues could say. One of them had however heard rumours about a scandal involving a psychiatrist in the US, but not being interested neither knew his city nor his name.

Alistair was sitting alone in his flat, brooding, smoking and drinking. To brood was something alien to someone who had always been content with his life, his golf, his work, his friends and his political prejudices. Yet after his return back from Sweden he missed Dina's not always comfortable presence and also many of his former friends, with whom he had lost contact in his isolated life on the shores of the Swedish lake.

He had been reading a lot recently as he had no other occupation except golf. The only reading matter for him was newspapers, mainly the Financial Times and two investor magazines, and for general news the International Herald Tribune, the Times and the Daily Telegraph. Of course it never crossed his mind to touch the Guardian, which was Rietberg's favourite newspaper.

Studying the press had always been part of his job as a banker. He was aware that his expertise in financial matters that people had expected from him was mainly based on newspaper articles. His clients in private banking or his superiors in Head Office, while he managed the British Orient Bank, were always impressed with his knowledge. If they had the time and the patience to read as he did, they would have been as knowledgeable as he was, he admitted once in a rare moment of self-criticism. Dina, who was always irritated by his usual arrogance, liked this unexpected insight and consoled him by saying that it was the same for scholars. The only difference was that the latter had their wisdom from books and the former from newspapers.

After their recent trip to Egypt he had resumed his former habit of reading everything related to Egyptian politics and finances. The Financial Times had reserved many pages in a recent edition for detailed reports about the Egyptian economy. Alistair read all of it, often shaking his head in disagreement, as if his former job many years ago made his judgement superior to that of contemporary journalists.

One thing that had not changed was the dire situation of Egypt's foreign currency reserves. She relied heavily on foreign loans and grants, about which the Financial Times gave a detailed survey. Although there was no lack of foreign donors or lenders, whose intention was less a capital investment than political gains in a country that could not service her loans anyway, there had been a rather mysterious case, when an important foreign donor backed out at the last minute.

The Arab-Islamic Development Cooperation, based in one of the Gulf states, was negotiating with Egypt for a loan to finance several infrastructure projects amounting to nearly one billion US-dollars, a sum for which the unanimous vote of the lender's Board of Directors was required. Until very recently there had been no doubt that all would sign. Egypt had already informally included the proceeds of this loan in her budget and her finance minister was ready to fly to the Gulf in order to sign for the Egyptian side.

Unfortunately, these preparations proved to be premature. One of the board members, the finance minister of the emirate of Umm Ghani, in a sudden volte-face reneged on his former promise and vetoed the project. It was a shock to everyone, mainly to the Egyptians. Considering the usual secrecy of the ballot it was surprising that the caster of the veto was mentioned, probably due to a leak by an irate member of the board. The reason for the Umm Ghani veto remained unknown. Their finance minister refused to give interviews, only mentioned his recent doubts in the viability of the intended projects.

Alistair had a feeling of nostalgia. During his active period he had been exposed to many strange, even bizarre events and persons, sometimes annoying, at other times encouraging, but in hindsight mostly entertaining. He would have liked to have been a closer witness or even be a part of this politico-economic scandal as before, but all he could do now was to read about it in the press.

At least he could discuss this with Rietberg, because the name Umm Ghani had been mentioned in Egypt in connection with Mona. He remembered that she had once said that her newest lover was a prince of Umm Ghani working as a diplomat in Cairo.

Yet he was soon to be fed more sensational news, and this time about a member of Dina's family.

His recent probe into Yusuf's American life through his former colleague, the CEO of the American mortgage bank, led to an astonishing result.

Yusuf had become a very bad risk in banker speak! He had been recently struck off the list of approved psychiatrists, and no longer had an accountable income. The reason was a veritable scandal that he had caused and which affected the reputation of the psychiatric profession in general. Yusuf had slept with two of his female patients, perhaps even with more!

The patients were not raped in the literal sense and had not denounced him to the police, nor were they minors. But that had not helped, when they mentioned it to relatives and friends, after which all came out. In former more easy-going times sleeping with patients used sometimes even to be considered a treatment, but no more in the neo-Victorian 21st century. The press and the police declared the women immediately as 'vulnerable', and vulnerable people were sacrosanct, and in case their sacrosanctity was not respected they could have potentially lucrative damage claims. With no income and probably facing hefty claims of indemnity by his vulnerable patients Yusuf was threatened with bankruptcy. His wife had moved out of their expensive mansion in a chic suburb of Philadelphia and had gone to live with her elderly parents. According to rumours taken up by a gleeful press she was particularly incensed because Yusuf had neglected her sexually for some time, while he treated his patients with his erotic services.

It was a catastrophe that had destroyed a comfortable family life and a successful career.

The CEO had sworn Alistair to secrecy, which he agreed to, although he intended to mention everything to the police. It seemed he had stumbled upon Yusuf's possible motive to murder his sister, which was to obtain much needed funds from the sale of the Cairo building.

"Jürgen, I want to talk with you about something that might be very interesting," said Alistair. "Why don't you come over? It's more comfortable in my flat, and I have cigars and drinks, and you can also smoke your stinking pipe, if you want."

"I have recently heard astonishing news about Yusuf," Alistair started their session.

"Same here," said Rietberg.

"You start and I will then add my own info."

Typical, he always tried to have the last word, thought Rietberg.

They exchanged their stories—the lie about attending the Amsterdam congress and the near-bankruptcy caused by Yusuf's abuse of female patients.

Both led them to the same conclusion.

"He was in urgent need of money—for surviving, paying the mortgage or as a silencer for his patients, whatever," said Alistair. "This money he hopes to obtain at least partly from his share in the sale of the building, and he could not wait much longer. It also explains why he was so well informed about the legal situation. He was assured by legal counsel that after Dina none of the beneficiaries of a possible last will could stand between him and more than the half million dollars he could expect from the sale."

As a side remark Alistair mentioned the Financial Times article about the veto of the Egyptian loan by Umm Ghani, coincidentally Mona's lover's emirate.

"I admit that I want to know more about the reasons. I have never stopped being interested in Egyptian finances," he said rather apologetically. "Do you think it appropriate for me to ask Mona about it?"

"Do so by all means. As you well know, my own interest in Egyptian finances does not extend beyond the 19th century. But coming back to our main subject, I still hesitate to believe that this pathetic brother of Dina's killed his own sister," said Rietberg after pensively blowing smoke rings into the air. "It would make a difference, though, if he was in fact the mysterious man with the hat. Without that proof we would not even know if he had ever entered her flat."

Alistair stood up and took a photograph from his desk.

"Look at this," he said, "I think you have seen it already."

It was the same photograph Rietberg had seen on Mona's desk. The picture with Yusuf and his hat! "How in God's name did you get hold of it?" asked Rietberg, who was utterly surprised and a bit jealous. "Did you steal it?"

Alistair smirked, proud of himself and of having outdone Rietberg.

"I got it from Mona, or to be precise, it is a copy made in a photo-shop of Mona's photograph. I told her that I wanted to have one showing the Ghalib family, who are also my own now. That's at least what I said."

"In that case she could have proposed to make a new one with everyone being present."

"Exactly," said Alistair, "and I would never have been able to get Yusuf's hat on it, because I would have to shoot inside the flat, where no one is wearing a hat. One more *felouka* trip was out of the question, of course. I was quite aware of that possibility. So I asked for a picture with their late father included, if possible. It could only be an old one, of course, which happened to be the photograph you told me about. By the way, Mona was very touched by my sentimental feelings for her family. She even thanked me for being much closer to them than Dina, her own cousin."

Rietberg had to admit that he would never have been able to reach this level of hypocrisy and said so.

"You know why?" asked Alistair with a friendly smile. "Because I am English and you are German."

With all the information about his bankruptcy, his lie about attending the congress and now with his picture that could be compared with the CCTV they had nearly everything to have Yusuf inculpated as the murderer.

Of the usual holy crime trinity—means, motive, and opportunity—the motive was the most obvious, *i.e.* getting more than half a million dollars in order to solve his immediate financial problems by eliminating Dina as the only obstacle to a sale of their building

Opportunity was nearly as probable. His lie about attending the Amsterdam congress could only mean that Yusuf had travelled to London instead. To know that for certain needed no more than a check with immigration. The photograph with his hat on would almost certainly help the police to identify him as the man accompanying Dina.

As to the means, Dina would have invited him into her flat, which explained the lack of any evidence for a break-in. The only question remaining was how he had managed to throw her out of the window. Although he was definitely the stronger, it could not have been easy for him to do that to a healthy grown-up woman. Except of course, if he had tricked her to step on her balcony and suddenly gripped her by the legs to throw her off balance.

Alistair and Rietberg spent some time discussing the pros and cons of their theory. In the end they came to an agreement that both had already wanted instinctively. Even though they could not identify the exact method as to how she had been pushed, the police would eventually find that out, if they were worthy of their name.

Alistair would have to go to the police with their information together with the photograph and the request to reopen the case. He must, furthermore, inform them about Dina's abduction and the probability that her brother Maguid had it arranged in order convince her that Egypt was no longer safe for her. If the CCTV-tape then allowed Yusuf's identification or at least did not contradict it, the police could not possibly refuse the request to open a case against Yusuf.

Rietberg eagerly awaited Alistair's report about his contact with the police. He devoted some time to thinking about the practical consequences, if the police were to be in accord with their theory about Yusuf being the main suspect. Dina's brother would have to be interrogated, but where? Perhaps he had returned to the US in the meantime, to live in his house, awaiting the inheritance money. For him to spend his future years in Egypt was out of the question, even if he faced police charges in the US or claims from his so-called victims. All that he could gain from his share in the sale of the building, and perhaps even more, would have to be spent buying another flat, leaving him as bankrupt as before.

Rietberg had no idea about transatlantic police work. Could Yusuf be summoned to an American police station, or according to a more US-like term a police precinct, or would he have to be extradited?

It was premature, anyway, to speculate about something he did not know. He decided therefore to complete an article on Red Sea trade in the 17th century, a topic that was as important for historical research as Dina's murder was for police work.

Rietberg's success as a professor of Middle Eastern history owed much to his talent of submerging himself in the old archives by excluding all thoughts of the present. When all of a sudden the telephone rang with Alistair on the line, it took him some time to realize what he was speaking about.

With a sigh of resignation at being distracted from writing down an important historical fact that had eluded the history profession so far, he agreed to go round to Alistair's flat once more.

...

Alistair received him, showing his outrage and disgust at the way the police had received him.

"Imagine, they did not even look closely at the photograph with Yusuf. They dismissed out of hand my theory that he could be the murderer, let alone comparing his photograph with the man on the CCTV-tape."

Alistair could hardly breathe with all the anger he had bottled up inside him.

"Have you ever had the urge to slap someone in his face?" he asked Rietberg. "I had that urge with the inspector who I had the

misfortune to meet this time. An arrogant youth who even continued chewing his gum to show his contempt for a grey-haired old
man like me. I wonder why they didn't employ him on a street-
crossing to replace the traffic lights instead of promoting him to
inspector."

Rietberg laughed.

"I think I got the picture. Chewing gum is a primordial sign of
an aggressor wanting to eat you, a psychiatrist once told me, and
to slap his face would be your legitimate self-defence! But tell
me—did he explain why they refused even to consider Yusuf's
involvement?"

"Yes, he did, this incompetent bastard!" Alistair was still
fuming. "He talked at length about the police having scrutinised
the CCTV-tapes once more, where they pretended to have found
something that pointed to other suspects."

"And that is?"

"They found a pizza-delivery man with a biker's helmet who
entered the building the evening of Dina's murder, and another
unidentifiable man entering soon after him. As no one in the building remembered having ordered a pizza, the police concocted their
own theory that the pizza-man gained access by pressing several
entry buttons, after which one inadvertent tenant must have
pressed the buzzer for the main door. The pizza-man then let the
other man in, and both waited inside, before Dina arrived a short
time later as shown on the tape. Forcing her to open the door of
her flat and throwing her out of the window would then have been
easy, according to the imaginative police."

Rietberg had first to digest this unexpected version of what
had happened that night. A killing like this clearly pointed to
other suspects than her family.

He needed a drink before discussing it and poured himself a
double Tamdhu from Alistair's bar. Fortunately, he remembered
his good manners and offered to pour one for Alistair as well, who
gladly accepted a drink from his own malt supply.

"Let us assume for a moment that the police are right,"
Rietberg started, while Alistair had slumped down in his armchair
exhausted by his anger. "Did any one of the tenants admit to

having opened the door to the pizza-man? Second question: how did the two so-called killers time their arrival so exactly as to arrive only a little earlier than Dina? The police cannot believe that these two guys could have lingered inside the building waiting in front of her flat a long time without being spotted and suspected by one of the tenants?"

"I was asking them exactly the same questions," retorted Alistair. "But they have their own way of dealing with those who doubt their conclusions. This bloody inspector treated me with hardly disguised disdain, only telling me that people are never likely to admit a mistake like opening the door to strangers. This answers your first question, and as to the second: anyone: someone waiting patiently outside Dina's office during the usual end of office hours could have alerted the pizza-man by a call on his mobile to set their plans into action. They also dismissed the possibility that Yusuf himself could have opened the main door after ringing Dina's bell on that night. The CCTV showed a pizza-man, but no Yusuf. I got the impression that apart from everything else they were never willing to contemplate the idea that her own brother could have killed her."

"This third man must have waited a couple of hours then; Dina was always working overtime," Rietberg remarked.

"Not an argument that would change police opinion," said Alistair. "To wait for hours is a small price to be paid for a murder. It is exactly as I said before! They want a balcony murder committed by two unknown and unidentifiable foreigners—even three now, if we include the mystery guard outside Dina's office. They can immediately file the case as they did with all previous balcony murders."

"Have you had any opportunity at all to discuss our suspicions against Yusuf?"

"I tried, but they would not listen. According to them, even if he was in fact the man on the tape, that would only prove his presence the morning before the night of the murder, because no other man with a hat was filmed later."

"Another argument that does not stand," said Rietberg. "He might have paid Dina a first visit for another reason, perhaps asking for money, which is quite probable. The neighbour told you that they did not seem to be on good terms, which is understandable enough, if she had refused such a request. Because Yusuf is not stupid and must know about the ubiquitous CCTV in London he needed to change his look if he wanted to return for murder. He would certainly not have worn his Humphrey Bogart hat then, which made him stand out from most other men. Perhaps he was the pizza-man himself, this time only with a biker's helmet instead of a hat. If it was not him, how could they dismiss offhand the idea that he or Maguid had arranged for the visit of a hit squad from the beginning, knowing that Yusuf alone would be reluctant or not be able to push his sister out of the window alone? It is common knowledge that most murders are family affairs."

"All this cannot help if you look more closely at the options available to Her Majesty's efficient police," replied a completely disillusioned Alistair. "One is closing the case as a politically motivated and therefore insoluble balcony murder. The other is investigating our suspect in the US through diplomatic channels or Interpol, trusting that our transatlantic brothers are willing to interrogate an American citizen and even extradite him to be sentenced here. Do you have any idea by the way how extradition works between the two nations?"

"No," said Rietberg, "how would I?"

"But I know, because I got some revealing statistics from the internet," said Alistair. "From 2004 to 2011 the UK extradited 33 British nationals to the US, while the US extradited seven of their citizens! Relative to population numbers that means a statistic of 24:1 in favour of America! Do you think that our police will try this unpromising channel, when they can close the case immediately, without anyone complaining except me or you?"

"Perhaps you Brits commit more crimes in or against America than Americans do against the UK. That could explain the discrepancy in figures," said Rietberg.

"Please do not try your German humour on me," replied Alistair, "the case is much too serious."

Their hopeful exploration trip to Egypt had resulted in a lot of speculation, but in no concrete result. The police made no secret of their intention to close the case as one more insoluble balcony murder made for mysterious reasons by equally mysterious agents of the Egyptian government. What was left was their resigned conviction that Dina's murder would never be solved, let alone be revenged.

Alistair and Rietberg had their own, individual ways of dealing with the situation. Rietberg started another article about something that had happened in the Middle East centuries ago and Alistair improved his excellent golf handicap by spending hours at his golf club. He even intended to run for board membership at the next election, a small consolation for having lost both Birgit and Dina.

During this quiet interim period Rietberg was contacted by a very old friend from his university days. Rupert Fischer had studied the same subjects as Rietberg, but had chosen a very different career as a journalist, which had landed him, after the many ups and downs typical of his profession, as the trusted Middle East correspondent of an independent newspaper, *i.e.* a newspaper without a pro-American or pro-Israeli or pro-Saudi or pro-Qatari or pro-whatever-else agenda. He was based in Dubai, travelled widely in the region, mainly in the Gulf, and every now and then went to Europe, whenever he missed the opera, concerts, German beer and sausages, and conversations with friends, whose main interest was not money.

Because Rietberg was one of them, he never missed an opportunity to visit him during his European holidays.

As usual they were relaxing in the comfortable armchairs that were Rietberg's most valued furniture, after a dinner prepared by Marie-Anne that made them look forward impatiently to their smoking sessions, with Rietberg's pipe and Rupert's expensive Havana cigars that he bought duty-free in Dubai.

Marie-Anne, who could not stand the thick tobacco smoke, retired soon and left the two men enjoying their bachelor habits.

After covering a wide variety of Rietberg's recent topics—from Dina's death, British police work, Egyptian politics to Dina's family—they remained silent for a while, smoking and drinking contentedly.

"Now we have only talked about me and not about you," said Rietberg. "Tell me what you have been doing recently."

Rupert laughed.

"You won't believe it, but recently I have turned into a society *vulgo* gossip journalist. Everyone else out there in my profession writes about oil, finance and politics, but no one writes about the anecdotal side of living in the Gulf, like supply of alcohol and whores, religious police, personal idiosyncrasies, expatriate peccadilloes and the follies of our sheikhs, etc. Therefore, I am writing, in addition to my serious articles, under my pen name Sheherazade, a special column titled "The Gulf Private Eye" about the funnier side of our society. Very popular with my readers—more so than the serious stuff!"

"Are you not afraid doing that? I cannot imagine that your princes or the religious establishment would tolerate being ridiculed easily or to have their weaknesses exposed in public." "I never mention names! Where I am living now, you do not have to do this anyway, because everyone knows everyone else. That's also a kind of protection, believe it or not. Or do you think that anyone would betray himself if I report—just to cite an example—a nightclub brawl in Rome between an unnamed prince and a Russian whore's pimp, who wanted her back for a Berlusconi bonga-bonga party?"

"You make it sound like a true story," remarked Rietberg drily.

"No one—least of all that prince—will be criticizing me! And of course I would never publish a photo of a princess lying on the beach with her top off, if I could ever catch her in the nude, which I have not done yet unfortunately. Moreover, I always make sure that I have the support of someone influential if I touch someone else's sensibilities, which is not too difficult because they are all jealous of one another. Besides, all my readers in Europe and the Middle East, including the sheikhs, like gossip, and when you reach a certain level of prominence in that field, as I have done, you gain a sort of immunity."

"Well," said Rietberg, "I envy you. You were always an adventurer and that's why your life is certainly more interesting than mine. Perhaps also more dangerous. But because you mentioned idiosyncrasies—could you perhaps provide me with some gossip about the finance minister of Umm Ghani? I heard his name recently in connection with Dina's Egyptian family, and also that for yet unknown reasons he has vetoed a loan for Egypt against the vote of the fellow board members of his bank."

Rupert looked at him with an amused grin.

"Jürgen, you are like the hedgehog in Grimm's fairytale, always arriving before the hare. In fact, I did visit Umm Ghani recently, where I heard about the finance minister's unexplained veto. Umm Ghani has always been the poor cousin of the other emirates, before they struck oil themselves, and they are still lacking the savvy of their cousins. You have to realise this in order to understand what follows. The story behind the veto is again jealousy. When the finance minister—the emir's brother by the way—heard about all the museums the other emirates are founding in order to gain an international reputation, he wanted to create a special chess museum in Umm Ghani. Its centrepiece was to be a unique artefact from Islamic Egypt, which he found on the market and which would make his museum unique amongst all the others. He even started negotiating with the chess museum in Amsterdam to reach a cooperation agreement, similar to the one the Louvre has with the sheikh's much envied Abu Dhabi. For reasons I do not know yet it did not work, however, and he holds the Egyptian government responsible. That, in a nutshell, is the explanation given to me in Umm Ghani. I am waiting for more details from a member of the ruling family, who hates the finance minister, and then I will write one more anecdote for the Gulf Private Eye."

"Which as usual you are not afraid to publish," remarked Rietberg.

Rietberg had recently received another visitor, although he had not been in much demand since his retirement:

"Martin Laird here," a man said on the phone. "Am I talking to Professor Rietberg?"

"Yes, you are," replied Rietberg, ready to put the receiver down if that person was a claim lawyer or another nuisance caller wanting to sell him something.

"You do not know me, but I was a friend of Dina's who unfortunately died recently. I understood from her that you were her closest friend, so I got your phone number from SOAS to express my most heartfelt condolences. We shall all miss her."

"In fact I do know who you are. Dina mentioned you once as the man, who had prompted her to go on her campaign to save Egyptian antiquities. Thank you for your condolences, but I guess that you did not call me for that only?"

"No, I did not," said Martin. "Dina never needed anyone to push her into action, however; all that she needed was restraint, which brings me my main reason for calling. As you know, I deal in Islamic antiquities and therefore I came across something recently that might interest you."

"Not that I want to sell you anything," he added with a little laugh. "I want to show you an article published in an art magazine that could perhaps explain what has happened to her."

"So you know how she died?"

"Of course, everyone in the art field knows. Dina was quite famous."

The man sounded respectable enough and Rietberg invited him to come over for a drink.

The first thing Rietberg saw was the chessboard on the cover of a magazine that Martin had brought along.

"That's a chessboard," he exclaimed.

Martin grinned his Cheshire cat grin.

"Yes, it obviously rings a bell, doesn't it?"

Martin was a subscriber to the same art-magazine that had written the article about Dina. He asked Rietberg to read it and give his comments.

"My God," said Rietberg after he had finished reading, "that is worse than I thought."

Martin scrutinized him. His Cheshire cat grin had vanished.

"Yes, she must have made enemies with this article. But was there even more? What is worse than you thought?"

"I am afraid that this magazine could have caused her murder," said Rietberg, still shocked by what he had read.

"What do you mean?" asked Martin, now clearly shocked himself. "Her attacks were certainly incautious, but a cause for murder? Was she even murdered? I was told she committed suicide."

"Then you have been misinformed," said Rietberg. "Who told you so?"

"Chrosby's. They said that she had been depressed recently, feeling lonely and frustrated with her work."

This time the wasp had missed the plum cake.

"She was in fact feeling depressed at times following her separation from her husband," said Rietberg, "but at other times she was quite glad to have been rid of him. No, she could not have killed herself. She was definitely murdered, and after seeing this magazine I can also imagine by whom."

He told Martin about the warnings she had received in Egypt.

"She had been warned in Cairo not to continue with her crusade and seemed to have understood. That's what a trustworthy person confirmed to a friend of mine. The people who threatened her, if she did not keep silent, probably considered the matter to be closed, after she gave in. The article in this magazine was therefore a slap in their face and an affront that could not remain unpunished."

"But they must have known that the article was written some time before she could have received her warning and that it was only published recently. How could she prevent the magazine from coming out at this stage?"

"I am afraid that she had to deal with people, who, as the saying goes, shoot first and ask questions later," replied Rietberg. "Personal excuses, attenuating circumstances and other niceties are not part of their vocabulary. There had been clear hints that the chessboard had somehow become a matter of national security, although no one, including me, her ex-husband and probably herself as well, could make any sense of it."

Martin reached for his glass—as usual a vodka-tonic—and finally came out with a suggestion.

"We have to look more closely at the fate of the chessboard," he said. "Perhaps that could help to solve this riddle. When I contacted Dina it was offered together with other items by a Syrian dealer in Dubai. I had heard that there was feverish competition amongst the bidders, most of them private collectors, including a particularly eager one from a Gulf emirate, who finally bought it."

"According to my information it was the finance minister of Umm Ghani, a member of the ruling family, who wanted it for his own chess museum," confirmed Rietberg.

"Impossible after this article about its theft by the Egyptian archaeologist!" emphasized Martin. "No one would touch it of course after that came out. It would have been like buying the bust of Nefertiti—you could do nothing with it except hide it in a secluded place. Yet contrary to common belief most collectors are not that autistic—they are proud and want to show their treasures to friends and to the world, exactly like the finance minister you just mentioned. He can only try to return it to the Syrian dealer requesting a refund. If you ask me he might just as well scrap it altogether."

"That is truly a sad story," said Rietberg. "All efforts to have it repatriated were in vain unless the Egyptians finally wake up and try to reclaim it from the finance minister. I would see the chances of that happening to be near zero as well. The sheikh has even vetoed a loan that Egypt expected from the Gulf to punish them for his disappointment, so he will doubtless keep the chessboard just out of spite, even if he cannot display it."

A lot of background information had been gathered, but who had committed the murder? Rietberg decided to contact Alistair once more; two brains were always better than one to find a solution.

Therefore, he proposed a meeting at home with Alistair and also Marie-Anne. She had been saddened and shocked by Dina's death as much as they had. Rietberg was grateful to her, because another woman could have resented the deep feelings her husband had for an old flame.

Alistair was glad of the invitation. He and Rietberg had formed a loose bond during the last few weeks. Somehow Dina's magical personality had brought her former husband and her unsuccessful suitor together, even after death. Her memory was stronger than the former near-animosity between the two men.

"Do you think, what I am thinking?" asked Rietberg.

"Yes, I do," answered Alistair, "and if it is true what we are both thinking, the police could be right after all."

"Truly unbelievable," said Rietberg after a moment of incredulity. "Only because Dina proved that his damned chessboard was stolen, this madman takes revenge against Egypt. The loan must have been the matter of 'national interest' that Dina and Mahmoud are supposed to have violated.."

Alistair cut the tip off another Cohiba with his Davidoff cutter and lit the cigar with a match he took from a large dedicated cigar match box. Rietberg refilled his pipe with the cheap Erinmore mixture and stuffed it unceremoniously with his finger.

After some moments of puffing very different tobaccos Alistair remarked: "I still tend to believe that Dina was murdered by her brothers for purely financial reasons. Anything else smacks too much of a conspiracy theory of which I have already heard far too many during my working days in Cairo. And we should not forget that her abduction in Cairo had evidently nothing to do with a chessboard, but a lot to do with her refusal to sell the building."

"Whatever the case, Dina was the victim of a conspiracy," said Rietberg, "only which one is still not clear."

"Have you any idea how we could make sure?" asked Alistair. "Because I don't. We cannot possibly ask the Egyptian government or His Royal - or is it Emiral? - Highness these questions and neither could our police request the British ambassadors to do so."

Rietberg knew no answer, the two amateur detectives continued drinking expensive whisky, and smoking cheap tobacco and expensive cigars for a while in silence.

After a while Rietberg said:

"We will have to leave it to Ahmed to sort out."

Further efforts to come to any conclusion were in vain. They just continued smoking and drinking several toasts to Dina's memory.

Several weeks passed without any news from Cairo. Rietberg was impatient to hear from Ahmed, but could not possibly discuss Dina's murder with him over the phone.

He had not seen Alistair for a while either. His relationship with him that had been problematic from the beginning had its ups and downs, but was never close enough to make them friends, who want to see each other without a special reason. One day he was sure he had seen Alistair accompanied by a blonde woman in a department store, but avoided them by taking another direction in order not to cause embarrassment.

He spoke to Marie-Anne about it.

"I wouldn't put it past him to bring his Birgit back in spite of everything that happened between them and in spite of whatever feelings he might have had for Dina. With her gone, he could now even make Birgit the beneficiary of his latest will, which would probably be enough to make her faithful to him for a while."

Marie-Anne laughed.

"It seems that you have forgotten what the Bible says about casting the first stone."

"Meaning what?"

"May I remind you that you married me shortly after my first husband died? You cannot possibly go on mourning for a long time if life presents you with an alternative, and I am not so different from Alistair, nor are you, my dear."

"It seems you, like all medical doctors, are a cynic," said Rietberg.

As usual Marie-Anne had the last word.

"It's just self-defence in order to remain normal when dealing with death all the time." she said. "It does not need much stamina to write about people, who died centuries ago, as is your privilege, but you cannot treat the terminally ill, as I have to do, and continue to live a normal life with too much sensitivity."

Rietberg picked up the mail thrown through their door. While Marie-Anne was at work, it was his role as her retired husband to go through the mail in the morning, separating his few and Marie-Anne's many letters from the junk-mail. Junk-mail represented the largest part of their postage and he always threw it into the bin. This time he found a large and embossed invitation card to attend a lecture carrying the unappealing but scholarly sounding title 'Ambivalence in Egypt's Identity', organized by the Royal Middle-East Society, of which he was a member.

'One more empty title of a lecture to impress,' he thought.

Identity coupled with ambivalence could mean anything or nothing, and a lecture with these buzzwords promised to be boring. Normally he would have thrown the card into the bin, but a name caught his interest. Someone had his name underlined.

The speaker was 'Ahmed Selim—Delta Research Association'!

Ahmed had announced his arrival by email a few days earlier, so Rietberg was not surprised that Ahmed seemed to be a trusted servant of the Egyptian government in spite of his scathing remarks. His lecture left no other conclusion. Anyone else living in Egypt would not dare to make a public lecture about a political subject for fear of later reprisals.

Rietberg wondered what he would have to say and what the Delta Research Association stood for. He did not expect much of his lecture, except a positive résumé of Sisi's rule, together with minor criticisms to make it more convincing. He had to attend, however, if only to get more information about the only subject that truly mattered.

In spite of his feelings about Alistair, he decided to tell him about Ahmed's lecture. Alistair had at least as much right as he had to know if Ahmed brought news about Dina's murder.

When he called, a woman with a Scandinavian accent answered the phone. It was true then—Birgit had returned!

She called Alistair to the phone, announcing "there is a call for you, darling."

When darling came to the phone, he was matter-of-fact without any attempt to explain the female presence in his home. He had received an email from Ahmed as well and wondered if he had the right to attend his lecture. Rietberg immediately put him at his ease.

"The society is not one of your posh clubs with non-members excluded," he said, "they are quite happy to have as many attendees as possible. Just wear a tie, because their venue is the Royal Automobile Club. As I am a member of the Royal Middle-East Society, I will ask them to send you an invitation card."

"No need for that," said Alistair, "I happen to be a member of the RAC itself."

It was the usual crowd attending to Ahmed's lecture. Expatriate professional Egyptians, for whose life and career modern London had proved to be the best place in the world, and some British and a few other European nostalgic lovers of Egypt's past.

Rietberg and Alistair had taken their seats in one of the front rows, because they wanted Ahmed to know that they were there.

After the chairwoman of the Royal Middle-East Society had welcomed everybody, the secretary introduced the speaker. Ahmed Selim, the unassuming lawyer without an office as Dina had called him, was an important man, a member of several law societies and honorary professor at Cairo University, who had served for many years in a prominent position in the Egyptian Ministry of Justice. The Royal Middle-East Society knew about him, but neither Rietberg nor Alistair had any idea until then how prominent their co-investigator was.

It did not matter therefore that his lecture was a typical example of political conformism as expected by Rietberg. In a *tour d'horizon* Ahmed covered the Tahrir revolution in moderately positive terms, deplored the betrayal of its aims by the Muslim Brothers and heaped well-measured praise on the army—without forgetting to mention Sisi—who came to the rescue of all Egyptians, regardless of class and religion.

It was exactly what the politically conservative audience wanted to hear, and Ahmed was given an enthusiastic applause. After a few questions, as usually made less to gain information than to show intimate knowledge of Egyptian affairs, the official part ended.

Rietberg and Alistair retreated with Ahmed, who had acknowledged with a short nod during his lecture their presence, into the club's impressive library. It was large, with an astonishing array of the latest magazines and newspapers in addition to well-stocked bookshelves, and was equipped with large leather arm-chairs that invited low-voiced serious discussions, which they could have at their ease, because there was no one else using the library.

Of course, politeness requested some praise for Ahmed's lecture initially. He looked amused at Rietberg, who managed to say something about how interesting it was.

"My dear Professor Rietberg," he said, "I know exactly what you mean. In England you call something interesting, if it is at best boring and at worst absurd. But let me put you at ease—my position in Egypt requires a show of allegiance to the people in power but it never clouds my own judgment. All those who live under a less liberal regime than yours must develop a healthy degree of schizophrenia that is needed to survive. My lecture had bored me myself, when I wrote it, and I saw you nearly falling asleep while you were pretending to listen, but the man from the Egyptian embassy, who I spotted in the audience, will certainly write a positive report."

Alistair and Rietberg could not help laughing. After Ahmed's remark there was no need for hypocrisy any more. They could talk freely now about the news of Dina's murder, and the involvement of a government that Ahmed had mentioned so favourably in his speech.

"It's quite a long story, but it will not bore you as my lecture did, I hope," he started.

"First of all I wanted to make really sure that someone in the army was behind poor Dina's abduction, as I had guessed, and possibly also behind what else happened, including her murder. To investigate anything concerning the army in Egypt can be life-threatening though. I could not ask friends I have in the army of course. The only military source I had was Dina's brother Maguid, who had probably instigated all this. Yet I was sure that he would not betray anything, even if my assumption was correct."

He paused, looking at his partners waiting for their suggestions.

"It seems like a dead end, but knowing you and your opinion about yourself I am sure you found a solution," commented Alistair dryly.

"Ts, ts," replied Ahmed waggling one finger at Alistair, "that was not very kind. But of course you are right. I found a means of blackmailing him."

"And how could you blackmail him?" asked Rietberg. "Did your Delta Research Association spy upon him and find lurid details about his sex life?"

"Your sense of humour is quite remarkable for a German," said Ahmed, "but totally inappropriate with regard to that harmless, not to say useless association. No, my blackmail was based on my experience with Egyptian courts alone. You once told me about the legal dispute you had with Yusuf about Alistair's share in the Ghalib building. As you were saying correctly yourself, even as the beneficiary of her will, Alistair does not inherit anything in Egypt because one third of her total estate, which the Sharia allows him as his share, is already eaten up by what he inherited in England. Based on the correct assumption that Alistair had inherited a lot in London, he therefore had no share left in the building so Dina's siblings started their final negotiations with the army. Do you follow me so far?"

"Of course," replied Rietberg slightly irritated by this schoolmasterly lesson, "that's how I myself convinced Alistair to give it a miss."

"It is still only an assumption that has to be proven in court, if the parties don't agree," said Ahmed. "And the onus of proof is on Dina's brothers, if Alistair claims his share in the building. He has only to state—falsely of course—that he inherited nothing abroad! Can you imagine what that means? To prove him wrong they would need to procure documents—legalized even—about Dina's British property to present them to the Egyptian court. In other words: finding and paying a British solicitor to obtain probate, title deeds etc., while the Egyptian court stops further proceedings, pending the outcome of the search for Dina's estate."

He laughed happily.

"Such a delay could last a long time in our courts. In the meantime, the army would lose patience, revoke their offer or simply expropriate the building with a lot of damage to Maguid's finances and his career. You will agree that this constitutes ideal blackmail material! When I met Maguid I showed him this stick, but also waved my carrot. If he told me frankly and completely everything about his own involvement, for which I pretended to have sufficient proof already, Alistair would not jeopardize his property deal with the army and he as well as Yusuf would get their ready money. I also swore that in this case all further steps from my side would stop and that I would not accuse him or anyone amongst his friends of eventual murder. It was his choice—either carrot or stick!"

Alistair showed signs of indignation.

"My dear Mr Selim, with all respect for your shrewd investigation methods I am not happy that you spoke on my behalf without consulting me first. I will not hesitate for one second to denounce the murder or the murderers whoever they are if I know them—from you or from someone else."

Ahmed's friendly report threatened to create a dispute. He stopped for a while, and then told Alistair with a cold smile:

"Now you force me to blackmail you. Either you swear that nothing that I tell you leaves this room, or I will leave immediately and you will be kept in the dark forever, because no one else will give you that information. I am surprised that with all your experience in Egypt you think that accusing an army officer of a crime can lead to more than the arrest of the accuser."

"Ok, ok, I swear," said Alistair, rather morosely though, "I did not want to cause offence."

Rietberg was glad of his reaction. They needed Ahmed's assistance and if he saw fit to give a promise of indemnity to Maguid—so be it.

"No offence taken," said Ahmed, now smiling in a more friendly manner again. "As I expected, Maguid confessed to having arranged her abduction by some of the soldiers under his command, but nothing more than that! He wanted to convince his sister that she had no interest in keeping a flat in a dangerous country like Egypt, which she would visit rarely anyway. That was all he did, and he had no other reason to warn or frighten her. Just as I suspected, he did know about her antiquities campaign from reading Mahmoud al-Allamy's article, and made it look like the cause of her abduction by drafting the warning made by the kidnappers accordingly. He almost succeeded in shifting any suspicion away from her family. I have no reason to doubt this explanation. He begged me to believe him that he never wanted to cause his sister any serious harm. It was all very tragic, but we have to look for Dina's murderers elsewhere."

All this did not come as a surprise. Ahmed had already mentioned the reasons for an acquittal for Dina's family from a murder accusation before. Still Maguid's statement changed everything from speculation to near proof.

Rietberg and Alistair had to digest this news and were silent for a while.

Then Rietberg remembered something.

"You will be pleased to hear that I have my own argument to support your opinion," he said to Ahmed. "During our first visit to the Ghalib family something in one of Maguid's reactions pointed in this same direction. Of all the possible reasons for Dina's death Maguid seemed to fear suicide more than an accident or even a murder. It was quite obvious as Alistair will certainly agree."

"In fact I do," said Alistair. "It did seem rather odd to exclude suicide much more vehemently as a possibility than murder or an accident, but I did not pay much attention to it at the time."

"Neither did I," continued Rietberg, "but with hindsight it can probably be explained that in the case of a suicide he could be somehow responsible for her death, but not in the case of a murder. The shock of her abduction, which he had arranged, might well have triggered a suicide, and Maguid dreaded being indirectly responsible for his sister's death. But, if neither he nor Yusuf were the murderers, his more indifferent reaction to the murder theory can be explained. That's what I would like to back Ahmed's theory."

"It does make sense," Alistair admitted in all fairness and then asked Ahmed: "Has Maguid said anything about Yusuf's alleged visit to the World Psychiatric Congress?"

"Until I mentioned it, he had no idea about that. He knew however about his brother's desperate situation and also the reason for it. It was also a strong motive for him to force Dina to take the only sensible decision and agree to the sale of the building."

It was quite late now, and Rietberg was wondering if they should not continue elsewhere. Alistair reassured him, with a big smile.

"The club is open 24/7, so no one will disturb us. But we should at least get some drinks at the bar in order to fortify us for further news from our amazing Ahmed."

It was wrong of course for Alistair to practise his irony on Ahmed, but he never liked to be at the receiving end of a discussion.

Ahmed let it pass, Rietberg smiled, they had their drinks and Ahmed continued.

"Now comes the truly interesting part. If neither Maguid, Yusuf nor the army caused her death, who did?"

"Some other dark forces in the deep state who punished her for violating national security?" speculated Rietberg. "Possibly the British police were right from the beginning. We have already heard about the Umm Ghani finance minister's veto and its probable cause—his anger about the scandal of the Fatimid chessboard that Dina had made public. Yet can we prove that this veto caused her murder, instead of suspicion?"

"Of course all of us want that, but unfortunately there is no database available for the public, listing murders committed by the state," said Ahmed..

"My obvious and only choice was to contact Mustafa Fezzani, as we agreed before, He was the only person I could think of, who might have some information, because it was he, who warned both Dina and Mahmoud al-Allamy. I explained to him that I had obtained his phone number from Dina. The reason I gave for my visit was that I represented her husband Alistair, who wanted to know more about the difficulties she had in Egypt trying to repatriate Islamic antiquities."

"Sorry," he said to Alistair, "but I had once more to refer to you as my client. I hope you do not mind."

Alistair said nothing.

Mustafa Fezzani's office reminded Ahmed of many other offices he had entered.

"Then I was in for a surprise," continued Ahmed with his report. "I had expected to meet a stolid government employee with no intellectual leanings in spite of his job in the antiquities department, the like of those I had to frequently face during my professional career as a lawyer. On the wall hung a photograph of President Sisi and on his desk the equally obligatory Koran. Also, his physique, his demeanour and even his clothes were those of a bureaucrat, who had landed a secure job in an office. Yet in addition to these there was also an opened book that looked like a museum catalogue, a sign that he was interested in culture. I am telling you all this, because it helps to explain what happened later.

"I started by thanking Mustafa 'Bey' profusely for taking his valuable time to meet me. He seemed to be quite nervous and probably in order to gain time he offered me a Turkish coffee ordered from an office boy. Judging by this reception and the special service of a secretary and an office boy, he was quite important, yet also eager to please. He asked me how Dina was and to convey his best wishes to her."

Ahmed stopped, and after a dramatic pause asked:

"What do you make of that?"

Both Alistair and Rietberg sat there like students searching for the correct answer during an exam.

"He did not know about her murder! At the start I suspected that he just pretended not to know. When I told him, he nearly collapsed, however. After recovering from his shock that he could not have feigned, he said that to throw her from her balcony could only mean that the real murderer wanted the Egyptian government to be blamed in view of all the rumours concerning previous so-called balcony murders."

"And what happened next?"

"Well, after already having excluded Maguid and Yusuf from our list of suspects, there was no other suspect left. To accuse the government in spite of Mustafa Bey's assurances would have led to nothing, except possibly to my arrest. As he had already told me enough, I just thanked him for his hospitality and left the office."

Ahmed made one more of his studious pauses. Alistair and Rietberg, who knew from previous experience that there was more to come, waited patiently.

"Seconds after taking my leave, he came scurrying after me and proposed a chat in a nearby coffee shop. I agreed, of course. There he divulged more of the truth. He respected and had liked Dina too much to let me go without giving me all the facts, he explained. All that he told me then more or less corroborated what we had suspected. Following orders from above he had advised both Dina and Mahmoud al-Allamy strongly not to continue with their campaign and that it would harm national interests. To me he was rather more explicit. They were in grave danger of infuriating one of Egypt's big donors. That donor had bought an authentic Fatimid chessboard for his own museum, trusting Egyptian assurances that everything was legitimate, and he was not to be disappointed. As a former university class mate, Mustafa was believed to be the best person to issue a friendly yet stern warning for Dina to drop the matter. While the journalist obeyed, intimidated by his arrest that was of course part of their strategy, Dina with her well-known stubbornness continued and made everything worse by her last interview given to the Gulf TV-station. The consequence, *i.e.* the veto of a billion dollar loan to Egypt, certainly did hurt national interests, where it hurt most- in their finances. Yet in spite of all that no one - and he repeated 'no one' - in the Egyptian government went so far as to order her murder. It could only have been someone else who wanted to implicate the government in yet another balcony murder. He pleaded with me to believe him, almost with tears in his eyes."

"And do you believe him?" asked Alistair.

"Yes I do," replied Ahmed firmly. "He could not possibly feign his obvious shock after I gave him the news, and moreover he admitted the warnings including Mahmoud's short arrest, so he did not simply deny everything. In fact, a government killing as a punishment for Dina's actions could of course never be ruled out, but it is still highly improbable. He told me the truth, I am sure of that—this time the Egyptian government is innocent."

"I am thirsty again," said Rietberg. "Let us continue at the bar."

They stayed there for a few more hours getting slowly drunk and repeating what had been said before. To Alistair's and Rietberg's relief the Muslim Ahmed's love of whisky had created a sort of booze-inspired bondage between the three of them. Once Rietberg made a call to Marie-Anne, well after midnight, to explain why he would be late, to which she answered in a sleepy voice that for heaven's sake he could stay where he was as long as he wanted and even longer.

Ahmed returned to Cairo and it was now up to Alistair to inform the police of their findings. The police, the former objects of his contempt, had got one thing right after all from the beginning—it was not a family affair.

"They told me that they have finally found a clue that could be decisive," Alistair reported after his visit to them, "*i.e.* the identity of the pizza-man."

"We could have come to the same conclusion," agreed Rietberg. "Pretending to deliver a pizza needs a job with a pizza bakery, or at least a bike, and both can be traced."

"But we didn't think of that," said Alistair drily. "Let me continue. The police started by contacting the pizza bakeries in London—starting from those in Dina's neighbourhood. Before asking the thousand others in London they hit the jackpot with number thirteen. A man with a Lithuanian passport and a Lithuanian driver's licence had been employed a couple of days before the murder as a temporary replacement for another employee on sick leave. What is more, he did not show up the following day. He had left the bike on the pavement in front of the bakery, and returned the keys through the letterbox."

"Our man!" exclaimed Rietberg.

"Of course," said Alistair. "Only the police did not know how to continue from there. The address he had given did not exist, and they could not find anyone answering to his name elsewhere in Britain. So once more a dead end."

"No—it needn't be," said Rietberg. "They could find out where this mysterious Lithuanian returned to after the murder, which he surely did. We know that Cairo and Umm Ghani are obvious choices. We ourselves cannot check with immigration or the airlines, but the police can. They should get the hint to do so as soon as possible."

"This is a clever remark, as Ahmed would say," laughed Alistair. "Also if he did not travel to the Middle East, it could perhaps be Vilnius, which would make things even easier."

At Scotland Yard they met a DCI CID, after announcing their visit with valuable information concerning the Dina Ghalib case. Rietberg was no longer confused by the bewildering amount of acronyms in the British police, because he had watched crime movies and always googled a still unknown one for its correct meaning. The detective chief inspector of the criminal investigation department—a title that made his acronym nearly indispensable—was quite reserved initially. At least he was not the young gum chewing arrogant inspector whom Alistair had met before, but a bespectacled grey-haired man who also looked as a senior police officer should look like. He was probably informed about Alistair's constant police pestering and apparently did not expect too much from their information.

Rietberg's presence helped to change his attitude. His professorial title, his unassuming ways and quiet voice quickly defused any reserve the DCI CID might have had.

Their advice to trace the murderer's escape route by checking flights to Cairo and Dubai out of London was indeed very welcome.

"Why these two cities in particular, may I ask?"

They had prepared their answer to this expected question beforehand. There was no need for detailed speculation about a murder committed by the Egyptian government or a government member in Umm Ghani. That would probably be shrugged off as the mad idea of eager spy novel readers.

"Dina had serious trouble with her own family in Cairo as you probably know already, who were threatening her in an inheritance case, and she had also accused an important collector in Umm Ghani of stealing a precious antiquity. So he probably returned to Cairo or Umm Ghani that can only be reached by plane from Dubai," said Alistair, to whom lying came easily enough.

It was a very good answer. The police had found a lot about Dina's fight with the antiquities mafia on her computer, and a family murder could still not be discounted definitely in spite of their first reaction..

The now friendly DCI CID accompanied them to the door and promised to keep Alistair informed about both lines of enquiry.

Their feedback came soon. After Alistair's and Rietberg's visit to the police they were obviously motivated to follow any lead in the case once more.

The Lithuanian had booked a flight to Dubai the day after the murder, and the police had already informed the authorities in Umm Ghani via Interpol that he was a murder suspect.

"That's all very fine and we should be grateful to the police," said Alistair during a new post-murder meeting with Rietberg. "But how can we or they prove on whose instructions he murdered our Dina? Most probably it was the Umm Ghani finance minister—at least I do not imagine anyone of importance in Lithuania having a grudge against Dina. Still I do not have much hope that the authorities in Umm Ghani will ever admit to that."

"I have an idea how we could make sure—with a little luck," Rietberg said, after puffing on his pipe for a few seconds and blowing smoke rings into the air. "Provided that Mona can learn what happened in Umm Ghani from her diplomat lover and provided she is willing to share her news with me, which I do not doubt for one minute, we can discover more. I will simply phone her and invite her to come to London."

After the usual exclamations of joy to hear each other's voices and the assurance that each one was fine and in good health he said:

"Mona, you have to do me a favour."

"Just ask," said Mona, "I am at your service."

"Come to London for a visit. I miss you."

At the other end of the line there was a short pause, then a laugh.

"My dear professor or Jürgen, as I may call you after your invitation, you are certainly not looking for an affair with me. I like you and could even fall for you, but you do not give me the impression that your interests in that kind of thing are more than moderate at most."

She giggled once more, while he pretended to be amused, feeling slightly hurt by her reaction.

"No, Mona, you are quite right. I only want to resume our last conversation that I found very interesting and refreshing, and to hear the latest news from Cairo and Umm Ghani."

"I thought so," answered Mona, "you are after my gossip and not after my body."

That woman could make a Casanova blush, thought Rietberg, although being even remotely suspected of carnal desires flattered him a lot.

"If you put it that way—yes!" he said.

"Ok," said Mona, "I can agree to that. You are lucky: I plan to come to London anyway for some shopping after a stop-over in Zurich next Thursday, when we can talk. I have one condition however."

"Which is?"

"You have to invite me for dinner in the Gordon Ramsay restaurant, where I will order the most expensive dish on the menu. At least you should bleed, when you want to hear my latest gossip."

"A restaurant of that vulgar chef, who always uses the f-word?"

"The very same!" said Mona. "A vulgar type has a certain sex appeal, which decent people like you never understand. Besides I was told that his food is seriously good."

Rietberg agreed. Even the most expensive dinner in a Gordon Ramsey restaurant would be cheaper and more comfortable than making one more trip to Cairo in order to listen to Mona's storytelling.

Mona and Rietberg sat at their table, where they had been served their starters, a prawn cocktail for Mona and a *vitello tonato* for Rietberg, which were remarkable mainly for their sophisticated arrangement on larger than necessary plates. He had decided to splurge beyond his means to take that ironic smile off her face, after she had asked him, if he could afford it. As first drinks she had a glass of champagne and he a Pernod. All that was more show than substance, which they could have found at a lower price in a less fashionable restaurant, but on Rietberg's agenda were the antics of a finance minister and rather less the food.

She kept him in suspense by choosing her meal very slowly and asking him which wines he would recommend and why. Rietberg, who did not understand much about wines, but had come to like Mona's capriciousness, uttered some nonsense about vintage and terroir of the wines to be selected or refused, and waited patiently for her to spill the beans.

It did not last long, her love of gossip was too strong.

For a while they were occupied attacking their main courses and drinking a vintage Barolo that would cost Rietberg a fortune.

"There is something important, but I am not sure if I should tell you," Mona continued-

"Then don't," answered Rietberg, without meaning it. He knew she was unable to hold back an important piece of information, when she had a chance to gossip, otherwise she would suffer from severe constipation.

"Before I do you have to tell me more about the cause of Dina's death," said Mona after a short pretence at hesitation. "You told us that she fell from a window in her flat, either by suicide, accident or even murder. Knowing you I am certain that you are hiding something from us. What really happened?"

"I cannot imagine why you need to know all that before you tell me more about whatever you have in mind. But if it satisfies you: I swear that I do not know more than I told you."

"In that case murder is still a possibility," said Mona. "You have to know that Jasim's uncle was particularly angry with the Egyptians in general and Dina in particular," she continued. "His obsession was collecting Egyptian and recently mainly Islamic art.

He wanted to create his own private museum and in it a special wing for everything connected with chess-playing in the Islamic world. Apparently he had a lot of material, but nothing yet that could compare with the chess museums in Amsterdam or Moscow. When he was offered the Fatimid chessboard, he knew instantly that it would upgrade his own museum to an international standard. He even compared it with the importance of the Tutankhamen treasures in the Egyptian museum. He had to have it by all means and bought it from a Syrian dealer. As a public figure he had to make sure, however, that its provenance was not tainted by anything illegal, especially when put on display in his museum."

"Well," remarked Rietberg, "as Dina has told me once herself, nearly all rare objects of Islamic art appearing on the market now have a doubtful provenance, even in the absence of concrete proof, and Jasim's uncle must have been aware of that."

"But that's what makes all the difference, don't you see?" said Mona. "Without knowing as much as you do about this subject, I think that museums everywhere would be emptied of most of their treasures, if all that is required is doubts, and not concrete proof of theft. It's the absence of proof that matters."

"You do seem to know a lot," said Rietberg.

"I have only the mind of a playgirl, who has a playgirl's talent to spot hypocrisy, however," laughed Mona. "But let us come back to Jasim's uncle and his dilemma between his obsession and his caution. Before buying he contacted various sources, including the Egyptian ambassador to find out if a Fatimid chessboard was missing from Egypt. Everyone assured him that there was not. He moreover requested the ambassador to make sure that no one in Egypt, including the restitution department, would accuse him at a later date of acquiring the chessboard illegally. He had heard about a recent article in an obscure Egyptian newspaper that vaguely mentioned a chessboard amongst other missing items. In order to save his reputation if he bought it, he did not want any more details to become known and then be forced to defend himself, like Western museums have to when faced with a third world country's request to return their antiquities. The ambassador told him again not to worry, his government would make sure that the chessboard would not be mentioned again."

"Jasim's uncle is indeed a moderately sincere collector, we have to give him that," remarked Rietberg, smiling ironically.

"More sincere than many others, as you will see when I tell you what happened next. Imagine his shock when a Gulf-based TV-station, which everyone watches in the Arab world, interviewed Dina, who told her interviewers in great detail how the chessboard had vanished from a known archaeological site in Aswan to be sold later by the Egyptian archaeologist supervising the excavation. Jasim's uncle was particularly incensed by the deviousness of the Egyptian authorities. According to what Dina said in her interview they had wanted at first everyone to believe that the chessboard Jasim's uncle had acquired was a copy, without telling him. After the truth came out, it became clear that he had bought a stolen object, and no one had told him either. All that in spite of the assurances given to him by the Egyptian ambassador, who must have consulted the antiquities department through his own Foreign Office. Jasim's uncle did not like to be taken for a fool at all. Now you know why he was so angry with Egypt and Dina. He once even called her an Egyptian whore who had betrayed her country by marrying a foreigner and as a Copt attacking Muslim collectors of Islamic art —imagine!"

"Why do you always use the past tense—he 'had' or he 'was'?" asked Rietberg. "Has he died?"

Mona made a studious pause. She relished her role as the messenger of important news. Finally, she dropped a bombshell.

"Jasim's uncle has been put under house arrest—fortunately, as even Jasim says now. Apparently he tried to smuggle one of his workers, who had been arrested, out of prison and even out of the country. He nearly succeeded, because the prison officials did not dare oppose a member of the ruling family. Their car was stopped at the last moment near the border to the next emirate, because the ministers of interior and justice—of course also members of the ruling house—were alerted and outraged at this encroachment on their domain by their own cousin."

Rietberg was too surprised to react immediately. That was his luck, because the pause following Mona's story allowed him to think carefully, before asking her what he wanted to know.

"You said one of the sheikh's workers. I wonder why and for what he employed workers."

"It's always his bloody museum. The company building it has not stopped their work; Jasim's uncle still has a large art collection to display, in spite of his disappointment over the chessboard."

"Of course," said Rietberg. "Probably one of the construction companies active in the Gulf with Bangladeshi or Nepalese workers, I presume?"

"No," laughed Mona, "he only trusts Europeans or Americans. It's a Polish company with workers from Eastern Europe. The worker Jasim's uncle sprang from prison was apparently from Lithuania, and he already had a ticket for a one-way flight from Dubai to Vilnius in his pocket when both were stopped near the border."

"Is that so?" was the only thing Rietberg could say.

The British police had done their homework as had the Umm Ghani police. There was no doubt that Jasim's uncle had ordered Dina's murder in a fit of rage and sent his Lithuanian worker and two as yet unknown others to London to do the job for him.

It was also clear that with his worker in prison he ran a big risk. The Lithuanian could denounce him as the instigator of the murder or blackmail him to get him released. To help him escape to his home country Lithuania, probably with a thick wad of banknotes, was the best solution.

Mona did not seem to know the reason for the worker's arrest, although it had to be a major crime to explain the interference by a minister. That could be anything from smuggling drugs or human trafficking for his account, beating one of the minister's enemies to pulp, even a murder. There was no need to give her all the facts, though. To know for sure that Jasim's relative had murdered her admired cousin, would cause her too much distress and possibly endanger her love affair with her completely innocent diplomat.

Mona had remarked that Rietberg was hiding something from her.

"Tell me, Jürgen, is there anything I should know?"

"No, nothing at all," was the quick answer, "I am only shocked. Does all this affect your friend Jasim?"

"No, why should it? The minister is only his uncle, and even

in Umm Ghani they do not believe in automatic extension of lia-
bility to relatives. Of course his uncle lost his job and remains now
incommunicado under police guard in his own palace to be ques-
tioned about his relation to the Lithuanian."

With an ironic smile she added:

"Whatever that is, I doubt that he will suffer more than the
loss of his post. The whole lot of them are above the law. Jasim
got the news during his last visit to Umm Ghani. He was shocked
of course, but he had already expected the worse after his uncle's
previous erratic behaviour and his hysterical reaction to the chessboard deal that made everyone doubt his mental sanity."

"Please excuse one totally unrelated question," said Rietberg.
"What has happened to the sale of the Ghalib family building?"

"My dear Jürgen, I think I have already given you too much
for a dinner," Mona protested mockingly. "You owe me more,
and before I answer your question you have to promise to give me
something else in exchange."

Mona wanted to see a musical.

"They are playing Chicago at the Adelphi theatre and you will
invite me there tomorrow night. They have been playing it for
long time already, so there should be no problem buying tickets.
The most expensive ones, of course."

Rietberg promised to go to a musical, instead of a classical
concert that he would have much preferred, and Mona answered
his question.

"It appears that the army is no longer so keen to buy the
building," she said, not without Schadenfreude. "The reason
seems to be that the General behind the idea has been transferred
to a post in Sinai to combat terrorism there and has been replaced
by another one, who is not keen on having the building. As you
well know, in our country projects that are started during the
tenure of one official are almost never approved by his successor.
Yet in case the building is sold to someone else Maguid would lose
the chance of getting his grace-and-favour apartment—I told you
what that is. He is therefore no longer so keen to sell. Yusuf and
Halim would like to proceed, of course, but have no chance
without Maguid. Poor sods as they are."

A few days later Rietberg received a letter with a colourful stamp depicting a palm tree and an oil rig. Inside were two newspaper articles. The first was the latest article written by his friend Rupert Fischer ('Sheherazade') for the Gulf Private Eye:

*Morning dawned and when the caliph woke up he called for Sheherazade to continue with her tale of the previous night about the fallen woman. She obeyed his command and said:*

*"Oh auspicious king and master, please listen to what the jinn told me after I released him from his bottle by rubbing it with my pearl white fingers. The Magic-Carpet Airline departing from Baghdad to the kingdom of the mighty conqueror, the fair-headed William, had lately on board a chained slave from the faraway lands of Baltica, who was wanted by the Qadi of the fair headed William to be punished for a heinous crime. Your august Majesty's scribes sent a message accompanying the human cargo to the aforementioned fair-headed William that no rumours or lies made by the slave about any member of your illustrious family should ever be published or commented upon by the slanderous market criers and heralds, for whom his capital is famous. If he does not obey the command of the Commander of the Faithful and benevolent stoker of the chimneys in his cold and damp land, the mighty and rich kingdom of Baghdad will no longer buy swords and lances from him, but from one of his many rivals from the Maghrib to the Mashriq. The code word of the message was Yamamah, which, as I regret to say, has no meaning to me, your ignorant and humble slave."*

*"Yamamah is my secret weapon for stifling slanders by the heralds of the fair-headed William, and it never fails to beat his nation of shopkeepers," smirked the mighty ruler of Baghdad.*

The other was a small article in the Financial Times titled "Negotiations between the UK and the emirate of Umm Ghani about the sale of 30 Tornado fighters."

## Epilogue

A Lithuanian labourer, who had originally come to the UK for work, was given a lifelong prison sentence for murdering the owner of a flat in Chelsea during a burglary...

Lightning Source UK Ltd.
Milton Keynes UK
UKHW01f1841080818
326958UK00001B/3/P